How Jerusalem Was Won

W.T. Massey

Table of Contents

How Jerusalem Was Won

W.T. Massey

How Jerusalem Was Won
        Being the Record of Allenby's Campaign in Palestine

HOW JERUSALEM WAS WON

BEING THE RECORD OF ALLENBY'S CAMPAIGN IN PALESTINE

by

W.T. MASSEY

OFFICIAL CORRESPONDENT OF THE LONDON NEWSPAPERS WITH THE EGYPTIAN EXPEDITIONARY FORCE

WITH ILLUSTRATIONS AND MAPS

LONDON 1919

PREFACE.

This narrative of the work accomplished for civilisation by General Allenby's Army is carried only as far as the occupation of Jericho. The capture of that ancient town, with the possession of a line of rugged hills a dozen miles north of Jerusalem, secured the Holy City from any Turkish attempt to retake it. The book, in fact, tells the story of the twenty–third fall of Jerusalem, one of the most beneficent happenings of all wars, and marking an epoch in the wonderful history of the Holy Place which will rank second only to that era which saw the birth of Christianity. All that occurred in the fighting on the Gaza–Beersheba line was part and parcel of the taking of Jerusalem, the freeing of which from four centuries of Turkish domination was the object of the first part of the campaign. The Holy City was the goal sought by every officer and man in the Army; and though from the moment that goal had been attained all energies were concentrated upon driving the Turk out of the war, there was not a member of the Force, from the highest on the Staff to the humblest private in the ranks, who did not feel that Jerusalem was the greatest prize of the campaign.

In a second volume I shall tell of that tremendous feat of arms which overwhelmed the Turkish Armies, drove them through 400 miles of country in six weeks, and gave cavalry an opportunity of proving that, despite all the arts and devices of modern warfare, with fighters and observers in the air and an entirely new mechanism of war, they continued as indispensable a part of an army as when the legions of old took the field. This is too long a story to be told in this volume, though the details of that magnificent triumph are so firmly impressed on the mind that one is loth to leave the narration of them to a future date. For the moment Jerusalem must be sufficient, and if in the telling of the British work up to that point I can succeed in giving an idea of the immense value of General Allenby's Army to the Empire, of the soldier's courage and fortitude, of his indomitable will and self–sacrifice and patriotism, it will indeed prove the most grateful task I have ever set myself.

April 1919.

CHAPTER I. PALESTINE'S INFLUENCE ON THE WAR

In a war which involved the peoples of the four quarters of the globe it was to be expected that on the world's oldest battleground would be renewed the scenes of conflict of bygone ages. There was perhaps a desire of some elements of both sides, certainly it was the unanimous wish of the Allies, to avoid the clash of arms in Palestine, and to leave untouched by armies a land held in reverence by three of the great religions of the world. But this ancient cockpit of warring races could not escape. The will of those who broke the peace prevailed. Germany's dream of Eastern Empires and world domination, the lust of conquest of the Kaiser party, required that the tide of war should once more surge across the land, and if the conquering hosts left fewer traces of war wreckage than were to be expected in their victorious march, it was due not to any anxiety of our foes to avoid conflict about, and damage to, places with hallowed associations, but to the masterly strategy of the British Commander–in–Chief who manoeuvred the Turkish Armies out of positions defending the sacred sites.

The people of to–day who have lived through the war, who have had their view bewildered by ever–recurring anxieties, by hopes shattered and fears realised, by a succession of victories and defeats on a colossal scale, and by a sudden collapse of the enemy, may fail to see the Palestine campaign in true perspective. But in a future generation the calm judgment of the historian in reviewing the greatest of all wars will, if I mistake not, pay a great tribute to General Allenby's strategy, not only as marking the commencement of the enemy's downfall, but as preserving from the scourge of war those holy places which symbolise the example by which most people rule their lives. Britons who value the good name of their country will appreciate what this means to those who shall come after us—that the record of a great campaign carried out exclusively by British Imperial troops was unsullied by a single act to disturb the sacred monuments, and left the land in the full possession of those rich treasures which stand for the principles that guided our actions and which, if posterity observes them, will make a better and happier world.

A few months after the Turks entered the war it was obvious that unaided they could never realise the Kaiser's hope of cutting the Suez Canal communications of the British Empire. The German commitments in Europe were too overwhelming to permit of their rendering the Turks adequate support for a renewed effort against Egypt after the failure of the attack on the Canal in February 1915. There was an attempt by the Turks in August 1916, but it was crushed by Anzac horse and British infantry at Romani,[1] a score of miles from Port Said, and thereafter the Turks in this theatre were on the defensive. Some declare the Dardanelles enterprise to have been a mistake; others believe that had we not threatened the Turks there Egypt would have had to share with us the anxieties that war brings alike upon attackers and defenders. Gallipoli and Mesopotamia, however we regard those expeditions in the first years of the struggle, undoubtedly prevented the Turks employing a large army against Egypt, and the possibilities resulting from a defeat there were so full of danger to us, not merely in that half—way house of the Empire but in India and the East generally, that if Gallipoli served to avert the disaster that ill—starred expedition was worth undertaking. We had to drive the Turks out of the Sinai Peninsula—Egyptian territory—and, that accomplished, an attack on the Turks through Palestine was imperative since the Russian collapse released a large body of Turkish troops from the Caucasus who would otherwise be employed in Mesopotamia.

[Footnote 1: *The Desert Campaigns*: London, Constable and Co., Ltd.]

When General Allenby took over the command of the Egyptian Expeditionary Force the British public as a whole did not fully realise the importance of the Palestine campaign. Most of them regarded it as a 'side show,' and looked upon it as one of those minor fields of operations which dissipated our strength at a time when it was imperative we should concentrate to resist the German effort on the Western Front. They did not know the facts. In our far—flung Empire it was essential that we should maintain our prestige among the races we governed, some of them martial peoples who might remain faithful to the British flag only so long as we could impress them with our power to win the war. They were more influenced by a triumph in Mesopotamia, which was nearer their doors, than by a victory in France, and the occupation of Bagdad was a victory of greater import to the King's Indian subjects than the German retirement from the Hindenburg line. If there ever was a fear of serious trouble in India the advance of General Maude in Mesopotamia dispelled it, and made it easier not only to release a portion of our white garrison in India for active service elsewhere, but to recruit a large force of Indians for the Empire's work in other climes. Bagdad was a tremendous blow to German ambitions. The loss of it spelt ruin to those hopes of Eastern conquest which had prompted the German intrigues in Turkey, and it was certain that the Kaiser, so long as he believed in ultimate victory, would refuse to accept the loss of Bagdad as final. Russia's withdrawal as a belligerent released a large body of Turkish troops in the Caucasus, and set free many Germans, particularly 'technical troops' of which the Turks stood in need, for other fronts. It was then that the German High Command conceived a scheme for retaking Bagdad, and the redoubtable von Falkenhayn was sent to Constantinople charged with the preparations for the undertaking. Certain it is that it would have been put into execution but for the situation created by the presence of a large British Army in the Sinai Peninsula. A large force was collected about Aleppo for a march down the Euphrates valley, and the winter of 1917–18 would have witnessed a stern struggle for supremacy in Mesopotamia if the War Cabinet had not decided to force the Turks to accept battle where they least wanted it.

The views of the British War Cabinet on the war in the East, at any rate, were sound and solid. They concentrated on one big campaign, and, profiting from past mistakes which led to a wastage of strength, allowed all the weight they could spare to be thrown into the Egyptian Expeditionary Force under a General who had proved his high military capacity in France, and in whom all ranks had complete confidence, and they permitted the Mesopotamian and Salonika Armies to contain the enemies on their fronts while the Army in Palestine set out to crush the Turks at what proved to be their most vital point. As to whether the force available on our Mesopotamia front was capable of defeating the German scheme I cannot offer an opinion, but it is beyond all question that the conduct of operations in Palestine on a plan at once bold, resolute, and worthy of a high place in military history saved the Empire much anxiety over our position in the Tigris and Euphrates valleys, and probably prevented unrest on the frontiers of India and in India itself, where mischief makers were actively working in the German cause. Nor can there be any doubt that the brilliant campaign in Palestine prevented British and French influence declining among the Mahomedan populations of those countries' respective spheres of control in Africa. Indeed I regard it as incontrovertible that the Palestine strategy of General Allenby, even apart from his stupendous rush through Syria in the autumn of the last year of war, did as much to end the war in 1918 as the great battles on the Western Front, for if there had been failure or check in Palestine some British and French troops in France might have had to be detached to other fronts, and the Germans' effort in the Spring might have pushed their line farther towards the Channel and Paris. If Bagdad was not actually saved in Palestine, an expedition against it was certainly stopped by our Army operating on the old battlegrounds in Palestine. We lost many lives, and it cost us a vast amount of money, but the sacrifices of brave men contributed to the saving of the world from German domination; and high as the British name stood in the East as the upholder of the freedom of peoples, the fame of Britain for justice, fair dealing, and honesty is wider and more firmly established to–day because the people have seen it emerge triumphantly from a supreme test.

In the strategy of the world war we made, no doubt, many mistakes, but in Palestine the strategy was of the best, and in the working out of a far–seeing scheme, victories so influenced events that on this front began the final phase of the war—once Turkey was beaten, Bulgaria and Austria–Hungary submitted and Germany acknowledged the inevitable. Falkenhayn saw that the Bagdad undertaking was impossible so long as we were dangerous on the Palestine front, and General Allenby's attack on the Gaza line wiped the Bagdad enterprise out of the list of German ambitions. The plan of battle on the Gaza–Beersheba line resembled in miniature the ending of the war. If we take Beersheba for Turkey, Sheria and Hareira for Bulgaria and Austria, and Gaza for Germany, we get the exact progress of events in the final stage, except that Bulgaria's submission was an intelligent anticipation of the laying down of their arms by the Turks. Gaza–Beersheba was a rolling up from our right to left; so was the ending of the Hun alliance.

CHAPTER II. OLD BATTLEGROUNDS

It was in accordance with the fitness of things that the British Army should fight and conquer on the very spots consecrated by the memories of the most famous battles of old. From Gaza onwards we made our progress by the most ancient road on earth, for this way moved commerce between the Euphrates and the Nile many centuries before the East knew West. We fought on fields which had been the battlegrounds of Egyptian and Assyrian armies, where Hittites, Ethiopians, Persians, Parthians, and Mongols poured out their blood in times when kingdoms were strong by the sword alone. The Ptolemies invaded Syria by this way, and here the Greeks put their colonising hands on the country. Alexander the Great made this his route to Egypt. Pompey marched over the Maritime Plain and inaugurated that Roman rule which lasted for centuries; till Islam made its wide irresistible sweep in the seventh century. Then the Crusaders fought and won and lost, and Napoleon's ambitions in the East were wrecked just beyond the plains.

Up the Maritime Plain we battled at Gaza, every yard of which had been contested by the armies of mighty kings in the past thirty-five centuries, at Akir, Gezer, Lydda, and around Joppa. All down the ages armies have moved in victory or flight over this plain, and General Allenby in his advance was but repeating history. And when the Turks had been driven beyond the Plain of Philistia, and the Commander-in-Chief had to decide how to take Jerusalem, we saw the British force move along precisely the same route that has been taken by armies since the time when Joshua overcame the Amorites and the day was lengthened by the sun and moon standing still till the battle was won. Geography had its influence on the strategy of to-day as completely as it did when armies were not cumbered with guns and mechanical transport. Of the few passes from the Maritime Plain over the Shephelah into the Judean range only that emerging from the green Vale of Ajalon was possible, if we were to take Jerusalem, as the great captains of old took it, from the north. The Syrians sometimes chose this road in preference to advancing through Samaria, the Romans suffered retreat on it, Richard Coeur de Lion made it the path for his approach towards the Holy City, and, precisely as in Joshua's day and as when in the first century the Romans fell victims to a tremendous Jewish onslaught, the fighting was hardest about the Beth-horons, but with a different result—the invaders were victorious. The corps which actually took Jerusalem advanced up the new road from Latron through Kuryet el Enab, identified by some as Kirjath-jearim where the Philistines returned the Ark, but that road would have been denied to us if we had not made good the ancient path from the Vale of Ajalon to Gibeon. Jerusalem was won by the fighting at the Beth-horons as surely as it was on the line of hills above the wadi Surar which the Londoners carried. There was fighting at Gibeon, at Michmas, at Beeroth, at Ai, and numerous other places made familiar to us by the Old Testament, and assuredly no army went forth to battle on more hallowed soil.

How Jerusalem Was Won

Of all the armies which earned a place in history in Palestine, General Allenby's was the greatest—the greatest in size, in equipment, in quality, in fighting power, and not even the invading armies in the romantic days of the Crusades could equal it in chivalry. It fought the strong fight with clean hands throughout, and finished without a blemish on its conduct. It was the best of all the conquering armies seen in the Holy Land as well as the greatest. Will not the influence of this Army endure? I think so. There is an awakening in Palestine, not merely of Christians and Jews, but of Moslems, too, in a less degree. During the last thirty years there have grown more signs of the deep faiths of peoples and of their veneration of this land of sacred history. If their institutions and missions could develop and shed light over Palestine even while the slothful and corrupt Turk ruled the land, how much faster and more in keeping with the sanctity of the country will the improvement be under British protection? The graves of our soldiers dotted over desert wastes and cornfields, on barren hills and in fertile valleys, ay, and on the Mount of Olives where the Saviour trod, will mark an era more truly grand and inspiring, and offer a far greater lesson to future generations than the Crusades or any other invasion down the track of time. The Army of General Allenby responded to the happy thought of the Commander–in–Chief and contributed one day's pay for the erection of a memorial near Jerusalem in honour of its heroic dead. Apart from the holy sites, no other memorial will be revered so much, and future pilgrims, to whatever faith they belong, will look upon it as a monument to men who went to battle to bring lasting peace to a land from which the Word of Peace and Goodwill went forth to mankind.

In selecting General Sir Edmund Allenby as the Palestine Army's chief the War Cabinet made a happy choice. General Sir Archibald Murray was recalled to take up an important command at home after the two unsuccessful attempts to drive the Turks from the Gaza defences. The troops at General Murray's disposal were not strong enough to take the offensive again, and it was clear there must be a long period of preparation for an attack on a large scale. General Allenby brought to the East a lengthy experience of fighting on the Western Front, where his deliberate methods of attack, notably at Arras, had given the Allies victories over the cleverest and bravest of our enemies. Palestine was likely to be a cavalry, as well as an infantry, campaign, or at any rate the theatre of war in which the mounted arm could be employed with the most fruitful of results. General Allenby's achievements as a cavalry leader in the early days of the war marked him as the one officer of high rank suited for the Palestine command, and his proved capacity as a General both in open and in trench warfare gave the Army that high degree of confidence in its Commander–in–Chief which it is so necessary that a big fighting force should possess. A tremendously hard worker himself, General Allenby expected all under him to concentrate the whole of their energies on their work. He had the faculty for getting the best out of his officers, and on his Staff were some of the most enthusiastic soldiers in the service. There was no room for an inefficient leader in any branch of the force, and the knowledge that the Commander–in–Chief valued the lives and the health of his men so highly that he would not risk a failure, kept all the staffs tuned up to concert pitch. We saw many changes, and the best men came to the top. His own vigour infected the whole command, and within a short while of arriving at the front the efficiency of the Army was considerably increased.

The Palestine G.H.Q. was probably nearer the battle front than any G.H.Q. in other theatres of operations, and when the Army had broken through and chased the enemy beyond the Jaffa–Jerusalem line, G.H.Q. was opened at Bir Salem, near Ramleh, and for several months was actually within reach of the long–range guns which the Turks possessed. The rank and file were not slow to appreciate this. They knew their Commander–in–Chief was on the spot, keeping his eye and hand on everything, organising with his organisers, planning with his operation staff, familiar with every detail of the complicated transport system, watching his supply services with the keenness of a quartermaster–general, and taking that lively interest in the medical branch which betrayed an anxious desire for the welfare and health of the men. The rank and file knew something more than this. They saw the Commander–in–Chief at the front every day. General Allenby did not rely solely on reports from his corps. He went to each section of the line himself, and before practically every major operation he saw the ground and examined the scheme for attack. There was not a part of the line he did not know, and no one will contradict me when I say that the military roads in Palestine were known by no one better than the driver of the Commander–in–Chief's car. A man of few words, General Allenby always said what he meant with soldierly directness, which made the thanks he gave a rich reward. A good piece of work brought a written or oral message of thanks, and the men were satisfied they had done well to deserve congratulations. They were proud to have the confidence of such a Chief and to deserve it, and they in their turn had such unbounded faith in the military judgment of the General and in the care he took to prevent unnecessary risk of life, that there was nothing which he sanctioned that they would not attempt. Such mutual confidence breeds strength, and it was the Commander–in–Chief's example, his tact, energy, and military genius which made his Army a potent power for Britain and a strong pillar of the Allies' cause.

How Jerusalem Was Won

Let it not be imagined that General Allenby in his victorious campaign shone only as a great soldier. He was also a great administrator. In England little was known about this part of the General's work, and owing to the difficulties of the task and to the consideration which had, and still has, to be shown to the susceptibilities of a number of friendly nations and peoples, it may be long before the full story of the administration of the occupied territory in Palestine is unfolded for general appreciation. It is a good story, worthy of Britain's record as a protector of peoples, and though from the nature of his conquest over the Turks in the Bible country the name of General Allenby will adorn the pages of history principally as a victor, it will also stand before the governments of states as setting a model for a wise, prudent, considerate, even benevolent, administration of occupied enemy territory. In days when Powers driven mad by military ambition tear up treaties as scraps of paper, General Allenby observed the spirit as well as the letter of the Hague Convention, and found it possible to apply to occupied territory the principles of administration as laid down in the Manual of Military Law.

The natives marvelled at the change. In place of insecurity, extortion, bribery and corruption, levies on labour and property and all the evils of Turkish government, General Allenby gave the country behind the front line peace, justice, fair treatment of every race and creed, and a firm and equitable administration of the law. Every man's house became his castle. Taxes were readily paid, the tax gatherers were honest servants, and, none of the revenue going to keep fat pashas in luxury in Constantinople, there came a prospect of expenditure and revenue balancing after much money had been usefully spent on local government. Until the signing of peace international law provided that Turkish laws should apply. These, properly administered, as they never were by the Turks, gave a basis of good government, and, with the old abuses connected with the collection of revenue removed, and certain increased taxation and customs dues imposed by the Turks during the war discontinued, the people resumed the arts of peace and enjoyed a degree of prosperity none of them had ever anticipated. What the future government of Palestine may be is uncertain at the time of writing. There is talk of international control—we seem ever ready to lose at the conference table what a valiant sword has gained for us—but the careful and perfectly correct administration of General Allenby will save us from the criticism of many jealous foreigners. Certainly it will bear examination by any impartial investigator, but the best of all tributes that could be paid to it is that it satisfied religious communities which did not live in perfect harmony with one another and the inhabitants of a country which shelters the people of many different races.

How Jerusalem Was Won

The Yilderim undertaking, as the Bagdad scheme was described, did not meet with the full acceptance of the Turks. The 'mighty Jemal', as the Germans sneeringly called the Commander of the Syrian Army, opposed it as weakening his prospects, and even Enver, the ambitious creature and tool of Germany, postponed his approval. It would seem the taking over of the command of the Egyptian Expeditionary Force by General Allenby set the Turks thinking, and made the German Military Mission in Constantinople reconsider their plans, not with a view to a complete abandonment of the proposal to advance on Bagdad, as would have been wise, but in order to see how few of the Yilderim troops they could allot to Jemal's army to make safe the Sinai front. There was an all–important meeting of Turkish Generals in the latter half of August, and Jemal stood to his guns. Von Falkenhayn could not get him to abate one item of his demands, and there can be no doubt that Falkenhayn, obsessed though he was with the importance of getting Bagdad, could see that Jemal was right. He admitted that the Yilderim operation was only practicable if it had freedom for retirement through the removal of the danger on the Palestine front. With that end in view he advocated that the British should be attacked, and suggested that two divisions and the 'Asia Corps' should be sent from Aleppo to move round our right. Jemal was in favour of defensive action; Enver procrastinated and proposed sending one division to strengthen the IVth Army on the Gaza front and to proceed with the Bagdad preparations. The wait–and–see policy prevailed, but long before we exerted our full strength Bagdad was out of the danger zone. General Allenby's force was so disposed that any suggestion of the Yilderim operation being put into execution was ruled out of consideration.

Several documents captured at Yilderim headquarters at Nazareth in September 1918, when General Allenby made his big drive through Syria, show very clearly how our Palestine operations changed the whole of the German plans, and reading between the lines one can realise how the impatience of the Germans was increasing Turkish stubbornness and creating friction and ill–feeling. The German military character brooks no opposition; the Turks like to postpone till to–morrow what should be done to–day. The latter were cocksure after their two successes at Gaza they could hold us up; the Germans believed that with an offensive against us they would hold us in check till the wet season arrived.[1]

[Footnote 1: See Appendices I., II., and III.]

11

How Jerusalem Was Won

Down to the south the Turks had to bring their divisions. Their line of communications was very bad. There was a railway from Aleppo through Rayak to Damascus, and onwards through Deraa (on the Hedjaz line) to Afule, Messudieh, Tul Keram, Ramleh, Junction Station to Beit Hanun, on the Gaza sector, and through Et Tineh to Beersheba. Rolling stock was short and fuel was scarce, and the enemy had short rations. When we advanced through Syria in the autumn of 1918 our transport was nobly served by motor–lorry columns which performed marvels in getting up supplies over the worst of roads. But as we went ahead we, having command of the sea, landed stores all the way up the coast, and unless the Navy had lent its helping hand we should never have got to Aleppo before the Turk cried 'Enough.' Every ounce of the Turks' supplies had to be hauled over land. They managed to put ten infantry divisions and one cavalry division against us in the first three weeks, but they were not comparable in strength to our seven infantry divisions and three cavalry divisions. In rifle strength we outnumbered them by two to one, but if the enemy had been well led and properly rationed he, being on the defensive and having strong prepared positions, should have had the power to resist us more strongly. The Turkish divisions we attacked were: 3rd, 7th, 16th, 19th, 20th, 24th, 26th, 27th, 53rd, and 54th, and the 3rd Cavalry Division. The latter avoided battle, but all the infantry divisions had heavy casualties. That the moral of the Turkish Army was not high may be gathered from a very illuminating letter written by General Kress von Kressenstein, the G.O.C. of the Sinai front, to Yilderim headquarters on September 29, 1917.[1]

[Footnote 1: See Appendix IV.]

The troops who won Palestine and made it happier than it had been for four centuries were exclusively soldiers of the British Empire. There was a French detachment and an Italian detachment with General Allenby's Army. The Italians for a short period held a small portion of the line in the Gaza sector, but did not advance with our force; the French detachment were solely employed as garrison troops. The French battleship *Requin* and two French destroyers cooperated with the ships of the Royal Navy in the bombardment of the coast. Our Army was truly representative of the Empire, and the units composing it gave an abiding example that in unity rested our strength. From over the Seven Seas the Empire's sons came to illustrate the unanimity of all the King's subjects in the prosecution of the war. English, Scottish, Irish, and Welsh divisions of good men and true fought side by side with soldiers of varying Indian races and castes. Australia's valiant sons constituted many brigades of horse and, with New Zealand mounted regiments, became the most hardened campaigners in the Egyptian and Palestine theatre of operations. Their powerful support in the day of anxiety and trial, as well as in the time of triumph, will be remembered with gratitude. South Africa contributed good gunners; our dark–skinned brethren in the West Indies furnished infantry who, when the fierce summer heat made the air in the Jordan Valley like a draught from a furnace, had a bayonet charge which aroused an Anzac brigade to enthusiasm (and Colonial free men can estimate bravery at its true value). From far–away Hong Kong and Singapore came mountain gunners equal to any in the world, Kroomen sent from their homes in West Africa surf boatmen to land stores, Raratongas from the Southern Pacific vied with them in boat craft and beat them in physique, while Egypt contributed a labour corps and transport corps running a long way into six figures. The communion of the representatives of the Mother and Daughter nations on the stern field of war brought together people with the same ideals, and if there are any minor jealousies between them the brotherhood of arms will make the soldiers returning to their homes in all quarters of the globe the best of missionaries to spread the Imperial idea. Instead of wrecking the British Empire the German–made war should rebuild it on the soundest of foundations, affection, mutual trust, and common interest.

CHAPTER III. DIFFICULTIES OF THE ATTACK

General Allenby's first problem was of vital consequence. He had to pierce the Gaza line. Before his arrival there had been, as already stated, two attempts which failed. A third failure, or even a check, might have spelt disaster for us in the East. The Turks held commanding positions, which they strengthened and fortified under the direction of German engineers until their country, between the sea and Beersheba, became a chain of land works of high military value, well adapted for defence, and covering almost every line of approach. The Turk at the Dardanelles had shown no loss of that quality of doggedness in defence which characterised him in Plevna, and though we know his commanders still cherished the hope of successfully attacking us before we could attempt to crush his line, it was on his system of defence that the enemy mainly relied to break the power of the British force. On arriving in Egypt General Allenby was given an appreciation of the situation written by Lieut.–General Sir Philip Chetwode, who had commanded the Desert Column in various stages across the sands of Sinai, was responsible for forcing the Turks to evacuate El Arish, arranged the dash on Magdaba by General Sir Harry Chauvel's mounted troops, and fought the brilliant little battle of Rafa.

How Jerusalem Was Won

This appreciation of the position was the work of a master military mind, taking a broad comprehensive view of the whole military situation in the East, Palestine's position in the world war, the strategical and tactical problems to be faced, and, without making any exorbitant demands for troops which would lessen the Allies' powers in other theatres, set out the minimum necessities for the Palestine force. General Allenby gave the fullest consideration to this document, and after he had made as complete an examination of the front as any Commander–in–Chief ever undertook—the General was in one or other sector with his troops almost every day for four months—General Chetwode's plan was adopted, and full credit was given to his prescience in General Allenby's despatch covering the operations up to the fall of Jerusalem.

It was General Chetwode's view at the time of writing his appreciation, that both the British and Turkish Armies were strategically on the defensive. The forces were nearly equal in numbers, though we were slightly superior in artillery, but we had no advantage sufficient to enable us to attack a well–entrenched enemy who only offered us a flank on which we could not operate owing to lack of water and the extreme difficulty of supply. General Chetwode thought it was possible the enemy might make an offensive against us—we have since learned he had such designs—but he gave weighty reasons against the Turk embarking upon a campaign conducted with a view to throwing us beyond the Egyptian frontier into the desert again. If the enemy contemplated even minor operations in the Sinai Desert he had not the means of undertaking them. We should be retiring on positions we had prepared, for, during his advance across the desert, General Chetwode had always taken the precaution of having his force dug in against the unlikely event of a Turkish attack. Every step we went back would make our supply easier, and there was no water difficulty, the pipe line, then 130 miles long, which carried the purified waters of the Nile to the amount of hundreds of thousands of gallons daily, being always available for our troops. It would be necessary for the Turks to repair the Beersheba–Auja railway. They had lifted some of the rails for use north of Gaza, and a raid we had carried out showed that we could stop this railway being put into a state of preparedness for military traffic. An attack which aimed at again threatening the Suez Canal was therefore ruled as outside the range of possibilities.

On the other hand, now that the Russian collapse had relieved the Turk of his anxieties in the Caucasus and permitted him to concentrate his attention on the Mesopotamian and Palestine fronts, what hope had he of resisting our attack when we should be in a position to launch it? The enemy had a single narrow–gauge railway line connecting with the

How Jerusalem Was Won

Jaffa–Jerusalem railway at Junction Station about six miles south–east of Ramleh. This line ran to Beersheba, and there was a spur line running past Deir Sineid to Beit Hanun from which the Gaza position was supplied. There was a shortage of rolling stock and, there being no coal for the engines, whole olive orchards had been hacked down to provide fuel. The Hebron road, which could keep Beersheba supplied if the railway was cut, was in good order, but in other parts there were no roads at all, except several miles of badly metalled track from Junction Station to Julis. We could not keep many troops with such ill–conditioned communications, but Turkish soldiers require far less supplies than European troops, and the enemy had done such remarkable things in surmounting supply difficulties that he was given credit for being able to support between sixty and seventy battalions in the line and reserve, with an artillery somewhat weaker than our own.

If we made another frontal attack at Gaza we should find ourselves up against a desperately strong defensive system, but even supposing we got through it we should come to another halt in a few miles, as the enemy had selected, and in most cases had prepared, a number of positions right up to the Jaffa–Jerusalem road, where he would be in a land of comparative plenty, with his supply and transport troubles very considerably reduced. No one could doubt that the Turks intended to defend Jerusalem to the last, not only because of the moral effect its capture would have on the peoples of the world, but because its possession by us would threaten their enterprise in the Hedjaz, and the enormous amount of work we afterwards found they had done on the Judean hills proved that they were determined to do all in their power to prevent our driving them from the Holy City. The enemy, too, imagined that our progress could not exceed the rate at which our standard gauge railway could be built. Water–borne supplies were limited as to quantity, and during the winter the landing of supplies on an open beach was hazardous. In the coastal belt there were no roads, and the wide fringe of sand which has accumulated for centuries and still encroaches on the Maritime Plain can only be crossed by camels. Wells are few and yield but small volumes of water. With the transport allotted to the force in the middle of 1917 it was not possible to maintain more than one infantry division at a distance of twenty to twenty–five miles beyond railhead, and this could only be done by allotting to them all the camels and wheels of other divisions and rendering these immobile. This was insufficient to keep the enemy on the move after a tactical success, and he would have ample time to reorganise.

How Jerusalem Was Won

General Chetwode held that careful preliminary arrangements, suitable and elastic organisation of transport, the collection of material at railhead, the training of platelaying gangs provided by the troops, the utilisation of the earthwork of the enemy's line for our own railway, luck as regards the weather and the fullest use of sea transport, should enable us to give the enemy less breathing time than appeared possible on paper. It was beyond hope, however, whatever preparations were made, that we should be able to pursue at a speed approaching that which the river made possible in Mesopotamia. General Chetwode considered it would be fatal to attempt an offensive with forces which might permit us to attack and occupy the enemy's Gaza line but which would be insufficient to inflict upon him a really severe blow, and to follow up that blow with sufficient troops. No less than seven infantry divisions at full strength and three cavalry divisions would be adequate for the purpose, and they would be none too many. Further, if the Turks began to press severely in Mesopotamia, or even to revive their campaign in the Hedjaz, a premature offensive might be necessitated on our part in Palestine.

The suggestion made by General Chetwode for General Allenby's consideration was that the enemy should be led to believe we intended to attack him in front of Gaza, and that we should pin him down to his defences in the centre, while the real attack should begin on Beersheba and continue at Hareira and Sheria, and so force the enemy by manoeuvre to abandon Gaza. That plan General Allenby adopted after seeing all the ground, and the events of the last day of October and the first week of November supported General Chetwode's predictions to the letter. Indeed it would be hard to find a parallel in history for such another complete and absolute justification of a plan drawn up several months previously, and it is doubtful if, supposing the Turks had succeeded in doing what their German advisers advocated, namely forestalling our blow by a vigorous attack on our positions, there would have been any material alteration in the working out of the scheme. The staff work of General Headquarters and of the staffs of the three corps proved wholly sound. Each department gave of its best, and from the moment when Beersheba was taken in a day and we secured its water supply, there was never a doubt that the enemy could be kept on the move until we got into the rough rocky hills about Jerusalem. And by that time, as events proved, his moral had had such a tremendous shaking that he never again made the most of his many opportunities.

The soundness of the plan can quite easily be made apparent to the unmilitary eye. Yet the Turk was absolutely deceived as to General Allenby's intentions. If it be conceded that to deceive the enemy is one of the greatest accomplishments in the soldier's art, it must be admitted that the battle of Gaza showed General Allenby's consummate generalship, just as it was proved again, and perhaps to an even greater extent, in the wonderful days of September 1918, in Northern Palestine and Syria. A glance at the map of the Gaza–Beersheba line and the country immediately behind it will show that if a successful attack were delivered against Gaza the enemy could withdraw his whole line to a second and supporting position where we should have to begin afresh upon an almost similar operation. The Turk would still have his water and would be slightly nearer his supplies.

Since the two unsuccessful attacks in March and April, Gaza had been put into a powerful state of defence. The houses of the town are mostly on a ridge, and enclosing the place is a mass of gardens fully a mile deep, each surrounded by high cactus hedges affording complete cover and quite impossible for infantry to penetrate. To reduce Gaza would require a prolonged artillery bombardment with far more batteries than General Allenby could ever expect to have at his command, and it is certain that not only would the line in front of the town have had to be taken, but also the whole of the western end of the Turks' trench system for a length of at least 12,000 yards. And, as has been said, with Gaza secured we should still have had to face the enemy in a new line of positions about the wadi Hesi. Gaza was the Turks' strongest point. To attack here would have meant a long–drawn–out artillery duel, infantry would have had to advance over open ground under complete observation, and, while making a frontal attack, would have been exposed to enfilade fire from the 'Tank' system of works to the south–east. It would have proved a costly operation, its success could only have been partial in that it did not follow that we should break the enemy's line, and it would not have enabled us to contain the remainder of the Turkish force.

Nor would an attack on the centre have promised more favourably. Here the enemy had all the best of the ground. At Atawineh, Sausage Ridge, Hareira, and Teiaha there were defences supporting each other on high ground overlooking an almost flat plain through which the wadi Ghuzze runs. All the observation was in enemy possession, and to attack over this ground would have been inviting disaster. There was little fear that the Turks would attack us across this wide range of No Man's Land, for we held secure control of the curiously shaped heaps of broken earth about Shellal, and the conical hill at Fara gave an uninterrupted view for several miles northward and eastward. The position was very different about Beersheba. If we secured that place with its water supply, and in this dry country the battle really amounted to a fight for water, we should be attacking from high ground and against positions which had not been prepared on so formidable a scale as elsewhere, with the prospect of compelling the enemy to abandon the remainder of the line for fear of being enveloped by mounted troops moving behind his weakened left. That, in brief outline, was the gist of General Chetwode's report, and with its full acceptance began the preparations for the advance. These preparations took several months to complete, and they were as thorough as the energy of a capable staff could make them.

CHAPTER IV. TRAINING THE ARMY

Those of us who were fortunate enough to witness the nature of the preparations for the first of General Allenby's great and triumphant moves in Palestine can speak of the debt Britain and her Allies owe not merely to the Commander–in–Chief and his Headquarters Staff, but to the three Corps Commanders, the Divisional Commanders, the Brigadiers, and the officers responsible for transport, artillery, engineer, and the other services. The Army had to be put on an altogether different footing from that which had twice failed to drive the Turks from Gaza. It serves nothing to ignore the fact that the moral of the troops was not high in the weeks following the second failure. They had to be tuned up and trained for a big task. They knew the Turk was turning his natural advantages of ground about Gaza into a veritable fortress, and that if their next effort was to meet with more success than their last, they had to learn all that experience on the Western Front had taught as to systems of trench warfare.

And, more than that, they had to prepare to apply the art of open warfare to the full extent of their powers.

A couple of months before General Allenby took over command, General Chetwode had taken in hand the question of training, and in employing the knowledge gained during the strenuous days he had spent in France and Flanders, he not only won the confidence of the troops but improved their tone, and by degrees brought them up to something approaching the level of the best fighting divisions of our Army in France.

This was hard work during hot weather when our trench systems on a wide front had to be prepared against an active enemy, and men could ill be spared for the all–important task of training behind the front line. It was not long, however, before troops who had got

18

into that state of lassitude which is engendered by a belief that they were settling down to trench warfare for the duration of the war—that, in fact, there was a stalemate on this front—became inspired by the energy of General Chetwode. They saw him in the front line almost every day, facing the risks they ran themselves, complimenting them on any good piece of work, suggesting improvements in their defences, always anxious to provide anything possible for their comfort, and generally looking after the rank and file with a detailed attention which no good battalion commander could exceed.

The men knew that the long visits General Chetwode paid them formed but a small part of his daily task. It has been said that a G.O.C. of a force has to think one hour a day about operations and five hours about beef. In East Force, as this part of the Egyptian Expeditionary Force was then called, General Chetwode, having to look months ahead, had also six worrying hours a day to think about water. For any one who did not love his profession, or who had not an ardent soldierly spirit within him, such a daily task would have been impossible. I had the privilege of living in General Chetwode's camp for some time, and I have seen him working at four o'clock in the morning and at nine o'clock at night, and the notes on a writing tablet by the side of his rough camp–bed showed that in the hours when sleep forsook him he was planning the next day's work.

His staff was entirely composed of hard workers, and perhaps no command in this war ever had so small a staff, but there was no officer in East Force who laboured so long or with such concentration and energy and determination as its Chief. This enthusiasm was infectious and spread through all ranks. The sick rate declined, septic sores, from which many men suffered through rough life in the desert on Army rations, got better, and the men showed more interest in their work and were keener on their sport. The full effects had not been wholly realised when the War Cabinet selected General Allenby for the control of the big operations, but the improvement in the condition of the troops was already most marked, and when General Allenby arrived and at once directed that General Headquarters should be moved from Cairo, which was pleasant but very far away from the front, to Kelab, near Khan Yunus, there was not a man who did not see in the new order of things a sign that he was to be given a chance of testing the Briton's supremacy over the Turk.

The improvement in the moral of the troops, the foundations of which were thus begun and cemented by General Chetwode, was rapidly carried on under the new Chief. Divisions like the 52nd, 53rd, and 54th, which had worked right across the desert from

19

the Suez Canal, toiling in a torrid temperature, when parched throats, sun–blistered limbs, and septic sores were a heavy trial, weakened by casualties in action and sickness, were brought up to something like strength. Reinforcing drafts joined a lot of cheery veterans. They were taught in the stern field of experience what was expected of them, and they worked themselves up to the degree of efficiency of the older men.

The 74th Division, made up of yeomanry regiments which had been doing excellent service in the Libyan Desert, watching for and harassing the elements of the Senussi Army, had to be trained as infantry. These yeomen did not take long to make themselves first–rate infantry, and when, after the German attack on the Somme in March 1918, they went away from us to strengthen the Western Front, a distinguished General told me he believed that man for man the 74th would prove the finest division in France. They certainly proved themselves in Palestine, and many an old yeomanry regiment won for itself the right to bear 'Jerusalem, 1917' on its standard.

The 75th Division had brought some of the Wessex Territorials from India with two battalions of Gurkhas and two of Rifles. The 1/4th Duke of Cornwall's Light Infantry joined it from Aden, but for some months the battalion was not itself. It had spent a long time at that dreary sunburnt outpost of the Empire, and the men did not regain their physical fitness till close upon the time it was required for the Gaza operations.

The 60th Division came over from Salonika and we were delighted to have them, for they not only gave us General Bulfin as the XXIst Corps Commander, but set an example of efficiency and a combination of dash and doggedness which earned for them a record worthy of the best in the history of the great war. These London Territorials were second–line men, men recruited from volunteers in the early days of the war, when the County of London Territorial battalions went across to France to take a part on a front hard pressed by German legions. The 60th Division men had rushed forward to do their duty before the Derby scheme or conscription sought out the cream of Britain's manhood, and no one had any misgivings about that fine cheery crowd.

The 10th Division likewise came from Salonika. Unfortunately it had been doing duty in a fever–stricken area and malaria had weakened its ranks. A little while before the autumn operations began, as many as 3000 of its men were down at one time with malaria, but care and tonic of the battle pulled the ranks together, and the Irish Division, a purely Irish division, campaigned up to the glorious traditions of their race. They worked like gluttons with rifle and spade, and their pioneer work on roads in the Judean hills will always be remembered with gratitude.

The cavalry of the Desert Mounted Corps were old campaigners in the East. The Anzac Mounted Division, composed of six regiments of Australian Light Horse and three regiments of New Zealand Mounted Rifles, had been operating in the Sinai Desert when they were not winning fame on Gallipoli, since the early days of the war. They had proved sterling soldiers in the desert war, hard, full of courage, capable of making light of the longest trek in waterless stretches of country, and mobile to a degree the Turks never dreamed of. There were six other regiments of Australian Light Horse and three first–line regiments of yeomanry in the Australian Mounted Division, and nine yeomanry regiments in the Yeomanry Mounted Division. The 7th Mounted Brigade was attached to Desert Corps, as was also the Imperial Camel Corps Brigade, formed of yeomen and Australians who had volunteered from their regiments for work as camelry. They, too, were veterans.

All these divisions had to be trained hard. Not only had the four infantry divisions of XXth Corps to be brought to a pitch of physical fitness to enable them to endure a considerable period of open fighting, but they had to be trained in water abstinence, as, in the event of success, they would unquestionably have long marches in a country yielding a quite inadequate supply of drinking water, and this problem in itself was such that fully 6000 camels were required to carry drinking water to infantry alone. Water–abstinence training lasted three weeks, and the maximum of half a gallon a man for all purposes was not exceeded, simply because the men had been made accustomed to deny themselves drink except when absolutely necessary. But for a systematic training they would have suffered a great deal. The disposition of the force is given in the Appendix.[1]

[Footnote 1: See Appendix v].

CHAPTER V. RAILWAYS, ROADS, AND THE BASE

To ease the supply problem a spur line was laid from Rafa to Shellal, on the wadi Ghuzze. In that way supplies, stores, and ammunition were taken up to our right flank. Shellal was a position of great strategic importance. At one time it appeared as if we should have to fight hard to gain it. The Turks had cut an elaborate series of trenches on

How Jerusalem Was Won

Wali Sheikh Nuran, a hill covering Shellal, but they evacuated this position before we made the first attack on Gaza, and left an invaluable water supply in our hands.

At Shellal the stony bed of the wadi Ghuzze rests between high mud banks which have been cut into fantastic shapes by the rushing waters descending from the southern extremities of the Judean range of hills during the winter rains. In the summer months, when the remainder of the wadi bed is dry, there are bubbling springs of good water at Shellal, and these have probably been continuously flowing for many centuries, for close above the spot where the water issues Anzac cavalry discovered a beautiful remnant of the mosaic flooring of an ancient Christian church, which, raised on a hundred–feet mound, was doubtless the centre of a colony of Christians, hundreds of years before Crusaders were attracted to the Holy Land. Our engineers harnessed that precious flow. A dam was put across the wadi bed and at least a million gallons of crystal water were held up by it, whilst the overflow went into shallow pools fringed with grass (a delightfully refreshing sight in that arid country) from which horses were watered. Pumping sets were installed at the reservoir and pipes were laid towards Karm, and from these the Camel Transport Corps were to fill fanatis—eight to twelve gallon tanks—for carriage of water to troops on the move.

The railway staff, the department which arranged the making up and running of trains, as well as the construction staff, had heavy responsibilities. It was recognised early in 1917 that if we were to crush the Turk out of the war, provision would have to be made for a larger army than a single line from the Suez Canal could feed. It was decided to double the track. The difficulties of the Director of Railway Transport were enormous. There was great shortage of railway material all over the world. Some very valuable cargoes were lost through enemy action at sea, and we had to call for more from different centres, and England deprived herself of rolling stock she badly needed, to enable her flag of freedom to be carried (though it was not to be hoisted) through the Holy Land. And incidentally I may remark that, with the solitary exception of a dirty little piece of Red Ensign I saw flying in the native quarter in Jerusalem, the only British flag the people saw in Palestine and Syria was a miniature Union Jack carried on the Commander–in–Chief's motor car and by his standard–bearer when riding. Thus did the British Army play the game, for some of the Allied susceptibilities might have been wounded if the people had been told (though indeed they knew it) that they were under the protection of the British flag. They had the most convincing evidence, however, that they were under the staunch protection of the British Army. The doubling of the railway track went on apace. To save pressure at the Alexandria docks and on the Egyptian State railway, which, giving some of its rolling stock and, I think, the whole of its reserve of material for the use of the military line east of the Canal, was worked to its utmost capacity, and also to economise money by saving railway freights, wharves were built on the Canal at Kantara, and as many as six ocean–going steamers could be unloaded there at one time. By and by a railway bridge was thrown over the Canal, and when the war was over through trains could be run from Cairo to Jerusalem and Haifa. Kantara grew into a wonderful town with several miles of Canal frontage, huge railway sidings and workshops, enormous stores of rations for man and horse, medical supplies, ordnance and ammunition dumps, etc. Probably the enemy knew all about this vast base. Any one on any ship passing through the Canal could see the place, and it is surprising, and it certainly points to a lack of enterprise on the part of the Germans, that no attempt was made to bomb Kantara by the super–Zeppelin which in November 1917 left its Balkan base and got as far south as the region of Khartoum on its way to East Africa, before being recalled by wireless. This same Zeppelin was seen about forty miles from Port Said and a visit by it was anticipated. Aeroplanes with experienced pilots and armed with the latest anti–Zeppelin devices were stationed at Port Said and Aboukir ready to ascend on any moonlight night when the hum of aerial motor machinery could be heard. The super–Zeppelin never came and Kantara's progress was unchecked.

The doubled railway track was laid as far as El Arish by the time operations commenced, and this was a great aid to the railway staff. Every engine and truck was used to its fullest capacity, and an enormous amount of time was saved by the abolition of passing stations for some ninety miles of the line's length. Railhead was at Deir el Belah, about eight miles short of Gaza, and here troops and an army of Egyptian labourers were working night and day, week in week out, off–loading trucks with a speed that enabled the maximum amount of service to be got out of rolling stock. There were large depots down the line too. At Rafa there was a big store of ammunition, and at Shellal large quantities not only of supplies but of railway material were piled up in readiness for pushing out railhead immediately the advance began. A Decauville, or light, line ran out towards Gamli from Shellal to make the supply system easier, and I remember seeing some Indian pioneers lay about three miles of light railway with astonishing rapidity the day after we took Beersheba. Every mile the line advanced meant time saved in getting up supplies, and the radius of action of lorries, horse, and camel transport was considerably increased.

23

How Jerusalem Was Won

To supply the Gaza front we called in aid a small system of light railways. From the railhead at Deir el Belah to the mouth of the wadi Ghuzze, and from that point along the line of the wadi to various places behind the line held by us, we had a total length of 21 kilometres of light railway. Before this railway got into full operation horses had begun to lose condition, and during the summer ammunition–column officers became very anxious about their horses. The light railway was almost everywhere within range of the enemy's guns, and in some places it was unavoidably exposed, particularly where it ran on the banks of the wadi due south of Gaza. I recollect while the track was being laid speaking to an Australian in charge of a gang of natives preparing an earthwork, and asked why it was that a trench was dug before earth was piled up. He pointed to the hill of Ali Muntar, the most prominent feature in the enemy's system, and said that from the Turks' observation post on that eminence every movement of the labourers could be seen, and the men were often forced by gunfire to the refuge of the trenches.

When the railway was in running order trains had to run the gauntlet of shell–fire on this section on bright moonlight nights, and no camouflage could hide them. But they worked through in a marvellously orderly and efficient fashion, and on one day when our guns were hungry this little line carried 850 tons of ammunition to the batteries. The horses became fit and strong and were ready for the war to be carried into open country. In christening their tiny puffing locomotives the Tommy drivers showed their strong appreciation of their comrades on the sea, and the 'Iron Duke' and 'Lion' were always tuned up to haul a maximum load. But the pride of the engine yard was the 'Jerusalem Cuckoo'—some prophetic eye must have seen its future employment on the light line between Jerusalem and Ramallah—though in popularity it was run close by the 'Bulfin–ch,' a play upon the name of the Commander of the XXIst Corps, for which it did sterling service.

The Navy formed part of the picture as well. Some small steamers of 1000 to 1500 tons burden came up from Port Said to a little cove north of Belah to lighten the railway's task. They anchored about 150 yards off shore and a crowd of boats passed backwards and forwards with stores. These were carried up the beach to trucks on a line connected with the supply depots, and if you wished to see a busy scene where slackers had no place the Belah beach gave it you. The Army tried all sorts of boatmen and labourers. There were Kroo boys who found the Mediterranean waters a comparative calm after the turbulent surf on their own West African shore. The Maltese were not a success. The Egyptians were, both here and almost everywhere else where their services were called for. The best of all the fellows on this beach, however, were the Raratongas from the Cook Islands, the islands from which the Maoris originally came. They were first employed at El Arish, where they made it a point of honour to get a job done well and quickly, and, on a given day, it was found that thirty of them had done as much labourers' work as 170 British soldiers. They were men of fine physical strength and endurance, and some one who knew they had the instincts of sportsmen, devised a simple plan to get the best out of them. He presented a small flag to be won each day by the crew accomplishing the best work with the boats. The result was amazing. Every minute the boats were afloat the Raratongas strained their muscles to win the day's competition, and when the day's task was ended the victorious crew marched with their flag to their camp, singing a weird song and as proud as champions. Some Raratongas worked at ammunition dumps, and it was the boast of most of them that they could carry four 60–pounder shells at a time. A few of these stalwart men from Southern Seas received a promotion which made them the most envied men of their race—they became loading numbers in heavy howitzer batteries, fighting side by side with the Motherland gunners.

However well the Navy and all associated with it worked, only a very small proportion of the Army's supplies was water borne. The great bulk had to be carried by rail. Enormously long trains, most of them hauled by London and South–Western locomotives, bore munitions, food for men and animals, water, equipment, medical comforts, guns, wagons, caterpillar tractors, motor cars, and other paraphernalia required for the largest army which had ever operated about the town of Gaza in the thousands of years of its history. The main line had thrown out from it great tentacles embracing in their iron clasp vital centres for the supply of our front, and over these spur lines the trains ran with the regularity of British main–line expresses. Besides 96,000 actual fighting men, there was a vast army of men behind the line, and there were over 100,000 animals to be fed. There were 46,000 horses, 40,000 camels, 15,000 mules, and 3500 donkeys on Army work east of the Canal, and not a man or beast went short of rations. We used to think Kitchener's advance on Khartoum the perfection of military organisation. Beside the Palestine expedition that Soudan campaign fades into insignificance. In fighting men and labour corps, in animals and the machinery of war, this Army was vastly larger and more important, and the method by which it was brought to Palestine and was supplied, and the low sick rate, constitute a tribute to the master minds of the organisers. The Army had fresh meat, bread, and vegetables in a country which under the lash of war yielded nothing, but which under our rule in peace will furnish three times the produce of the best of past years of plenty.

How Jerusalem Was Won

A not inconsiderable portion of the front line was supplied with Nile water taken from a canal nearly two hundred miles away. But the Army once at the front depended less upon the waters of that Father of Rivers than it had to do in the long trek across the desert. Then all drinking water came from the Nile. It flowed down the sweet–water canal (if one may be pardoned for calling 'sweet' a volume of water so charged with vegetable matter and bacteria that it was harmful for white men even to wash in it), was filtered and siphoned under the Suez Canal at Kantara, where it was chlorinated, and passed through a big pipe line and pumped through in stages into Palestine. The engineers set about improving all local resources over a wide stretch of country which used to be regarded as waterless in summer. Many water levels were tapped, and there was a fair yield. The engineers' greatest task in moving with the Army during the advance was always the provision of a water supply, and in developing it they conferred on the natives a boon which should make them be remembered with gratitude for many generations.

In the months preceding our attack Royal Engineers were also concerned in improving the means of communication between railway depots and the front line. Before our arrival in this part of Southern Palestine, wheeled traffic was almost unknown among the natives. There was not one metalled roadway, and only comparatively light loads could be transported in wheeled vehicles. The soil between Khan Yunus and Deir el Belah, especially on the west of our railway line, was very sandy, and after the winter rains had knitted it together it began to crumble under the sun's heat, and it soon cut up badly when two or three limbers had passed over it. The sandy earth was also a great nuisance in the region between Khan Yunus and Shellal, but between Deir el Belah and our Gaza front, excepting on the belt near the sea which was composed of hillocks of sand precisely similar to the Sinai Desert, the earth was firmer and yielded less to the grinding action of wheels. For ordinary heavy military traffic the engineers made good going by taking off about one foot of the top soil and banking it on either side of the road. These tracks lasted very well, but they required constant attention. Ambulances and light motor cars had special arrangements made for them. Hundreds of miles of wire netting were laid on sand in all directions, and these wire roads, which, stretching across bright golden sand, appeared like black bands to observers in aircraft, at first aroused much curiosity among enemy airmen, and it was not until they had made out an ambulance convoy on the move that they realised the purpose of the tracks.

The rabbit wire roads were a remarkable success. Motor wheels held firmly to the surface, and when the roads were in good condition cars could travel at high speed. Three or four widths of wire netting were laced together, laid on the sand and pegged down. After a time loose pockets of sand could not resist the weight of wheels and there became many holes beneath the wire, and the jolting was a sore trial alike to springs and to a passenger's temper. But here again constant attention kept the roads in order, and if one could not describe travelling over them as easy and comfortable they were at least sure, and one could be certain of getting to a destination at an average speed of twelve miles an hour. In sand the Ford cars have performed wonderful feats, but remarkable as was the record of that cheap American car with us—it helped us very considerably to win the war—you could never tell within hours how long a journey would take off the wire roads. Once leave the netting and you might with good luck and a skilful driver get across the sand without much trouble, but it often meant much bottom–gear work and a hot engine, and not infrequently the digging out of wheels. The drivers used to try to keep to the tracks made by other cars. These were never straight, and the swing from side to side reminded you of your first ride on a camel's back. The wire roads were a great help to us, and the officer who first thought out the idea received our daily blessings. I do not know who he was, but I was told the wire road scheme was the outcome of a device suggested by a medical officer at Romani in 1916, when infantry could not march much more than six miles a day through the sand. This officer made a sort of wire moccasin which he attached to the boot and doubled the marching powers of the soldier. A sample of those moccasins should find a place in our War Museum.

CHAPTER VI. PREPARING FOR 'ZERO DAY'

About the middle of August it was the intention that the attack on the Turks' front line in Southern Palestine should be launched some time in September. General Allenby knew his force would not be then at full strength, but what was happening at other points in the Turkish theatres of operations might make it necessary to strike an early blow at Gaza to spoil enemy plans elsewhere. However, it was soon seen that a September advance was not absolutely necessary. General Allenby decided that instead of making an early attack it would be far more profitable to wait until his Army had been improved by a longer period of training, and until he had got his artillery, particularly some of his heavy batteries, into a high state of efficiency. He would risk having to take Jerusalem after bad weather had set in rather than be unable, owing to the condition of his troops, to exploit an initial success to the fullest extent. How wholly justified was this decision the subsequent fighting proved, and it is doubtful if there was ever a more complete

How Jerusalem Was Won

illustration of the wisdom of those directing war policy at home submitting to the cool, balanced calculations of the man on the spot. The extra six weeks spent in training and preparation were of incalculable service to the Allies. I have heard it said that a September victory in Palestine would have had its reflex on the Italian front, and that the Caporetto disaster would not have assumed the gigantic proportions which necessitated the withdrawal to Italy of British and French divisions from the Western Front and prevented Cambrai being a big victory. That is very doubtful. On the contrary, a September battle in Palestine before we were fully ready to follow the Turks after breaking and rolling up their line, even if we had succeeded in doing this completely, might have deprived us of the moral effect of the capture of Jerusalem and of the wonderful influence which that victory had on the whole civilised world by reason of the sacrifices the Commander—in—Chief made to prevent any fighting at all in the precincts of the Holy City. Of this I shall speak later, giving the fullest details at my command, for there is no page in the story of British arms which better upholds the honour and chivalry of the soldier than the preservation of the Holy Place from the clash of battle.

That last six weeks of preparation were unforgettable. The London newspapers I had the honour to represent as War Correspondent knew operations were about to begin, but I did not cable or mail them one word which would give an indication that big things were afoot. They never asked for news, but were content to wait till they could tell the public that victory was ours. In accordance with their practice throughout the war the London Press set an example to the world by refraining from publishing anything which would give information of the slightest value to the enemy. It was a privilege to see that victory in the making. Some divisions which had allotted to them the hardest part of the attack on Beersheba were drawn out of the line, and forming up in big camps between Belah and Shellal set about a course of training such as athletes undergo. They had long marches in the sand carrying packs and equipment. They were put on a short allowance of water, except for washing purposes. They dug, they had bombing practice, and with all this extra exercise while the days were still very hot they needed no encouragement to continue their games. Football was their favourite sport, and the British Tommy is such a remarkable fellow that it was usual to see him trudge home to camp looking 'fed up' with exercise, and then, after throwing off his pack and tunic, run out to kick a ball. The Italian and French detachments used to look at him in astonishment, and doubtless they thought his enthusiasm for sport was a sore trial. He got thoroughly fit for marches over sand, over stony ground, over shifting shingle. During the period of concentration he had to cross a district desperately bad for marching, and it is more than probable the enemy never believed him capable of such endurance. He was often tired, no doubt, but he always got to his destination, was rarely footsore, and laughed at the worst parts of his journey. The sand was choking, the flies were an irritating pest, equipment became painfully heavy; but a big, brave heart carried Tommy through his training to a state of perfect condition for the heavy test.

To enable about two–thirds of the force to carry on a moving battle while the remainder kept half the enemy pinned down to his trench system on his right–centre and right, it was necessary to reinforce strongly the transport service for our mobile columns. The XXIst Corps gave up most of its lorries, tractors, and camels to XXth Corps. These had to be moved across from the Gaza sector to our right as secretly as possible, and they were not brought up to load at the supply depots at Shellal and about Karm until the moment they were required to carry supplies for the corps moving to attack.

It is not easy to convey to any one who has not seen an army on the move what a vast amount of transport is required to provision two corps. In France, where roads are numerous and in comparatively good condition, the supply problem could be worked out to a nicety, but in a roadless country where there was not a sound half–mile of track, and where water had to be developed and every gallon was precious, the question of supply needed most anxious consideration, and a big margin had to be allowed for contingencies. It will give some idea of the requirements when I state that for the supply of water alone the XXth Corps had allotted to it 6000 camels and 73 lorries. To feed these water camels alone needed a big convoy.

We got an impression of the might and majesty of an army in the field as we saw it preparing to take the offensive. The camp of General Headquarters where I was located was situated north of Rafa. The railway ran on two sides of the camping ground, one line going to Belah and the other stretching out to Shellal, where everything was in readiness to extend the iron road to the north–east of Karm, on the plain which, because the Turks enjoyed complete observation over it, had hitherto been No Man's Land. We saw and heard the traffic on this section of the line. It was enormous. Heavily laden trains ran night and day with a mass of stores and supplies, with motor lorries, cars, and tractors; and the ever–increasing volume of traffic told those of us who knew nothing of the date of 'Zero day' that it was not far off. The heaviest trains seemed to run at night, and the returning empty trains were hurried forward at a speed suggesting the urgency of clearing the line for a fully loaded train awaiting at Rafa the signal to proceed with its valuable load to railhead. Perfect control not only on the railway system but in the forward supply yards prevented congestion, and when a train arrived at its destination and was split up into several parts, well–drilled gangs of troops and Egyptian labourers were allotted to each truck, and whether a lorry or a tractor had to be unshipped and moved down a ramp, or a truck had to be relieved of its ten tons of tibbin, boxes of biscuit and bully, or of engineers' stores, the goods were cleared away from the vicinity of the line with a celerity which a goods–yard foreman at home would have applauded as the smartest work he had ever seen. There was no room for slackers in the Army, and the value of each truck was so high that it could not be left standing idle for an hour. The organisation was equally good at Kantara, where the loading and making up of trains had to be arranged precisely as the needs at the front demanded. Those remarkable haulers, the caterpillar tractors, cut many a passage through the sand, tugging heavy guns and ammunition, stores for the air and signal services, machinery for engineers and mobile workshops, and sometimes towing a weighty load of petrol to satisfy their voracious appetites for that fuel. The tractors did well. Sand was no trouble to them, and when mud marooned lorries during the advance in November the rattling, rumbling old tractor made fair weather of it. The mechanical transport trains will not forget the service of the tractors on the morning after Beersheba was taken. From railhead to the spot where Father Abraham and his people fed their flocks the country was bare and the earth's crust had yielded all its strength under the influence of the summer sun. Loaded lorries under their own power could not move more than a few yards before they were several inches deep in the sandy soil, but a Motor Transport officer devised a plan for beating down a track which all lorries could use. He got a tractor to haul six unladen lorries, and with all the vehicles using their own power the tractor managed to pull them through to Beersheba, leaving behind some wheel tracks with a hard foundation. A hundred lorries followed, the drivers steering them in the ruts, and they made such good progress that by the afternoon they had deposited between 200 and 300 tons of supplies in Beersheba. The path the tractor cut did not last very long, but it was sound enough for the immediate and pressing requirements of the Army.

Within a month of his arrival in Egypt, General Allenby had visited the whole of his front line and had decided the form his offensive should take. As soon as his force had been made up to seven infantry divisions and the Desert Mounted Corps, and they had been brought up to strength and trained, he would attack, making his main offensive against the enemy's left flank while conducting operations vigorously and on an extensive scale against the Turkish right–centre and right. The principal operation against the left was to be conducted by General Chetwode's XXth Corps, consisting of four infantry divisions and the Imperial Camel Brigade, and by General Chauvel's Desert Mounted Corps. General Bulfin's XXIst Corps was to operate against Gaza and the Turkish right–centre south–east of that ancient town. If the situation became such as to make it necessary to take the offensive before the force had been brought up to strength, the XXIst Corps would have had to undertake its task with only two divisions, but in those circumstances its operations were to be limited to demonstrations and raids. By throwing forward his right, the XXIst Corps Commander was to pin the enemy down in the Atawineh district, and on the left he would move against the south–western defences of Gaza so as to lead the Turks to suppose an attack was to come in this sector. That movement being made, the XXth Corps and Desert Mounted Corps were to advance against Beersheba, and, having taken it, to secure the valuable water supply which was known to have existed there since Abraham dug the well of the oath which gave its name to the town. Because of water difficulties it was considered vital that Beersheba should be captured in one day, a formidable undertaking owing to the situation of the town, the high entrenched hills around it and the long marches for cavalry and infantry before the attack; and in drawing up the scheme based on the Commander-in-Chief's plan, the commanders of XXth Corps and Desert Mounted Corps had always to work on the assumption that Beersheba would be in their hands by nightfall of the first day of the attack. General Barrow's Yeomanry Mounted Division was to remain at Shellal in the gap between XXth Corps and XXIst Corps in case the enemy should attempt to attack the XXth Corps' left flank. Having dealt with the enemy in Beersheba, General Chetwode with mounted troops protecting his right was to move north and north–west against the enemy's left flank, to drive him from his strong positions at Sheria and Hareira, enveloping his left flank and striking it obliquely.

While the XXth Corps was moving against this section of the enemy line, Desert Mounted Corps was to bring up the mounted division left at Shellal, and passing behind the XXth Corps to march on Nejile, where there was an excellent water supply, and the wadi Hesi, so as to threaten the left rear and the line of retreat of the Turkish Army.

It was always doubtful whether XXth Corps would be able to close up the gap between it and the XXIst Corps owing to the length of its marches and the distance it was from railhead, and the scheme therefore provided that the XXIst Corps should confirm successes gained on our right by forcing its way through the tremendously strong Gaza position to the line of the wadi Hesi and joining up with Desert Mounted Corps. A considerable number of XXth Corps troops would then return to the neighbourhood of railhead and release the greater part of its transport for the infantry of XXIst Corps moving up the Maritime Plain.

This, in summary form, was the scheme General Allenby planned before the middle of August, and though the details were not, and could not be, worked out until a couple of months had passed, it is noteworthy as showing that, notwithstanding the moves an enterprising enemy had at his command in a country where positions were entirely favourable to him, where he had water near at hand, where the transport of supplies was never so serious a problem for him as for us when we got on the move, and where he could make us fight almost every step of the way, the Commander–in–Chief foresaw and provided for every eventuality, and his scheme worked out absolutely and entirely 'according to plan,' to use the favourite phrase of the German High Command.

When the Corps Commanders began working out the details two of the greatest problems were transport and water. Only patience and skilful development of known sources of supply would surmount the water difficulty, and we had to wait till the period of concentration before commencing its solution. But to lighten the transport load which must have weighed heavily on Corps Staffs, the Commander–in–Chief agreed to allow the extension of the railway east of Shellal to be begun sooner than he had provided for. It was imperative that railway construction should not give the enemy an indication of our intentions. If he had realised the nature and scope of our preparations he would have done something to counteract them and to deny us that element of surprise which exerted so great an influence on the course of the battle. General Allenby, however, was willing to take some risks to simplify supply difficulties, and he ordered that the extension to a railway station north–east of Karm should be completed by the evening of the third day before the attack, that a Decauville line from Gamli, not to be begun before the sixth day prior to the attack, was to be completed to Karm by the day preceding the opening of the fighting at Beersheba, and that a new Decauville line should be started at Karm when fighting had begun, and should be carried nearly three miles in the Beersheba direction early on the following morning. These new lines, though of short length, were an inestimable boon to the conductors of supply trains. The new railheads both of the standard gauge and light lines were well placed, and they not only saved time and shortened the journeys of camel convoys and lorry transport columns, but prevented congestion at depots in one central spot.

How Jerusalem Was Won

A big effort was made to escape detection by enemy aircraft. For the first time since the Egyptian Expeditionary Force took the field we had obtained mastery in the air. On the 8th and 15th October two enemy planes were shot down behind our lines, and the keenness of our airmen for combat made the German aviators extremely careful. They had been bold and resolute, taking their observations several thousand feet higher than our pilots, it is true, but neither anti−aircraft fire nor the presence of our machines in the air had up to this time deterred them. However, just at the moment when airwork was of extreme importance to the Turks, the German flying men, recognising that our pilots had new battle planes and were full of resource and daring, showed an unusual lack of enterprise, and we profited from their inactivity. The concentration of the force in the positions from which it was to attack Beersheba was to have taken seven days, but owing to the difficulties attending the development of water at Asluj and Khalasa the time was extended to ten days. During this period the uppermost thought of commanders was to conceal their movements. All marching was done at night and no move of any kind was permitted till nearly six o'clock in the evening, when enemy aircraft were usually at rest and the light was sufficiently dull to prevent the Fritzes seeing much if they had made an exceptionally late excursion. All the tents and temporary shelters which had been occupied for weeks were left standing. Cookhouses, horse lines, canteens, and so on were untouched, and one had an eerie feeling in passing at night through these untenanted camping grounds, deserted and lifeless, and a prey to the jackal and pariah dog. A vast area of many square miles which had held tens of thousands of troops and animals almost became a wilderness again, and the few natives hereabouts who had made large profits from the sale of eggs, fruit, and vegetables looked disconsolate and bewildered at the change, hoping and believing that the empty tents merely denoted a temporary absence. But the great majority of the Army never came that way again.

When the infantry started on the march, divisions and brigades had allotted to them particular areas for their march routes, and all over that country, where scarcely a tree or native hut existed to make a landmark, there were dotted small arrow−pointed boards with the direction 'A road,' 'B road,' 'Z road,' as the case might be. Marching in the dark hours when a refreshing air succeeded the heat of the day, the troops halted as soon as a purple flush threw into high relief the southern end of the Judean hills, and they hid themselves in the wadis and broken ground; and on one unit vacating a bivouac area it was occupied by another, thus making the areas in which the troops rested as few as possible.

The concentration was worked to a time–table. Not only were brigades allotted certain marches each night, but they were given specified times to cover certain distances, and these were arranged according to the condition of the ground. In parts it was very broken and covered with loose stones, and the pace of infantry by night was very slightly more than one mile per hour. The routes for guns were not chosen until the whole country had been reconnoitred, and it was a highly creditable performance for artillery to get their field guns and heavy howitzer batteries through to the time–table. But the clockwork precision of the movements reflected even more highly on the staff working out the details than on the infantry and artillery, and it may be said with perfect truth that the staff made no miscalculation or mistake. The XXth Corps staff maps and plans, and the details accompanying them, were masterpieces of clearness and completeness. The men who fought out the plans to a triumphant finish were glad to recognise this perfection of staff work.[1]

[Footnote 1: See Appendix VI.]

CHAPTER VII. THE BEERSHEBA VICTORY

The XXth Corps began its movement on the night of 20–21st October. The whole Corps was not on the march, but a sufficient force was sent forward to form supply dumps and to store water at Esani for troops covering Desert Mounted Corps engineers engaged on the development of water at Khalasa and Asluj. Some of the Australian and New Zealand troops engaged on this work had previously been at these places.

In the early summer it was thought desirable to destroy the Turkish railway which ran from Beersheba to Asluj and on to Kossaima, in order to prevent an enemy raid on our communications between El Arish and Rafa, and the mounted troops with the Imperial Camel Corps had had a most successful day in destroying many miles of line and several bridges. The Turks were badly in need of rails for the line they were then constructing down to Deir Sineid, and they had lifted some of the rails between Asluj and Kossaima, but during our raid we broke every rail over some fifteen miles of track. Khalasa and Asluj being water centres became the points of concentration for two mounted divisions, and the splendid Colonials in the engineer sections worked at the wells as if the success of the whole enterprise depended upon their efforts, as, indeed, to a very large extent it did. Theirs was not an eight hours day. They worked under many difficulties, often thigh deep in water and mud, cleaning out and deepening wells and installing power pumps, putting up large canvas tanks for storage, and making water troughs. The results exceeded anticipations, and the Commander–in–Chief, on a day when the calls on his time were many and urgent, made a long journey to thank the officers and men for the work they had done and to express his high appreciation of their skill and energy.

The principal work carried out by the XXth Corps during the period of concentration consisted in laying the standard gauge line to Imara and opening the station at that place on October 28; prolonging the railway line to a point three–quarters of a mile north–north–east of Karm, where the station was opened on November 3; completing by October 30 the light railway from the east bank of the wadi Ghuzze at Gamli *via* Karm to Khasif; and developing water at Esani, Malaga, and Abu Ghalyun for the use first by cavalry detachments and then by the 60th Division. Cisterns in the Khasif and Imsiri area were stocked with 60,000 gallons of water to be used by the 53rd and 74th Divisions, and this supply was to be supplemented by camel convoys. Apparently the enemy knew very little about the concentration until about October 26, and even then he could have had only slight knowledge of the extent of our movements, and probably knew nothing at all of where the first blow was to fall. In the early hours of October 27 he did make an attempt to interfere with our concentration, and there was a spirited little action on our outpost line which had been pushed out beyond the plain to a line of low hills near the wadi Hanafish. The Turks in overwhelming force met a most stubborn defence by the Middlesex Yeomanry, and if the enemy took these London yeomen as an average sample of General Allenby's troops, this engagement must have given them a foretaste of what was in store for them.

The Middlesex Yeomanry (the 1st County of London Yeomanry, to give the regiment the name by which it is officially known, though the men almost invariably use the much older Territorial title) and the 21st Machine Gun Squadron, held the long ridge from El Buggar to hill 630. There was a squadron dismounted on hill 630, three troops on hill 720, the next and highest point on the ridge, and a post at El Buggar. At four o'clock in the morning the latter post was fired on by a Turkish cavalry patrol, and an hour later it was evident that the enemy intended to try to drive us off the ridge, his occupation of which would have given him the power to harass railway construction parties by shell–fire, even if it did not entirely stop the work. Some 3000 Turkish infantry, 1200 cavalry, and twelve guns had advanced from the Kauwukah system of defences to attack our outpost line on the ridge. They heavily engaged hill 630, working round both flanks,

35

and brought heavy machine–gun and artillery fire to bear on the squadron holding it. The Royal Flying Corps estimated that a force of 2000 men attacked the garrison, which was completely cut off.

A squadron of the City of London Yeomanry sent to reinforce was held up by a machine–gun barrage and had to withdraw. The garrison held out magnificently all day in a support trench close behind the crest against odds of twenty to one, and repeatedly beat off rushes, although the bodies of dead Turks showed that they got as close as forty yards from the defenders. Two officers were wounded, and four other ranks killed and twelve wounded.

The attack on hill 720 was made by 1200 cavalry supported by a heavy volume of shell and machine–gun fire. During the early morning two desperate charges were beaten off, but in a third charge the enemy gained possession of the hill after the detachment had held out for six hours. All our officers were killed or wounded and all the men were casualties except three. At six o'clock in the evening the Turks were holding this position in strength against the 3rd Australian Light Horse, but two infantry brigades of the 53rd Division were moving towards the ridge, and during the evening the enemy retired and we held the ridge from this time on quite securely. The strong defence of the Middlesex Yeomanry undoubtedly prevented the Turks establishing themselves on the ridge, and saved the infantry from having to make a night attack which might have been costly. Thereafter the enemy made no attempt to interfere with the concentration. The yeomanry losses in this encounter were 1 officer and 23 other ranks killed, 5 officers and 48 other ranks wounded, 2 officers and 8 other ranks missing.

On the night of October 30–31 a brilliant moon lit up the whole country. The day had been very hot, and at sunset an entire absence of wind promised that the night march of nearly 40,000 troops of all arms would be attended by all the discomforts of dust and heat. The thermometer fell, but there was not a breath of wind to shift the pall of dust which hung above the long columns of horse, foot, and guns. Where the tracks were sandy some brigades often appeared to be advancing through one of London's own particular fogs. Men's faces became caked with yellow dust, their nostrils were hot and burning, and parched throats could not be relieved because of the necessity of conserving the water allowance. A hot day was in prospect on the morrow, and the fear of having to fight on an empty water–bottle prevented many a gallant fellow broaching his supply before daybreak. Most of the men had had a long acquaintance with heat in the Middle

East, and the high temperature would have caused them scarcely any trouble if there had been wind to carry away the dust clouds. The cavalry marched over harder and more stony ground than the infantry. They advanced from Khalasa and Asluj a long way south of Beersheba to the east of the town. It was a big night march of some thirty miles, but it was well within the powers of the veterans of the Anzac Mounted Division and Australian Mounted Division, whose men and horses were in admirable condition.

The infantry were ordered to be on their line of deployment by four o'clock on the morning of October 31, and in every case they were before time. There had been many reconnaissances by officers who were to act as guides to columns, and they were quite familiar with the ground; and the guns and ammunition columns were taken by routes which had been carefully selected and marked. In places the banks of wadis had been cut into and ramps made to enable the rough stony watercourses to be practicable for wheels, and, broken as the country was, and though all previous preparations had to be made without arousing the suspicions of Turks and wandering Bedouins, there was no incident to check the progress of infantry or guns. Occasional rifle fire and some shelling occurred during the early hours, but at a little after three A.M. the XXth Corps advanced headquarters had the news that all columns had reached their allotted positions.

The XXth Corps plan was to attack the enemy's works between the Khalasa road and the wadi Saba with the 60th and 74th Divisions, while the defences north of the wadi Saba were to be masked by the Imperial Camel Corps Brigade and two battalions of the 53rd Division, the remainder of the latter division protecting the left flank of the Corps from any attack by enemy troops who might move south from the Sheria area. The first objective was a hill marked on the map as '1070,' about 6000 yards south—west of Beersheba. It was a prominent feature, 500 yards or perhaps a little more from a portion of the enemy's main line, and the Turks held it strongly and were supported by a section of German machine—gunners. We had to win this height in order to get good observation of the enemy's main line of works, and to allow of the advance of field artillery within wire—cutting range of an elaborate system of works protecting Beersheba from an advance from the west. At six the guns began to bombard 1070, and the volume of fire concentrated on that spot must have given the Turks a big surprise. On a front of 4500 yards we had in action seventy—six 18—pounders, twenty 4.5—inch howitzers, and four 3.7—inch howitzers, while eight 60—pounders, eight 6—inch howitzers, and four 4.5—inch howitzers were employed in counter battery work. The absence of wind placed us at a heavy disadvantage. The high explosive shells bursting about the crest of 1070 raised

37

enormous clouds of dust which obscured everything, and after a short while even the flames of exploding shells were entirely hidden from view. The gunners had to stop firing for three–quarters of an hour to allow the dust to settle. They then reopened, and by half–past eight, the wire–cutting being reported completed, an intense bombardment was ordered, under cover of which, and with the assistance of machine–gun fire from aeroplanes, the 181st Infantry Brigade of the 60th Division went forward to the assault. They captured the hill in ten minutes, only sustaining about one hundred casualties, and taking nearly as many prisoners. A German machine–gunner who fell into our hands bemoaned the fact that he had not a weapon left—every one of the machine guns had been knocked out by the artillery, and a number were buried by our fire.

The first phase of the operations having thus ended successfully quite early in the day, the second stage was entered upon. Field guns were rushed forward at the gallop over ground broken by shallow wadis and up and down a very uneven stony surface. The gun teams were generally exposed during the advance and were treated to heavy shrapnel fire, but they swung into action at prearranged points and set about wire–cutting with excellent effect. The first part of the second phase consisted in reducing the enemy's main line from the Khalasa road to the wadi Saba, though the artillery bombarded the whole line. The 60th Division on the right had two brigades attacking and one in divisional reserve, and the 74th Division attacking on the left of the 60th likewise had a brigade in reserve. The 74th, while waiting to advance, came under considerable shell–fire from batteries on the north of the wadi, and it was some time before their fire could be silenced. As a rule the enemy works were cut into rocky, rising ground and the trenches were well enclosed in wire fixed to iron stanchions. They were strongly made and there were possibilities of prolonged opposition, but by the time the big assault was launched the Turks knew they were being attacked on both sides of Beersheba and they must have become anxious about a line of retreat. General Shea reported that the wire in front of him was cut before noon, but General Girdwood was not certain that the wire was sufficiently broken on the 74th Division's front, though he intimated to the Corps Commander that he was ready to attack at the same time as the 60th. It still continued a windless day, and the dust clouds prevented any observation of the wire entanglements. General Girdwood turned this disadvantage to account, and ordering his artillery to raise their fire slightly so that it should fall just in front of and about the trenches, put up what was in effect a dust barrage, and under cover of it selected detachments of his infantry advanced almost into the bursting shell to cut passages through the wire with wire–cutters. The dismounted yeomanry of the 231st and 230th Infantry Brigades rushed through, and by half–past one the 74th Division had secured their objectives. The 179th and 181st Brigades of the 60th Division had won their trenches almost an hour earlier, and about 5000 yards of works were in our hands south of the wadi Saba. The enemy had 3000 yards of trenches north of the wadi, and though these were threatened from the south and west, it was not until five o'clock that the 230th Brigade occupied them, the Turks clearing out during the bombardment. During the day, on the left of the 74th Division, the Imperial Camel Corps Brigade and two battalions of the 53rd Division held the ground to the north of the wadi Saba to a point where the remainder of the 53rd Division watched for the approach of any enemy force from the north, while the 10th Division about Shellal protected the line of communications east of the wadi Ghuzze, and the Yeomanry Mounted Division was on the west side of the wadi Ghuzze in G.H.Q. reserve. The XXth Corps' losses were 7 officers killed and 42 wounded, 129 other ranks killed, 988 wounded and 5 missing, a light total considering the nature of the works carried during the day. It was obvious that the enemy was taken completely by surprise by the direction of the attack, and the rapidity with which we carried his strongest points was overwhelming. The Turk did not attempt anything in the nature of a counter–attack by the Beersheba garrison, nor did he make any move from Hareira against the 53rd Division. Had he done so the 10th Division and the Yeomanry Mounted Division would have seized the opportunity of falling on him from Shellal, and the Turk chose the safer course of allowing the Beersheba garrison to stand unaided in its own defences. The XXth Corps' captures included 25 officers, 394 other ranks, 6 guns, and numerous machine guns.

The Desert Mounted Corps met with stubborn opposition in their operations south–east and east of Beersheba, but they were carried through no less successfully than those of the XXth Corps. The mounted men had had a busy time. General Ryrie's 2nd Australian Light Horse Brigade and the Imperial Camel Corps Brigade had moved southwards on October 2, and on them and on the 1st and 2nd Field Squadrons Australian Engineers the bulk of the work fell of developing water and making and marking tracks which, in the sandy soil, became badly cut up. On the evening of October 30 the Anzac Mounted Division was at Asluj, the Australian Mounted Division at Khalasa, the 7th Mounted Brigade at Esani, Imperial Camel Brigade at Hiseia, and the Yeomanry Mounted Division in reserve at Shellal. The Anzac Division commanded by General Chaytor left Asluj during the night, and in a march of twenty–four miles round the south of Beersheba met with only slight opposition on the way to Bir el Hamam and Bir Salim abu Irgeig, between five and seven miles east of the town. The 2nd Australian Light Horse Brigade during the morning advanced north to take the high hill Tel el Sakaty, a little east of the

How Jerusalem Was Won

Beersheba—Hebron road, which was captured at one o'clock, and the brigade then swept across the metalled road which was in quite fair condition, and which subsequently was of great service to us during the advance of one infantry division on Bethlehem and Jerusalem. The 1st Australian Light Horse Brigade commanded by General Cox, and the New Zealand Mounted Rifles Brigade under General Meldrum, moved against Tel el Saba, a 1000—feet hill which rises very precipitously on the northern bank of the wadi Saba, 4000 yards due east of Beersheba. Tel el Saba is believed to be the original site of Beersheba. It had been made into a strong redoubt and was well held by a substantial garrison adequately dug in and supported by nests of machine—gunners. The right bank of the wadi Khalil was also strongly held, and between the Hebron road and Tel el Saba some German machine—gunners in three houses offered determined opposition. The New Zealanders and a number of General Cox's men crept up the wadi Saba, taking full advantage of the cover offered by the high banks, and formed up under the hill of Saba. They then dashed up the steep sides while the horse artillery lashed the crest with their fire, and driving the Turks from their trenches had captured the hill by three o'clock. At about the same time the 1st Light Horse Brigade suitably dealt with the machine—gunners in the houses. Much ground east of Beersheba had thus been made good, and the Hebron road was denied to the garrison of the town as a line of retreat. The Anzac Mounted Division was then reinforced by General Wilson's 3rd Australian Light Horse Brigade, and by six P.M. the Division held a long crescent of hills from Point 970, a mile north of Beersheba, through Tel el Sakaty, round south—eastwards to Bir el Hamam.

General Hodgson's Australian Mounted Division had a night march of thirty—four miles from Khalasa to Iswawin, south—east of Beersheba, and after the 3rd Light Horse Brigade had been detached to assist the Anzac Division, orders were given to General Grant's 4th Australian Light Horse Brigade to attack and take the town of Beersheba from the east. The orders were received at four o'clock, and until we had got an absolute hold on Tel el Saba an attack on the town from this direction would have been suicidal, as an attacking force would have been between two fires. The shelling of the cavalry during the day had been rather hot, and enemy airmen had occasionally bombed them. It was getting late, and as it was of the greatest importance that the town's available water should be secured that night, General Grant was directed to attack with the utmost vigour. His brigade worthily carried out its orders. The ground was very uneven and was covered with a mass of large stones and shingle. The trenches were well manned and strongly held, but General Grant ordered them to be taken at the gallop. The Australians carried them with an irresistible charge; dismounted, cleared the first line of all the enemy in it, ran on and captured the second and third system of trenches, and then, their horses having been brought up, galloped into the town to prevent any destruction of the wells. The first–line eastern trenches of Beersheba were eight feet deep and four feet wide, and as there were many of the enemy in them they were a serious obstacle to be taken in one rush. This charge was a sterling feat, and unless the town had been occupied that night most, if not all, of the cavalry would have had to withdraw many miles to water, and subsequent operations might have been imperilled. Until we had got Beersheba there appeared small prospect of watering more than two brigades in this area.

Luckily there had been two thunderstorms a few days before the attack, and we found a few pools of sweet water which enabled the whole of the Corps' horses to be watered during the night. These pools soon dried up and the water problem again became serious. The Commander–in–Chief rewarded General Grant with the D.S.O. as an appreciation of his work, and the brigade was gratified at a well–earned honour. The 7th Mounted Brigade was held up for some time in the afternoon by a flanking fire from Ras Ghannam, south of Beersheba, but this was silenced in time to enable the brigade to assist in the occupation of Beersheba at nightfall. The 4th Light Horse Brigade's captures in the charge were 58 officers, 1090 other ranks, and 10 field guns, and the total 'bag' of the Desert Mounted Corps was 70 officers and 1458 other ranks.

The loss of Beersheba was a heavy blow to the Turk. Yet he did not even then realise to the full the significance of our capture of the town. He certainly failed to appreciate that we were to use it as a jumping–off place to attack his main line from Gaza to Sheria by rolling it up from left to right. In this plan there is no doubt that General Allenby entirely deceived his enemy, for in the next few days there was the best of evidence to show that General Kress von Kressenstein believed we were going to advance from Beersheba to Jerusalem up the Hebron road, and he made his dispositions to oppose us here. It was not merely the moral effect of the loss of Beersheba that disturbed the Turks; they had been driven out of a not unimportant stronghold.

All through the many centuries since Abraham and his people led a pastoral life near the wells, Beersheba had been a meanly appointed place. There were no signs as far as I could see of any elaborate ruins to indicate anything larger than a native settlement. Elsewhere we saw crumbling walls of ancient castles and fortresses to tell of conquerors and glories long since faded away, of relics of an age when great captains led martial men into new worlds to conquer, of the time when the Crusading spirit was abroad and the

41

flower of Western chivalry came East to hold the land for Christians. Here the native quarter suggested that trade in Beersheba was purely local and not ambitious, that it provided nothing for the world's commerce save a few skins and hides, and that the inhabitants were content to live the rude, simple lives of their forefathers. But the enterprising German arrived, and you could tell by his work how he intended to compel a change in the unchanging character of the people. He built a handsome Mosque—but before he was driven out he wired and mined it for destruction. He built a seat of government, a hospital, and a barracks, all of them pretentious buildings for such a town, well designed, constructed of stone with red–tiled roofs, and the gardens were nicely laid out. There were a railway station and storehouses on a scale which would not yield a return on capital expenditure for many years, and the water tower and engine sheds were built to last longer than merely military necessities demanded. They were fashioned by European craftsmen, and the solidity of the structures offered strange contrast to the rough–and–ready native houses. The primary object of the Hun scheme was, doubtless, to make Beersheba a suitable base for an attack on the Suez Canal, and the manner of improving the Hebron road, of setting road engineers to construct zigzags up hills so that lorries could move over the road, was part of the plan of men whose vision was centred on cutting the Suez Canal artery of the British Empire's body. The best laid schemes....

When I entered Beersheba our troops held a line of outposts sufficiently far north of the town to prevent the Turks shelling it, and the place was secure except from aircraft bombs, of which a number fell into the town without damaging anything of much consequence. Some of the troops fell victims to booby traps. Apparently harmless whisky bottles exploded when attempts were made to draw the corks, and several small mines went up. Besides the mines in the Mosque there was a good deal of wiring about the railway station, and some rolling stock was made ready for destruction the instant a door was opened. The ruse was expected; some Australian engineers drew the charges, and the coaches were afterwards of considerable service to the supply branch.

CHAPTER VIII. GAZA DEFENCES

Meanwhile there were important happenings at the other end of the line. Gaza was about to submit to the biggest of all her ordeals. She had been a bone of contention for thousands of years. The Pharaohs coveted her and more than 3500 years ago made bloody strife within the environs of the town. Alexander the Great besieged her, and

How Jerusalem Was Won

Persians and Arabians opposed that mighty general. The Ptolemies and the Antiochi for centuries fought for Gaza, whose inhabitants had a greater taste for the mart than for the sword, and when the Maccabees were carrying a victorious war through Philistia, the people of Gaza bought off Jonathan, but the Jews occupied the city itself about a century before the Christian era. Later on the place was captured after a year's siege and destroyed, and for long it remained a mass of mouldering ruins. Pompey revived it, making it a free city, and Gabinius extended it close to the harbour, whilst under Caesar and Herod its prosperity and fame increased. In succeeding centuries Gaza's commerce flourished under the Greeks, who founded schools famous for rhetoric and philosophy, till the Mahomedan wave swept over the land in the first half of the seventh century, when the town became a shadow of its former self, though it continued to exist as a centre for trade. The Crusaders made their influence felt, and many are the traces of their period in this ancient city, but Askalon always had more Crusader support. Napoleon's attack on Gaza found Abdallah's army in a very different state of preparedness from von Kress's Turkish army. Nearly all Abdallah's artillery was left behind in a gun park at Jaffa owing to lack of transport, and though he had a numerically superior force he did not like Napoleon's dispositions, and retreated when Kleber moved up the plain to pass between Gaza and the sea, and the cavalry advanced east of the Mound of Hebron, or Ali Muntar, as we know the hill up which Samson is reputed to have carried the gates and bar of Gaza. For nearly a century and a quarter since Napoleon passed forwards and backwards through the town, Gaza pursued the arts of peace in the lethargic spirit which suits the native temperament, but in eight months of 1917 it was the cockpit of strife in the Middle East, and there was often crammed into one day as much fighting energy as was shown in all the battles of the past thirty–five centuries, Napoleon's campaign included.

Fortunately after the battles of March and April nearly all the civilian population left the town for quieter quarters. Some of them on returning must have had difficulty in identifying their homes. In the centre of the town, where bazaars radiated from the quarter of which the Great Mosque was the hub, the houses were a mass of stones and rubble, and the narrow streets and tortuous byways were filled with fallen walls and roofs. The Great Mosque had entirely lost its beauty. We had shelled it because its minaret, one of those delicately fashioned spires which, seen from a distance, lead a traveller to imagine a native town in the East to be arranged on an artistic and orderly plan, was used as a Turkish observation post, and the Mosque itself as an ammunition store. I am told our guns were never laid on to this objective until there was an accident within it which exploded the ammunition. Be that as it may, there was ample justification

43

for shelling the Mosque. I went in to examine the structure a few hours after the Turks had been compelled to evacuate the town, and whilst they were then shelling it with unpleasant severity. Amid the wrecked marble columns, the broken pulpit, the torn and twisted lamps and crumbling walls were hundreds of thousands of rounds of small–arms ammunition, most of it destroyed by explosion. A great shell had cut the minaret in half and had left exposed telephone wires leading direct to army headquarters and to the Turkish gunners' fire control station. Most of the Mosque furniture and all the carpets had been removed, but a few torn copies of the Koran, some of them in manuscript with marginal notes, lay mixed up with German newspapers and some typical Turkish war propaganda literature. That Mosque, which Saladin seized from the Crusaders and turned from a Christian into a Mahomedan place of worship, was unquestionably used for military purposes, and the Turks cared as little for its religious character or its venerable age as they did for the mosque on Nebi Samwil, where the remains of the Prophet Samuel are supposed to rest. Their stories of the trouble taken to avoid military contact with holy places and sites were all bunkum and eyewash. They would have fought from the walls of the Holy City and placed machine–gun nests in the Church of the Holy Sepulchre and the Mosque of Omar if they had thought it would spare them the loss of Jerusalem.

Gaza had, as I have said, been turned into a fortress with a mass of field works, in places of considerable natural strength. If our force had been on the defensive at Gaza the Germans would not have attacked without an army of at least three times our strength. It is doubtful if the Turks put as much material in use on Gallipoli as they did here. Their trenches were deeply cut and were protected by an immense amount of wire. In the sand–dune area they used a vast quantity of sandbags, and they met the shortage of jute stuffs by making small sacks of bedstead hangings and curtains which, in the dry heat of the summer, wore very well. Looking across No Man's Land one could easily pick out a line of trenches by a red, a vivid blue, or a saffron sandbag. The Turkish dug–outs were most elaborate places of security. The excavators had gone down into the hard earth well beneath the deep strata of sand, and they roofed these holes with six, eight, and sometimes ten layers of palm logs. We had seen these beautiful trees disappearing and had guessed the reason. But an even greater protection than the devices of military engineers had been provided for the Turks by Dame Nature. Along the southern outskirts of the town all the fields were enclosed by giant cactus hedges, sometimes with stems as thick as a man's body and not infrequently rearing their strong limbs and prickly leaves twenty feet above the ground. The hedges were deep as well as high. They were at once a screen for defending troops and a barrier as impenetrable as the walls of a fortress. If one

44

line of cactus hedges had been cut through, infantry would have found another and yet another to a depth of nearly two miles, and as the whole of these thorny enclosures were commanded by a few machine guns the possibility of getting through was almost hopeless. There were similar hedges on the eastern and western sides of Gaza, but they were not quite so deep as on the south. On the western side, and extending south as far as the desert which the Army had crossed with such steady, methodical, and one may also say painful progression, was a wide belt of yellow sand, sometimes settled down hard under the weight of heavy winds, and in other places yielding to the pressure of feet. The Turks had laboured hard in this mile and a half width of sand, right down to the sea, to protect their right flank. There was a point about 4000 yards due west from the edge of the West Town of Gaza which we called Sea Post. It was the western extremity of the enemy's exceedingly intricate system of defences. The beach was below the level of the Post. From Sea Post for about 1500 yards the Turkish front line ran to Rafa Redoubt. There were wired–in entrenchments with strong points here and there, and a series of communication trenches and redoubts behind them for 3000 yards to Sheikh Hasan, which was the port of Gaza, if you can so describe an open roadstead with no landing facilities. From Rafa Redoubt the contour of the sand dunes permitted the enemy to construct an exceedingly strong line running due south for 2000 yards, the strongest points being named by us Zowaid trench, El Burj trench, Triangle trench, Peach Orchard, and El Arish Redoubt, the nomenclature being reminiscent of the trials of the troops in the desert march. Behind this line there was many a sunken passageway and shelter from gunfire, while backing the whole system, and, for reasons I have given, an element of defence as strong as the prepared positions, were cactus hedges enclosing the West Town's gardens.

From El Arish Redoubt the line ran east again to Mazar trench with a prodigal expenditure of wire in front of it, and then south for several hundred yards, when it was thrown out to the south–west to embrace a position of high importance known as Umbrella Hill, a dune of blazing yellow sand facing, about 500 yards away, Samson's Ridge, which we held strongly and on which the enemy often concentrated his fire. This ended the Turks' right–half section of the Gaza defences. Close by passed what from time immemorial has been called the Cairo Road, a track worn down by caravans of camels moving towards Kantara on their way with goods for Egyptian bazaars. But there was no break in the trench system which ran across the plain, a beautiful green tinted with the blooms of myriads of wild flowers when we first advanced over it in March, now browned and dried up by absolutely cloudless summer days. In the gardens on the western slopes of the hills running south from Ali Muntar the Turk had achieved much spadework, but he had done far more work on the hills themselves, and these were a frame of fortifications for Ali Muntar, on which we once sat for a few hours, and the possession of which meant the reduction of Gaza. By the end of summer the hill of Muntar had lost its shape. When we saw it during the first battle of Gaza it was a bold feature surmounted by a few trees and the whitened walls and grey dome of a sheikh's tomb. In the earlier battles of 1917 much was done to ruffle Muntar's crest. We saw trees uprooted, others lose their limbs, and naval gunfire threatened the foundations of the old chief's burying place. But Ali Muntar stoutly resisted the heavy shells' attack. As if Samson's feat had endowed it with some of the strong man's powers, Muntar for a long time received its daily thumps stoically; but by degrees the resistance of the old hill declined, and when agents reported that the sheikh's tomb was used as an observation post, 8–inch howitzers got on to it and made it untenable. There was a bit of it left at the end, but not more than would offer protection from a rifle bullet, and the one tree left standing was a limbless trunk. The crest of the hill lost its roundness, and the soil which had worked out through the shell craters had changed the colour of the summit. Old Ali Muntar had had the worst of the bombardment, and if some future sheikh should choose the site for a summer residence he will come across a wealth of metal in digging his foundations.

To capture Gaza the Formidable it was proposed first to take the western defences from Umbrella Hill to Sea Post, to press on to Sheikh Hasan and thus turn the right flank of the whole position. That would compel the enemy to reinforce his right flank when he was being heavily attacked elsewhere, and if he had been transferring his reserves to meet the threat against the left of his main line after Beersheba had been won for the Empire he would be in sore trouble. Gaza had already tasted a full sample of the war food we intended it should consume. Before the attack on Beersheba had developed, ships of war and the heavy guns of XXIst Corps had rattled its defences. The warships' fire was chiefly directed on targets our land guns could not reach. Observers in aircraft controlled the fire and notified the destruction of ammunition dumps at Deir Sineid and other places. The work of the heavy batteries was watched with much interest. Some were entirely new batteries which had never been in action against any enemy, and they only arrived on the Gaza front five weeks before the battle. These were not allowed to register until shortly before the battle began, and they borrowed guns from other batteries in order to train the gun crews. So desirous was General Bulfin to conceal the concentration of heavies that the wireless code calls were only those used by batteries which were in position before his Corps was formed, and the volume of fire came as an absolute surprise to the enemy. It came as a surprise also to some of us in camp at G.H.Q. one night at the end of October. Suddenly there was a terrific burst of fire on about four miles of front. Vivid fan–shaped flashes stabbed the sky, the bright moonlight of the East did not dim the guns' lightning, and their thunderous voices were a challenge the enemy was powerless to refuse. He took it up slowly as if half ashamed of his weakness. Then his fire increased in volume and in strength, but it ebbed again and we knew the reason. We held some big 'stuff' for counter battery work, and our fire was effective.

The preliminary bombardment began on October 27 and it grew in intensity day by day. The Navy co–operated on October 29 and subsequent days. The whole line from Middlesex Hill (close to Outpost Hill) to the sea was subjected to heavy fire, all the routes to the front line were shelled during the night by 60–pounder and field–gun batteries. Gas shells dosed the centres of communication and bivouac areas, and every quarter of the defences was made uncomfortable. The sound–ranging sections told us the enemy had between sixteen and twenty–four guns south of Gaza, and from forty to forty–eight north of the town, and over 100 guns were disclosed, including more than thirty firing from the Tank Redoubt well away to the eastward. On October 29 some of the guns south of Gaza had been forced back by the severity of our counter battery work, and of the ten guns remaining between us and the town on that date all except four had been removed by November 2. For several nights the bombardment continued without a move by infantry. Then just at the moment von Kress was discussing the loss of Beersheba and his plans to meet our further advance in that direction, some infantry of the 75th Division raided Outpost Hill, the southern extremity of the entrenched hill system south of Ali Muntar, and killed far more Turks than they took prisoners. There was an intense bombardment of the enemy's works at the same time. The next night—November 1–2—was the opening of XXIst Corps' great attack on Gaza, and though the enemy did not leave the town or the remainder of the trenches we had not assaulted till nearly a week afterwards, the vigour of the attack and the bravery with which it was thrust home, and the subsequent total failure of counter–attacks, must have made the enemy commanders realise on the afternoon of November 2 that Gaza was doomed and that their boasts that Gaza was impregnable were thin air. Their reserves were on the way to their left where they were urgently wanted, there was nothing strong enough to replace such heavy wastage caused to them by the attack of the night of November 1 and the morning of the 2nd, and our big gains of ground were an enormous advantage to us for the second phase in the Gaza sector, for we had bitten deeply into the

Turks' right flank.

Like the concentration of the XXth Corps and the Desert Mounted Corps for the jump off on to Beersheba, the preparations against the Turks' extreme right had to be very secretly made. The XXIst Corps Commander had to look a long way ahead. He had to consider the possibility of the enemy abandoning Gaza when Beersheba was captured, and falling back to the line of the wadi Hesi. His troops had been confined to trench warfare for months, digging and sitting in trenches, putting out wire, going out on listening patrols, sniping and doing all the drudgery in the lines of earthworks. They were hard and strong, their health having considerably improved since the early summer, but at the end of September the infantry were by no means march fit. Realising that, if General Allenby's operations were successful, and no one doubted that, we should have a period of open warfare when troops would be called upon to make long marches and undergo the privations entailed by transport difficulties, General Bulfin brought as many men as he could spare from the trenches back to Deir el Belah and the coast, where they had route marches over the sand for the restoration of their marching powers. Gradually he accumulated supplies in sheltered positions just behind the front. In three dumps were collected seven days' mobile rations, ammunition, water, and engineers' material. Tracks were constructed, cables buried, concealed gun positions and brigade and battalion headquarters made, and from the 25th October troops were ready to move off with two days' rations on the man. Should the enemy retire, General Hill's 52nd (Lowland) Division was to march up the shore beneath the sand cliffs, get across the wadi Hesi at the mouth, detach a force to proceed towards Askalon, and then move eastward down to the ridge opposite Deir Sineid, and, by securing the bridge and crossings of the wadi Hesi, prevent the enemy establishing himself on the north bank of the wadi. The operations on the night of November 1–2 were conducted by Major–General Hare, commanding the 54th Division, to which General Leggatt's 156th Infantry Brigade was temporarily attached. The latter brigade was given the important task of capturing Umbrella Hill and El Arish Redoubt. Umbrella Hill was to be taken first, and as it was anticipated the enemy would keep up a strong artillery fire for a considerable time after the position had been taken, and that his fire would interfere with the assembly and advance of troops detailed for the second phase, the first phase was timed to start four hours earlier than the second. For several days the guns had opened intense fire at midnight and again at 3 A.M. so that the enemy should not attach particular importance to our artillery activity on the night of action, and a creeping barrage nightly swept across No Man's Land to clear off the chain of listening posts established 300 yards in front of the enemy's trenches. Some heavy banks of cloud moved across the sky when the Scottish Rifle Brigade assembled for the assault, but the moon shed sufficient light at intervals to enable the Scots to file through the gaps made in our wire and to form up on the tapes laid outside. At 11 P.M. the 7th Scottish Rifles stormed Umbrella Hill with the greatest gallantry. The first wave of some sixty–five officers and men was blown up by four large contact mines and entirely destroyed. The second wave passed over the bodies of their comrades without a moment's check and, moving through the wire smashed by our artillery, entered Umbrella Hill trenches and set about the Turks with their bayonets. They had to clear a maze of trenches and dug–outs, but they bombed out of existence the machine–gunners opposing them and had settled the possession of Umbrella Hill in half an hour.

The 4th Royal Scots led the attack on El Arish Redoubt. It was a bigger and noisier 'show' than the Royal Scots had had some months before, when in a 'silent' raid they killed with hatchets only, for the Scots had seen the condition of some of their dead left in Turkish hands and were taking retribution. Not many Turks in El Arish Redoubt lived to relate that night's story. The Scots were rapidly in the redoubt and were rapidly through it, cleared up a nasty corner known as the 'Little Devil,' and were just about to shelter from the shells which were to answer their attack when they caught a brisk fire from a Bedouin hut. A platoon leader disposed his men cleverly and rushed the hut, killing everybody in it and capturing two machine guns. The vigorous resistance of the Turks on Umbrella Hill and El Arish Redoubt resulted in our having to bury over 350 enemy dead in these positions.

The second phase was to attack the enemy's front–line system from El Arish Redoubt to the sea at Sea Post. At 3 A.M., after the enemy guns had plentifully sprinkled Umbrella Hill and had given it up as irretrievably lost, we opened a ten–minutes' intense bombardment of the front line, exactly as had been done on preceding mornings, but this time the 161st and 162nd Infantry Brigades followed up our shells and carried 3000 yards of trenches at once. Three–quarters of an hour afterwards the 163rd Infantry Brigade tried to get the support trenches several hundred yards in rear, but the difficulties were too many and the effort failed. Having secured Sea Post and Beach Post the 162nd Brigade completed the programme by advancing up the coast and capturing the 'port' of Gaza, Sheikh Hasan, with a considerable body of prisoners.

How Jerusalem Was Won

The enemy's guns remained active until seven o'clock, when they reserved their fire till the afternoon. Then a heavy counter–attack was seen to be developing by an aerial observer, whose timely warning enabled the big guns and warships to smash it up. Another counter–attack against Sheikh Hasan was repulsed later in the day, and a third starting from Crested Rock which aimed at getting back El Burj trench was a complete failure. After the second phase our troops buried 739 enemy dead. Without doubt there were many others killed and wounded in the unsuccessful counter–attacks, particularly the first against Sheikh Hasan, when many heavy shells were seen to fall in the enemy's ranks. We took prisoners 26 officers, including two battalion commanders, and 418 other ranks. Our casualties were 30 officers and 331 other ranks killed, 94 officers and 1869 other ranks wounded, and 10 officers and 362 other ranks missing. Considering the enormous strength of the positions attacked, the numbers engaged, and the fact that we secured enemy front 5000 yards long and 3000 yards deep, the losses were not more severe than might have been expected.

The Turks clung to their trenches with a tenacity equal to that which characterised their defences on Gallipoli, and officer prisoners told us they had been ordered to hold Gaza at all costs. That was good news, though even if they had got back to the wadi Hesi line it is doubtful if, when Sheria was taken, they could have done more than temporarily hold us up there. During the next few days the work against the enemy's right consisted of heavy bombardments on the line of hills running from the north–east to the south of Gaza, and on the prominent position of Sheikh Redwan, east of the port. The enemy made some spirited replies, notably on the 4th, but his force in Gaza was getting shaken, and prisoners reluctantly admitted that the heavy naval shells taking them in flank and rear were affecting the moral of the troops. The gunfire of Rear–Admiral Jackson's fleet of H.M.S. *Grafton*, *Raglan*, Monitors 15, 29, 31, and 32, river–gunboats *Ladybird* and *Amphis*, and the destroyers *Staunch* and *Comet*, was worthy of the King's Navy. They were assisted by the French battleship *Requin*. We lost a monitor and destroyer torpedoed by a submarine, but the marks of the Navy's hard hitting were on and about Gaza, and we heard, if we could not see, the best the ships were doing. On one day there was a number of explosions about Deir Sineid indicating the destruction of some of the enemy's reserve of ammunition, and while the Turks were still in Gaza they received a shock resembling nothing more than an earthquake. One of the ships—the *Raglan*, I believe—taking a signal from a seaplane, got a direct hit on an ammunition train at Beit Hanun, the railway terminus north of Gaza. The whole train went up and its load was scattered in fragments over an area of several hundred square yards, an extraordinary scene of wreckage of torn and twisted railway material and destroyed ammunition presenting itself to us when we got on the spot on November 7. There was another very fine example of the Navy's indirect fire a short distance northward of this railway station. A stone road bridge had been built over the wadi Hesi and it had to carry all heavy traffic, the banks of the wadi being too steep and broken to permit wheels passing down them as they stood. During our advance the engineers had to build ramps here. A warship, taking its line from an aeroplane, fired at the bridge from a range of 14,000 yards, got two direct hits on it and holed it in the centre, and there must have been thirty or forty shell craters within a radius of fifty yards. The confounding of the Turks was ably assisted by the Navy.

CHAPTER IX. CRUSHING THE TURKISH LEFT

Now we return to the operations of XXth Corps and Desert Mounted Corps on our right. After the capture of Beersheba this force was preparing to attack the left of the Turkish main line about Hareira and Sheria, the capture of which would enable the fine force of cavalry to get to Nejile and gain an excellent water supply, to advance to the neighbourhood of Huj and so reach the plain and threaten the enemy's line in rear, and to fall on his line of retreat. It was proposed to make the attack on the Kauwukah and Rushdi systems at Hareira on November 4, but the water available at Beersheba had not been equal to the demands made upon it and was petering out, and mounted troops protecting the right flank of XXth Corps had to be relieved every twenty–four hours. The men also suffered a good deal from thirst. The weather was unusually hot for this period of the year, and the dust churned up by traffic was as irritating as when the khamseen wind blew. The two days' delay meant much in favour of the enemy, who was enabled to move his troops as he desired, but it also permitted our infantry to get some rest after their long marches, and supplies were brought nearer the front. 'Rest' was only a comparative term. Brigades were on the move each day in country which was one continual rise and fall, with stony beds of wadis to check progress, without a tree to lend a few moments' grateful relief from a burning sun, and nothing but the rare sight of a squalid native hut to relieve the monotony of a sun–dried desolate land.

The troops were remarkably cheerful. They were on their toes, as the cavalry told them. They had drawn first blood profusely from the Turk after many weary months of waiting and getting fit, and they knew that those gaunt mountain ridges away on their right front held behind them Bethlehem and Jerusalem, goals they desired to reach more than any other prizes of war. They had seen the Turk, and had soundly thrashed him out of trenches which the British could have held against a much stronger force. Their confidence was based on the proof that they were better men, and they were convinced that once they got the enemy into the open their superiority would be still more marked. The events of the next six weeks showed their estimate of the Turkish soldier was justified.

The 53rd Division with the Imperial Camel Corps on its right moved to Towal Abu Jerwal on November 1 to protect the flank guard of the XXth Corps during the pending attack on the Kauwukah system. The infantry had some fighting on that day, but it was mild compared with the strenuous days before them. The 10th Division attacked Irgeig railway station north–west of Beersheba and secured it, and waited there with the 74th Division on its right while the Welsh Division went forward to fight for Khuweilfeh on November 3. The Welshmen could not obtain the whole of the position on that day, and it was not until the 6th that it became theirs. Khuweilfeh is about ten miles due east of Sheria, the same distance north of Beersheba, and some five miles west of the Hebron road. It is in the hill country, difficult to approach, with nothing in the nature of a road or track leading to it, and there was no element in the position to suggest the prospect of an easy capture. When General Mott advanced to these forbidding heights the strength of the enemy in these parts was not realised. Prisoners taken during the day proved that there were portions of three or four Turkish divisions in the neighbourhood, and the strong efforts made to prevent the Welsh troops gaining the position and the furious attempts to drive them out of it suggested that most of the Turkish reserves had been brought over to their left flank to guard against a wide movement intended to envelop it. It afterwards turned out that von Kressenstein believed General Allenby intended to march on Jerusalem up the Hebron road, and he threw over to his left all his reserves to stop us. That was a supreme mistake, for when we had broken through at Hareira and Sheria the two wings of his Army were never in contact, and their only means of communication was by aeroplane.

The magnificent fight the 53rd Division put up at Khuweilfeh against vastly superior forces and in the face of heavy casualties played a very important part in the overwhelming defeat of the Turks. For four days and nights the Welsh Division fought without respite and with the knowledge that they could not be substantially reinforced, since the plan for the attack on Hareira and Sheria entailed the employment of all the available infantry of XXth Corps. Attack after attack was launched against them with extreme violence and great gallantry, their positions were raked by gunfire, whilst water and supplies were not over plentiful. But the staunch Division held on grimly to what it had gained, and its tenacity was well rewarded by what was won on other portions of the field.

During the night of November 5–6 and the day of the 6th, the 74th, 60th, and 10th Divisions concentrated for the attack on the Kauwukah system. The enemy's positions ran from his Jerusalem–Beersheba railway about five miles south–east of Hareira, across the Gaza–Beersheba road to the wadi Sheria, on the northern bank of which was an exceedingly strong redoubt covering Hareira. The eastern portion of this line was known as the Kauwukah system, and between it and Hareira was the Rushdi system, all being connected up by long communication and support trenches, while a light railway ran from the Rushdi line to dumps south of Sheria. At the moment of assembly for attack our line from right to left was made up as follows: the 158th Infantry Brigade was on the right, south of Tel Khuweilfeh. Then came the 160th Brigade and 159th Brigade. The Yeomanry Mounted Division held a long line of country and was the connecting link between the 53rd and 74th Divisions. The latter division disposed from right to left the 231st Brigade, the 229th Brigade, and 230th Brigade, who were to march from the south–east to the north–west to attack the right of the Kauwukah system of entrenchments on the railway. The 181st Brigade, 180th Brigade, and 179th Brigade of the 60th Division were to march in the same direction to attack the next portion of the system on the left of the 74th Division's objectives, then swinging to the north to march on Sheria. The 31st Brigade, 30th Brigade, and 29th Brigade were to operate on the 60th Division's left, with the Australian Mounted Division watching the left flank of XXth Corps. The Turkish VIIth Army and 3rd Cavalry Division were opposing the XXth Corps, another Division was opposite the 53rd Division and the Imperial Camel Corps with the 12th Depot Regiment at Dharahiyeh on the Hebron road, the 16th Division opposite our 74th, the 24th and 26th Divisions opposite our 69th, and the 54th against the 10th Division. The 3rd, 53rd, and 7th Turkish Divisions were in the Gaza area.

At daybreak the troops advanced to the attack. The first part of the line in front of the 231st Brigade was a serious obstacle. Two or three small outlying rifle pits had to be taken before the Division could proceed with its effort to drive the enemy out of Sheria and protect the flank of the 60th Division, which had to cross the railway where a double line of trenches was to be tackled, the rear line above the other with the flank well thrown back and protected by small advanced pits to hold a few men and machine guns. The

How Jerusalem Was Won

Turks held on very obstinately to their ground east of the railway, and kept the 74th Division at bay till one o'clock in the afternoon, but the artillery of that Division had for some time been assisting in the wire–cutting in front of the trenches to be assaulted by the 60th Division, and the latter went ahead soon after noon, and with the assistance of one brigade of the 10th Division, had won about 4000 yards of the complicated trench system and most of the Rushdi system by half–past two. The Londoners then swung to the north and occupied the station at Sheria, while the dismounted yeomanry worked round farther east, taking a series of isolated trenches on the way, the Irish troops relieving the 60th in the captured trenches at Kauwukah. The 60th Division, having possession of the larger part of Sheria, intended to attack the hill there at nightfall, and the attack was in preparation when an enemy dump exploded and a huge fire lighted up the whole district, so that all troops would have been exposed to the fire of the garrison on the hill. General Shea therefore stopped the attack, but the hill was stormed at 4.30 next morning and carried at the point of the bayonet. A bridgehead was then formed at Sheria, and the Londoners fought all day and stopped one counter–attack when it was within 200 yards of our line. On that same morning the Irish troops had extended their gains westwards from the Rushdi system till they got to Hareira Tepe Redoubt, a high mound 500 yards across the top, which had been criss–crossed with trenches with wire hanging about some broken ground at the bottom. Here there was a hot tussle, but the Irishmen valiantly pushed through and not only gave XXth Corps the whole of its objectives and completed the turn of the enemy's left flank, but joined up with the XXIst Corps. The working of XXth Corps' scheme had again been admirable, and once more the staff work had enabled the movements to be timed perfectly.

The Desert Mounted Corps was thus able to draw up to Sheria in readiness to take up the pursuit and to get the water supply at Nejile. This ended the XXth Corps' task for a few days, though the 60th Division became temporarily attached to Desert Mounted Corps. XXth Corps had nobly done its part. The consummate ability, energy, and foresight of the corps commander had been supported throughout by the skill of divisional and brigade commanders. For the men no praise could be too high. The attention given to their training was well repaid. They bore the strain of long marches on hard food and a small allowance of water in a way that proved their physique to be only matched by their courage, and that was of a high order. Their discipline was admirable, their determination alike in attack and defence strong and well sustained. To say they were equal to the finest troops in the world might lay one open to a charge of exaggeration when it was impossible to get a fair ground of comparison, seeing the conditions of fighting on different fronts was so varied, but the trials through which the troops of XXth Corps passed up to the end of the first week of November, and their magnificent accomplishments by the end of the year, make me doubt whether any other corps possessed finer soldierly qualities. The men were indeed splendid. The casualties sustained by the XXth Corps from October 31 to November 16 were: killed, officers 63, other ranks 869; wounded, officers 198, other ranks 4246; missing, no officers, 108 other ranks—a total of 261 officers and 5223 other ranks.

During the period after Beersheba when the XXth Corps troops were concentrating to break up the Turks' defensive position on the left, the Desert Mounted Corps was busily engaged holding a line eight or ten miles north and north-east of Beersheba, and watching for any movement of troops down the Hebron road. The 2nd Australian Light Horse Brigade and 7th Mounted Brigade tried to occupy a line from Khuweilfeh to Dharahiyeh, but it was not possible to reach it—a fact by no means surprising, as in the light of subsequent knowledge it was clear that the Turks had put much of their strength there. A patrol of Light Horsemen managed to work round to the north of Dharahiyeh, a curious group of mud houses on a hill-top inhabited by natives who have yet to appreciate the evils of grossly overcrowded quarters as well as some of the elementary principles of sanitation, and they saw a number of motor lorries come up the admirably constructed hill road designed by German engineers. The lorries were hurrying from the Jerusalem area with reinforcements. Prisoners—several hundreds of them in all—were brought in daily, but no attempt was made to force the enemy back until November 6, when the 53rd Division, which for the time being was attached to the Desert Mounted Corps, drove the Turks off the whole of Khuweilfeh, behaving as I have already said with fine gallantry and inflicting severe losses. There were also counter-attacks launched against the 5th Mounted Brigade, the New Zealand Mounted Rifles Brigade, and the Imperial Camel Corps Brigade, but these were likewise beaten off with considerable casualties to the enemy. When the XXth Corps had captured the Khauwukah system, a detachment for the defence of the right flank of the Army was formed under the command of Major-General G. de S. Barrow, the G.O.C. Yeomanry Mounted Division, consisting of the Imperial Camel Corps Brigade, 53rd Division, Yeomanry Mounted Division, New Zealand Mounted Rifles Brigade, and two squadrons and eight machine guns of the 2nd Australian Light Horse Brigade. The Australian Mounted Division marched from Karm, whither it had been sent on account of water difficulties, to rejoin Desert Mounted Corps to whom the 60th Division was temporarily attached. The Desert Corps had orders on November 7 to push through as rapidly as possible to the line wadi

Jemmameh–Huj, and from that day the Corps commenced its long march to Jaffa, a march which, though strongly opposed by considerable bodies of troops, was more often interfered with by lack of water than by difficulty in defeating the enemy.

The scarcity of water was a sore trouble. There was an occasional pool here and there, but generally the only water procurable was in deep wells giving a poor yield. The cavalry will not forget that long trek. No brigade could march straight ahead. Those operating in the foothills on our right had to fight all the way, and they were often called upon to resist counter–attacks by strong rearguards issuing from the hills to threaten the flank and so delay the advance in order to permit the Turks to carry off some of their material. It was necessary almost every day to withdraw certain formations from the front and send them back a considerable distance to water, replacing them by other troops coming from a well centre. In this way brigades were not infrequently attached to divisions other than their own, and the administrative services were heavily handicapped. Several times whole brigades were without water for forty–eight hours, and though supplies reached them on all but one or two occasions they were often late, and an exceedingly severe strain was put on the transport. During that diagonal march across the Maritime Plain I heard infantry officers remark that the Australians always seemed to have their supplies up with them. I do not think the supplies were always there, but they generally were not far behind, and if resource and energy could work miracles the Australian supply officers deserve the credit for them. The divisional trains worked hard in those strenuous days, and the 'Q' staff of the Desert Mounted Corps had many a sleepless night devising plans to get that last ounce out of their transport men and to get that little extra amount of supplies to the front which meant the difference between want and a sufficiency for man and horse.

On the 7th November the 60th Division after its spirited attack on Tel el Sheria crossed the wadi and advanced north about two miles, fighting obstinate rearguards all the way. The 1st Australian Light Horse took 300 prisoners and a considerable quantity of ammunition and stores at Ameidat, and with the remainder of the Anzac Division reached Tel Abu Dilakh by the evening, and the Australian Mounted Division filled the gap between the Anzacs and the Londoners, but having been unable to water could not advance further. The 8th November was a busy and brilliantly successful day. The Corps' effort was to make a wide sweeping movement in order first to obtain the valuable and urgently required water at Nejile, and then to push across the hills and rolling downs to the country behind Gaza to harass the enemy retreating from that town. The Turks had a big rearguard south–west of Nejile and made a strong effort to delay the capture of that place, the importance of which to us they realised to the full, and they were prepared to sacrifice the whole of the rearguard if they could hold us off the water for another twenty–four hours. The pressure of the Anzac Division and the 7th Mounted Brigade assisting it was too much for the enemy, who though holding on to the hills very stoutly till the last moment had to give way and leave the water in our undisputed possession. The Sherwood Rangers and South Notts Hussars were vigorously counter–attacked at Mudweiweh, but they severely handled the enemy, who retired a much weakened body.

By the evening the Anzacs held the country from Nejile to the north bank of the wadi Jemmameh, having captured 300 prisoners and two guns. The Australian Mounted Division made an excellent advance round the north side of Huj, which had been the Turkish VIIIth Army Headquarters, and the 4th Australian Light Horse Brigade was in touch with the corps cavalry of XXIst Corps at Beit Hanun, while the 3rd Australian Light Horse Brigade had taken prisoners and two of the troublesome Austrian 5.9 howitzers.

It was the work of the 60th Division in the centre, however, which was the outstanding feature of the day, though the Londoners readily admitted that without the glorious charge of the Worcester and Warwickshire Yeomanry in the afternoon they would not have been in the neighbourhood of Huj when darkness fell. The 60th were in the centre, sandwiched between the Anzacs and Australian Mounted Division, and their allotted task was to clear the country between Sheria and Huj, a distance of ten miles. The country was a series of billowy downs with valleys seldom more than 1000 yards wide, and every yard of the way was opposed by infantry and artillery. Considering the opposition the progress was good. The Londoners drove in the Turks' strong flank three times, first from the hill of Zuheilika, then from the cultivated area behind it, and thirdly from the wadi–torn district of Muntaret el Baghl, from which the infantry proceeded to the high ground to the north. It was then between two and three o'clock in the afternoon, and maps showed that between the Division and Huj there was nearly four miles of most difficult country, a mass of wadi beds and hills giving an enterprising enemy the best possible means for holding up an advance. General Shea went ahead in a light armoured car to reconnoitre, and saw a strong body of Turks with guns marching across his front. It was impossible for his infantry to catch them and, seeing ten troops of Warwick and Worcester Yeomanry on his right about a mile away, he went over to them and ordered Lieut.–Colonel H. Cheape to charge the enemy. It was a case for instant action. The

57

enemy were a mile and a half from our cavalry. The gunners had come into action and were shelling the London Territorials, but they soon had to switch off and fire at a more terrifying target. Led by their gallant Colonel, a Master of Foxhounds who was afterwards drowned in the Mediterranean, the yeomen swept over a ridge in successive lines and raced down the northern slope on to the flat, at first making direct for the guns, then swerving to the left under the direction of Colonel Cheape, whose eye for country led him to take advantage of a mound on the opposite side of the valley. Over this rise the Midland yeomen spurred their chargers and, giving full–throated cheers, dashed through the Turks' left flank guard and went straight for the guns. Their ranks were somewhat thinned, for they had been exposed to a heavy machine–gun fire as well as to the fire of eight field guns and three 5.9 howitzers worked at the highest pressure. The gunners were nearly all Germans and Austrians and they fought well. They splashed the valley with shrapnel, and during the few moments' lull when the yeomanry were lost to view behind the mound they set their shell fuses at zero to make them burst at the mouth of the guns and act as case shot. They tore some gaps in the yeomen's ranks, but nothing could stop that charge. The Midlanders rode straight at the guns and sabred every artilleryman at his piece. The Londoners say they heard all the guns stop dead at the same moment and they knew they had been silenced in true Balaclava style. Having wiped out the batteries the yeomen again answered the call of their leader and swept up a ridge to deal effectively with three machine guns, and having used the white arm against their crews the guns were turned on to the retreating Turks and decimated their ranks. This charge was witnessed by General Shea, and I know it is his opinion that it was executed with the greatest gallantry and elan, and was worthy of the best traditions of British cavalry. The yeomanry lost about twenty–five per cent. of their number in casualties, but their action was worth the price, for they completely broke up the enemy resistance and enabled the London Division to push straight through to Huj. The Warwick and Worcester Yeomanry received the personal congratulations of the Commander–in–Chief, and General Shea was also thanked by General Allenby.

During this day General Shea accomplished what probably no other Divisional Commander did in this war. When out scouting in a light armoured car he was within 500 yards of a big ammunition dump which was blown up. He saw the three men who had destroyed it running away, and he chased them into a wadi and machine–gunned them. They held up their hands and were astonished to find they had surrendered to a General. These men were captured in the nick of time. But for the appearance of General Shea they would have destroyed another dump, which we captured intact.

How Jerusalem Was Won

I was with the Division the night after they had taken Huj. It was their first day of rest for some time, but the men showed few signs of fatigue. No one could move among them without being proud of the Londoners. They were strong, self–reliant, well–disciplined, brave fellows. I well remember what Colonel Temperley, the G.S.O. of the Division, told me when sitting out on a hill in the twilight that night. Colonel Temperley had been brigade major of the first New Zealand Infantry Brigade which came to Egypt and took a full share in the work on Gallipoli on its way to France. He had over two years of active service on the Western Front before coming out to Palestine for duty with the 60th Division, and his views on men in action were based on the sound experience of the professional soldier. Of the London County Territorials he said: 'I cannot speak of these warriors without a lump rising in my throat. These Cockneys are the best men in the world. Their spirits are simply wonderful, and I do not think any division ever went into a big show with higher moral. After three years of war it is refreshing to hear the men's earnestly expressed desire to go into action again. These grand fellows went forward with the full bloom on them, there never was any hesitation, their discipline was absolutely perfect, their physique and courage were alike magnificent, and their valour beyond words. The Cockney makes the perfect soldier.' I wrote at the time that 'whether the men came from Bermondsey, Camberwell or Kennington, or belonged to what were known as class corps, such as the Civil Service or Kensingtons, before the war, all battalions were equally good. They were trained for months for the big battle till their bodies were brought to such a state of fitness that Spartan fare during the ten days of ceaseless action caused neither grumble nor fatigue. The men may well be rewarded with the title "London's Pride," and London is honoured by having such stalwarts to represent the heart of the British Empire. In eight days the Londoners marched sixty–six miles and fought a number of hot actions. The march may not seem long, but Palestine is not Salisbury Plain. A leg–weary man was asked by an officer if his feet were blistered, and replied: "They're rotten sore, but my heart's gay." That is typical of the spirit of these unconquerable Cockneys. I have just left them. They still have the bloom of freshness and I do not think it will ever fade. Scorching winds which parched the throat and made everything one wore hot to the touch were enough to oppress the staunchest soldier, but these sterling Territorials, costers and labourers, artisans and tradesmen, professional men and men of independent means, true brothers in arms and good Britons, left their bivouacs and trudged across heavy country, fearless, strong, proud, and with the cheerfulness of good men who fight for right.' What I said in those early days of the great advance was more than borne out later, and in the capture of Jerusalem, in taking Jericho, and in forcing the passage of the Jordan this glorious Division of Londoners was always the same, a pride to its commander, a bulwark of the XXth Corps, and a great asset of the Empire.

CHAPTER X. THROUGH GAZA INTO THE OPEN

On the Gaza section of the front the XXIst Corps had been busily occupied with preparations for a powerful thrust through the remainder of the defences on the enemy's right when the XXth Corps should have succeeded in turning the main positions on the left. The 52nd Division on the coast was ready to go ahead immediately there was any sign that the enemy, seeing that the worst was about to happen, intended to order a general retirement, and then it would be a race and a fight to prevent his establishing himself on the high ground north of the wadi Hesi. Should he fail to do that there was scarcely a possibility of the Turks holding us up till we got to the Jaffa–Jerusalem road, though between Gaza and that metalled highway there were many points of strength from which they could fight delaying actions. It is very doubtful whether the Turkish General Staff gave the cavalry credit for being able to move across the Plain in the middle of November when the wadis are absolutely dry and the water–level in the wells is lower than at any other period of the year. Nor did they imagine that the transport difficulties for infantry divisions fed as ours were could be surmounted. They may have thought that if they could secure the wadi Hesi line before we got into position to threaten it in flank they would immobilise our Army till the rains began, and there was a possibility of sitting facing each other in wet uncomfortable trench quarters till the flowers showed themselves in the spring, by which time, the Bagdad venture of the German Higher Command proving hopeless before it was started, a great volume of reinforcements might be diverted to Southern Palestine with Turkish divisions from the Salonika front and a stiffening of German battalions spared from Europe in consequence of the Russian collapse.

Whatever they may have been, the Turkish calculations were completely upset. The cavalry's water troubles remained and no human foresight could have smoothed them over, but the transport problem was solved in this way. During the attack on Beersheba XXIst Corps came to the aid of XXth Corps by handing over to it the greater part of its camel convoys and lorries, so much transport, indeed, that a vast amount of work in the Gaza sector fell to be done by a greatly depleted supply staff. When Beersheba had been won and the enemy's left flank had been smashed and thrown back, the XXth Corps repaid the XXIst Corps, not only by returning what it had borrowed, but by marching back into the region of railhead at Karm, where it could live with a minimum of transport and send all its surplus to work in the coastal sector. The switching over of this transport was a fine piece of organisation. On the allotted day many thousands of camels were seen drawn out in huge lines all over the country intersected by the wadi Ghuzze, slowly converging on the spots at which they could be barracked and rested before loading for the advance. The lorries took other paths. There was no repose for their drivers. They worked till the last moment on the east, and then, caked with the accumulated dust of a week's weary labour in sand and powdered earth, turned westward to arrive just in time to load up and be off again in pursuit of infantry, some making the mistake of travelling between the West and East Towns of Gaza, while others took the longer and sounder but still treacherous route east of Ali Muntar and through the old positions of the Turks. These lorry drivers were wonderful fellows who laughed at their trials, but in the days and nights when they bumped over the uneven tracks and negotiated earth rents that threatened to swallow their vehicles, they put their faith in the promise of the railway constructors to open the station at Gaza at an early date. Even Gaza, though it saved them so many toilsome miles, did not help them greatly because of a terrible piece of road north–east of the station, but Beit Hanun was comfortable and for the relief brought by the railway's arrival at Deir Sineid they were profoundly grateful.

But this is anticipating the story of Gaza's capture. The XXIst Corps had not received its additional transport when it gained the ancient city of the Philistines, though it knew some of it was on the way and most of it about to start on its westward trek. On the day of November 4 and during the succeeding night the Navy co–operated with the Corps' artillery in destroying enemy trenches and gun positions, and the Ali Muntar Ridge was a glad sight for tired gunners' eyes. The enemy showed a disposition to retaliate, and on the afternoon of the 4th he put up a fierce bombardment of our front–line positions from Outpost Hill to the sea, including in his fire area the whole of the trenches we had taken from him from Umbrella Hill to Sheikh Hasan. Many observers of this bombardment by all the Turks' guns of heavy, medium, and small calibre declared it was the prelude not of an attack but of a retirement, and that the Turks were loosing off a lot of the ammunition they knew they could not carry away. They were probably right, though the enemy made no sign of going away for a couple of days, but if he thought his demonstration by artillery was going to hasten back to Gaza some of the troops assembling against the left of his main line he was grievously in error. The XXIst Corps was strong enough to deal with any attack the Turks could launch, and they would have been pleased if an attempt to reach our lines had been made.

Next day the Turks were much quieter. They had to sit under a terrific fire both on the 5th and 6th November, when in order to assist XXth Corps' operations the Corps' heavy artillery, the divisional artillery, and the warships' guns carried out an intense bombardment. The land guns searched the Turks' front line and reserve systems, while the Navy fired on Fryer's Hill to the north of Ali Muntar, Sheikh Redwan, a sandhill with a native chief's tomb on the crest, north of Gaza, and on trenches not easily reached by the Corps' guns.

During the night of November 6–7 General Palin's 75th Division, as a preliminary to a major operation timed for the following morning, attacked and gained the enemy's trenches on Outpost Hill and the whole of Middlesex Hill to the north of it, the opposition being less serious than was anticipated. At daylight the 75th Division pushed on over the other hills towards Ali Muntar and gained that dominating position before eight o'clock. The fighting had not been severe, and it was soon realised that the enemy had left Gaza, abandoning a stronghold which had been prepared for defence with all the ingenuity German masters of war could suggest and into which had been worked an enormous amount of material. It was obvious from the complete success of XXth Corps' operations against the Turkish left, which had been worked out absolutely 'according to plan,' that General Allenby had so thoroughly mystified von Kressenstein that the latter had put all his reserves into the wrong spot, and that the 53rd Division's stout resistance against superior numbers had pinned them down to the wrong end of the line. There was nothing, therefore, for the Turk to do but to try to hold another position, and he was straining every nerve to reach it. The East Anglian Division went up west of Gaza and held from Sheikh Redwan to the sea by seven o'clock, two squadrons of the Corps' cavalry rode along the seashore and had patrols on the wadi Hesi a little earlier than that, and the Imperial Service Cavalry Brigade, composed of troops raised and maintained by patriotic Indian princes, passed through Gaza at nine o'clock and went out towards Beit Hanun. To the Lowland Division was given the important task of getting to the right or northern bank of the wadi Hesi. These imperturbable Scots left their trenches in the morning delighted at the prospect of once more engaging in open warfare. They marched along the beach under cover of the low sand cliffs, and by dusk had crossed the mouth of the wadi and held some of the high ground to the north in face of determined opposition. The 157th Brigade, after a march through very heavy going, got to the wadi at five in the afternoon and saw the enemy posted on the opposite bank. The place was reconnoitred and the brigade made a fine bayonet charge in the dark, securing the position between ten and eleven o'clock. On this and succeeding days the division had to fight very hard indeed, and they often met the enemy with the bayonet. One of their officers told me the Scot was twice as good as the Turk in ordinary fighting, but with the bayonet his advantage was as five to one. The record of the Division throughout the campaign showed this was no too generous an estimate of their powers. After securing Ali Muntar the 75th Division advanced over Fryer's Hill to Australia Hill, so that they held the whole ridge running north and south to the eastward of Gaza. The enemy still held to his positions to the right of his centre, and from the Atawineh Redoubt, Tank Redoubt, and Beer trenches there was considerable shelling of Gaza and the Ali Muntar ridge throughout the day. A large number of shells fell in the plantations on the western side of the ridge; our mastery of the air prevented enemy aviators observing for their artillery, or they would have seen no traffic was passing along that way. We were using the old Cairo 'road,' and as far as I could see not an enemy shell reached it, though when our troops were in the town of Gaza there were many crumps and woolly bears to disturb the new occupation. But all went swimmingly. It was true we had only captured the well–cracked shell of a town, but the taking of it was full of promise of greater things, and those of us who looked on the mutilated remnants of one of the world's oldest cities felt we were indeed witnesses of the beginning of the downfall of the Turkish Empire. Next morning the 75th Division captured Beer trenches and Tank and Atawineh Redoubts and linked up with the Irish Division of XXth Corps on its right. They were shelled heavily, but it was the shelling of rearguards and not attackers, and soon after twelve o'clock we had the best of evidence that the Turks were saying good–bye to a neighbourhood they had long inhabited. I was standing on Raspberry Hill, the battle headquarters of XXIst Corps, when I heard a terrific report. Staff officers who were used to the visitations of aerial marauders came out of their shelters and searched the pearly vault of the heavens for Fritz. No machine could be found. Some one looking across the country towards Atawineh saw a huge mushroom–shaped cloud, and then we knew that one enormous dump at least contained no more projectiles to hold up an advance. This ammunition store must have been eight miles away as the crow flies, but the noise of the explosion was so violent that it was a considerable time before some officers could be brought to believe an enemy plane had not laid an egg near us. The blowing up of that dump was a signal that the Turk was off.

The Lowlanders had another very strenuous day in the sand–dune belt. First of all they repulsed a strong counter–attack from the direction of Askalon. Then the 155th Infantry

Brigade went forward and, swinging to the right, drove the Turks off the rising ground north–west of Deir Sineid, the possession of which would determine the question whether the Turk could hold on in this quarter sufficiently long to enable him to get any of his material away by his railway and road. The enemy put in a counter–attack of great violence and forced the Scots back.

The 157th Brigade in the early evening attacked the ridge and gained the whole of their objectives by eight o'clock. There ensued some sanguinary struggles on this sandy ground during the night. The Turks were determined to have possession of it and the Scots were willing to fight it out to a finish. The first counter–attack in the dark hours drove the Lowlanders off, but they were shortly afterwards back on the hills again. The Turks returned and pushed the Highland Light Infantry and Argyll and Sutherland Highlanders off a second time. A third attack was delivered with splendid vigour and the enemy left many dead, but they renewed their efforts to get the commanding ground and succeeded once more. The dogged Scots, however, were not to be denied. They re–formed and swept up the heavy shifting sand, met the Turk on the top with a clash and knocked him down the reverse slope. Soon afterwards there was another ding–dong struggle. The Turks, putting in all their available strength, for a fourth time got the upper hand, and the Lowlanders had to yield the ground, doing it slowly and reluctantly and with the determination to try again. They were Robert Bruces, all of them. It's the best that stays the longest. After a brief rest these heroic Scots once more swarmed up the ridge. Their cheers had the note of victory in them, they drove their bayonets home with the haymakers' lift, and what was left of the Turks fled helter–skelter down the hill towards Deir Sineid, broken, dismayed, beaten, and totally unable to make another effort. The H.L.I. Brigade's victory was bought at a price. The cost of that hill was heavy, but the Turks' tale of dead was far heavier than ours, and we had won and held the hills and consolidated them. The Turks then turned their faces to the north and the Scots hurried them on. The Imperial Service Cavalry Brigade had also met with considerable resistance, but they worked up to and on the ridge overlooking Beit Hanun from the east and captured a 5.9. By evening these Indian horsemen were linked up with the 4th Australian Light Horse Brigade on their right and the 52nd Division on their left, and pursued the enemy as far as Tumrah and Deir Sineid.

General Headquarters directed that two infantry divisions should advance to the line Julis–Hamameh in support of mounted troops, and the 75th Division was accordingly ordered from its position east of Gaza up to Beit Hanun. On the 9th November the 52nd

How Jerusalem Was Won

Division was again advancing. The 156th Brigade had moved forward from the Gaza trenches. One officer, five grooms, and two signallers mounted on second horses formed a little party to reconnoitre Askalon, and riding boldly into the ancient landing place of the Crusader armies captured the ruined town unaided. There are visible remains of its old strength, but the power of Askalon has departed. It still stands looking over the blue Mediterranean as a sort of watch tower, a silent, deserted outpost of the land the Crusaders set their hearts on gaining and preserving for Christianity, but behind it is many centuries' accumulation of sand encroaching upon the fertile plain, and no effort has been made to stop the inroad. The gallant half–dozen having reported to the 156th Brigade that Askalon was open to them—the Brigade occupied the place at noon—rode across the sand–dunes to the important native town of Mejdel, where there was a substantial bazaar doing a good trade in the essentials for native existence, beans and cereals in plenty, fruit, and tobacco of execrable quality. At Mejdel the six accepted the surrender of a body of Turks guarding a substantial ammunition dump and rejoined their units, satisfied with the day's adventure. The Turks had retired a considerable distance during the day. The principal body was moving up what is called the main road from Deir Sineid, through Beit Jerjal to Julis, to get to Suafir esh Sherkiyeh, Kustineh, and Junction Station, from which they could reach Latron by a metalled road, or Ramleh by a hard mud track by the side of their railway. They were clearly going to oppose us all the way or they would lose the whole of their material, and their forces east and west of the road were well handled in previously selected and partially prepared positions.

They left behind them the unpleasant trail of a defeated army. Turks had fallen by the way and the natives would not bury them. Our aircraft had bombed the road, and the dead men, cattle and horses, and smashed transport were ghastly sights and made the air offensive. There they lay, one long line of dead men and animals, and if a London fog had descended to blind the eyes of our Army the sense of smell would still have carried a scout on the direct line of the Turkish retreat.

I will break off the narrative of fighting at this point to describe a scene which expressed more eloquently than anything else I witnessed in Palestine how deeply engraved in the native mind was the conviction that Britain stood for fair dealing and freedom. The inhabitants, like the Arabs of the desert, do not allow their faces to betray their feelings. They preserve a stolid exterior, and it is difficult to tell from their demeanour whether they are friendly or indifferent to you. But their actions speak aloud. Early on the morning after the Lowlanders had entered Mejdel I was in the neighbourhood. Our guns banging away to the north were a reminder that there was to be no promenade over the Plain, and that we had yet to make good the formidable obstacle of the wadi Sukereir, when I passed a curious procession. People whom the Turks had turned out of Gaza and the surrounding country were trekking back to the spots where they and their forefathers had lived for countless generations. All their worldly goods and chattels were packed on overloaded camels and donkeys. The women bore astonishingly heavy loads on their heads, the men rode or walked carrying nothing, while patriarchs of families were either held in donkey saddles or were borne on the shoulders of younger men. Agriculturists began to turn out to plough and till the fields which had lain fallow while the Turkish scourge of war was on the land, and the people showed that, now they had the security of British protection, they intended at once to resume their industry. The troops had the liveliest welcome in passing through villages, though the people are not as a rule demonstrative; and one could point to no better evidence of the exemplary behaviour of our soldiers than the groups of women sitting and gossiping round the wells during the process of drawing water, just as they did in Biblical days, heedless of the passing troops whom they regarded as their protectors. The man behind a rude plough may have stopped his ill−matched team of pony and donkey to look at a column of troops moving as he had never seen troops march before, a head of a family might collect the animals carrying his household goods and hurry them off the line of route taken by military transport, but neither one nor the other had any fear of interference with his work, and the life of the whole country, one of the most unchanging regions of the world, had suddenly again become normal, although only yesterday two armies had disputed possession of the very soil on which they stood. The moment we were victorious old occupations were resumed by the people in the way that was a tradition from their forefathers. Our victory meant peace and safety, according to the native idea, and an end to extortion, oppression, and pillage under the name of requisitions. It also meant prosperity. The native likes to drive a bargain. He will not sell under a fair price, and he asks much more in the hope of showing a buyer who has beaten him down how cheaply he is getting goods. The Army chiefly sought eggs, which are light to carry and easy to cook, and give variety to the daily round of bully, biscuit, and jam. The soldier is a generous fellow, and if a child asked a piastre (2−1/2d.) for an egg he got it. The price soon became four to five for a shilling in cash, though the Turks wanted five times that number for an equivalent sum in depreciated paper currency. The law of supply and demand obtained in this old world just as at home, and it became sufficient for a soldier to ask for an article to show he wanted it and would pay almost anything that was demanded. It was curious to see how the news spread not merely among traders but also among villagers. The men who first occupied a place found oranges, vegetables, fresh bread, and eggs cheap. In Ramleh, for example, a market was opened for our troops immediately they got to the town, and the goods were sound and sold at fair rates. The next day prices were up, and the standards fixed behind the front soon ruled at the line itself. There was no real control attempted, and while the extortionate prices charged by Jews in their excellent agricultural colonies and by the natives made a poor people prosperous, it gave them an exaggerated idea of the size of the British purse, and they may be disappointed at the limitation of our spending powers in the future. Also it was hard on the bravest and most chivalrous of fighting men. But it opened the eyes of the native, whose happiness and contentment were obvious directly we reached his doors.

Our movements on November 9 were limited by the extent to which General Chauvel was able to use his cavalry of the Desert Mounted Corps. Water was the sole, but absolute handicap. The Yeomanry Mounted Division rejoined the Corps on that day and got south of Huj, but could not proceed further through lack of water and supply difficulties. The Australian Mounted Division also had to halt for water, and it was left to Anzac Mounted Division, plus the 7th Mounted Brigade, to march eighteen miles north–westwards to occupy the line Et Tineh–Beit Duras–Jemameh–Esdud (the Ashdod of the Bible). The 52nd Division occupied the area Esdud–Mejdel–Herbieh by the evening of the 10th, and on the way, Australian cavalry being held up on a ridge north of Beit Duras, the 157th Brigade made another of its fine bayonet charges at night and captured the ground, enabling the cavalry to get at some precious water. The brigade made the attack just after completing a fourteen miles' march in heavy going, achieving the remarkable record of having had three bayonet battles on three nights out of four. On this occasion the Turks again suffered heavy casualties in men and lost many machine guns. The 75th Division prolonged the infantry line through Gharbiyeh to Berberah. The 54th Division was in the Gaza defences with all its transport allotted to the divisions taking part in the forward move, but as the 54th had five days' rations in dumps close at hand it was able to maintain itself, and the railway was being pushed on from the wadi Ghuzze with the utmost speed. The iron road in war is an army's jugular vein, and each mile added to its length was of enormous value during the advance.

General Allenby, looking well ahead and realising the possibilities opened out by his complete success in every phase of the operations on the Turks' main defensive line, on the 10th November ordered the 52nd and 75th Divisions to concentrate on their advanced guards so as to support the cavalry on their front and to prevent the Turk consolidating on the line of the wadi Sukereir. The enemy was developing a more organised resistance on a crescent–shaped line from Et Tineh through Yasur to Beshshit, and it was necessary to adopt deliberate methods of attack to move him. The advance on the 11th was the preliminary to three days of stirring fighting. The Turks put up a very strong defence by their rearguards, and when one says that at this time they were fighting with courage and magnificent determination one is not only paying a just tribute to the enemy but doing justice to the gallantry and skill of the troops who defeated him. The Scots can claim a large share of the success of the next two days, but British yeomanry took a great part in it, and their charge at Mughar, and perhaps their charge at Abu Shushe as well, will find a place in military text–books, for it has confounded those critics who declared that the development of the machine gun in modern warfare has brought the uses of cavalry down to very narrow limits.

The 156th Brigade was directed to take Burkah on the 12th so as to give the infantry liberty of manoeuvre on the following day. Burkah was a nasty place to tackle. The enemy had two lines of beautifully sited trenches prepared before he fell back from Gaza. The Scots had to attack up a slope to the first line, and having taken this to pass down another slope for 1000 yards before reaching the glacis in front of the second line. The Scottish Rifles assaulted this position by day without much artillery support, but they took it in magnificent style. It looked as if the Turks had accepted the verdict, but at night they returned to a brown hill on the right and drove the 4th Royal Scots from it. This battalion came back soon afterwards and retook the hill with the assistance of some Gurkhas of General Colston's 233rd Infantry Brigade, and the Turk retired to another spot, hoping that his luck would change. While this fighting was going on about Burkah the 155th Brigade went ahead up a road which the cavalry said was strongly held. They got eight miles north of Esdud, and were in advance of the cavalry, intending to try to secure the two heights and villages of Katrah and Mughar on the following day. Katrah was a village on a long mound south of Mughar, native mud huts constituting its southern part, whilst separated from it on the northern side by some gardens was a pretty little Jewish settlement whose red–tiled houses and orderly well–cared–for orchards spoke of the industry of these settlers in Zion. All over the hill right up to the houses the cactus flourished, and the hedges were a replica of the terrible obstacles at Gaza. From Katrah the ground sloped down to the flat on all four sides, so that the village seemed to stand on an island in the plain. A mile due west of it was Beshshit, while one mile to the north across more than one wadi stood El Mughar at the southern end of an irregular line of hills which separated Yebnah and Akir, which will be more readily recognised, the former as the Jamnia of the Jews and the latter as Ekron, one of the famous Philistine cities. While the 75th Division was forcing back the line Turmus–Kustineh–Yasur and Mesmiyeh athwart the road to Junction Station the 155th Brigade attacked Katrah. The whole of the artillery of two divisions opened a bombardment of the line at eight o'clock, but the Turks showed more willingness to concede ground on the east than at Katrah, where the machine–gun fire was exceptionally heavy. General Pollak M'Call decided to assault the village with the bulk of his brigade, and seizing a rifle and bayonet from a wounded man, led the charge himself, took the village, and gradually cleared the enemy out of the cactus–enclosed gardens. The enemy losses at Katrah were very heavy. In crossing a rectangular field many Turks were caught in a cross fire from our machine guns, and over 400 dead were counted in this one field.

CHAPTER XI. TWO YEOMANRY CHARGES

In front of the mud huts of Mughar, so closely packed together on the southern slope of the hill that the dwellings at the bottom seemed to keep the upper houses from falling into the plain, there was a long oval garden with a clump of cypresses in the centre, the whole surrounded by cactus hedges of great age and strength. In the cypresses was a nest of machine guns whose crews had a perfect view of an advance from Katrah. The infantry had to advance over flat open ground to the edge of the garden. The Turkish machine–gunners and riflemen in the garden and village were supported by artillery firing from behind the ridge at the back of the village, and although the brigade made repeated efforts to get on, its advance was held up in the early afternoon, and it seemed impossible to take the place by infantry from the south in the clear light of a November afternoon. The 6th Mounted Brigade commanded by Brigadier–General C.A.C. Godwin, D.S.O., composed of the 1/1st Bucks Hussars, 1/1st Berkshire Yeomanry, and 1/1st Dorset Yeomanry, the Berkshire battery Royal Horse Artillery, and the 17th Machine Gun Squadron—old campaigners with the Egyptian Expeditionary Force—had worked round to the left of the Lowlanders and had reached a point about two miles south–west of Yebnah, that place having been occupied by the 8th Mounted Brigade, composed of the 1/1st City of London Yeomanry, 1/1st County of London Yeomanry, and the 1/3rd County of London Yeomanry. At half–past twelve the Bucks Hussars less one squadron and the Berks battery, which were in the rear of the brigade, advanced *via* Beshshit to the wadi Janus, a deep watercourse with precipitous banks running across the plain east of Yebnah and joining the wadi Rubin. One squadron of the Bucks Hussars had entered

How Jerusalem Was Won

Yebnah from the east, co–operating with the 8th Brigade. General Godwin was told over the telephone that the infantry attack was held up and that his brigade would advance to take Mughar. This order was confirmed by telegram a quarter of an hour later as the brigadier was about to reconnoitre a line of approach. The Berks battery began shelling Mughar and the ridge behind the village from a position half a mile north of Beshshit screened by some trees. Brigade headquarters joined the Bucks Hussars headquarters in the wadi Janus half a mile south–east of Yebnah, where Lieut.–Colonel the Hon. F. Cripps commanding the Bucks Hussars had, with splendid judgment, already commenced a valuable reconnaissance, the Dorset and Berks Yeomanry being halted in a depression out of sight a few hundred yards behind. The Turks had the best possible observation, and, knowing they were holding up the infantry, concentrated their attention upon the cavalry. Therein they showed good judgment, for it was from the mounted troops the heavy blow was to fall. Lieut. Perkins, Bucks Hussars, was sent forward to reconnoitre the wadi Shellal el Ghor, which runs parallel to and east of the wadi Janus. He became the target of every kind of fire, guns, machine guns, and rifles opening on him from the ridge whenever he exposed himself. Captain Patron, of the 17th Machine Gun Squadron, was similarly treated while examining a position from which to cover the advance of the brigade with concentrated machine–gun fire. It was not an easy thing to get cavalry into position for a mounted attack. Except in the wadis the plain between Yebnah and Mughar offered no cover and was within easy range of the enemy's guns. The wadi Janus was a deep slit in the ground with sides of clay falling almost sheer to the stony bottom. It was hard to get horses into the wadi and equally troublesome to get them to bank again, and the wadi in most places was so narrow that horses could only move in single file. The Dorsets were brought up in small parties to join the Bucks in the wadi, and they had to run the gauntlet of shell and rifle fire. The Berks were to enter the wadi immediately the Bucks had left it. Behind Mughar village and its gardens the ground falls sharply, then rises again and forms a rocky hill some 300 yards long. There is another decline, and north of it a conical shaped hill, also stony and barren, though before the crest is reached there is some undulating ground which would have afforded a little cover if the cunning Turks had not posted machine guns on it. The Dorset Yeomanry were ordered to attack this latter hill and the Bucks Hussars the ridge between it and Mughar village, the Berks Yeomanry to be kept in support. There seems to be no reason for doubting that Mughar would not have been captured that day but for the extremely brilliant charge of these home counties yeomen. The 155th Brigade was still held fast in that part of the wadi Janus which gave cover south–west and south of Mughar, and after the charge had been completely successful and the yeomanry were working forward to clear up the village a

70

message was received—timed 2.45 P.M., but received at 4 P.M.—which shows the difficulties facing that very gallant infantry brigade: '52nd Division unable to make progress. Co–operate and turn Mughar from the north.'

It was a hot bright afternoon. The dispositions having been made, the Bucks Hussars and Dorset Yeomanry got out of the wadi and commenced their mounted attack, the Berks battery in the meantime having registered on certain points. The Bucks Hussars, in column of squadrons extended to four yards interval, advanced at a trot from the wadi, which was 3000 yards distant from the ridge which was their objective. Two machine guns were attached to the Bucks and two to the Dorsets, and the other guns under Captain Patron were mounted in a position which that officer had chosen in the wadi El Ghor from which they could bring to bear a heavy fire almost up to the moment the Bucks should be on the ridge. This machine–gun fire was of the highest value, and it unquestionably kept many Turkish riflemen inactive. 'B' squadron under Captain Bulteel, M.C., was leading, and when 1000 yards from the objective the order was given to gallop, and horses swept over the last portion of the plain and up the hill at a terrific pace, the thundering hoofs raising clouds of dust. The tap–tap of machine guns firing at the highest pressure, intense rifle fire from all parts of the enemy position, the fierce storm of shells rained on the hill by the Berks battery, which during the charge fired with splendid accuracy no fewer than 200 rounds of shrapnel at a range of 3200 to 3500 yards, and the rapid fire of Turkish field guns, completely drowned the cheers of the charging yeomen. 'C' squadron, commanded by Lord Bosebery's son, Captain the Hon. Neil Primrose, M.C., who was killed on the following day, made an equally dashing charge and came up on the right of 'B' squadron. Once the cavalry had reached the crest of the hill many of the Turks surrendered and threw down their arms, but some retired and then, having discovered the weakness of the cavalry, returned to some rocks on the flanks and continued the fight at close range. Captain Primrose's squadron was vigorously attacked on his left flank, but Captain Bulteel was able to get over the ridge and across the rough, steep eastern side of it, and from this point he utilised captured Turkish machine guns to put down a heavy barrage on to the northern end of the village. 'A' squadron under Captain Lawson then came up from Yebnah at the gallop, and with his support the whole of the Bucks' objectives were secured and consolidated.

The Dorset Yeomanry on the left of the Bucks had 1000 yards farther to go, and the country they traversed was just as cracked and broken. Their horses at the finish were quite exhausted. At the base of the hills Captain Dammers dismounted 'A' squadron,

71

which charged on the left, and the squadron fought their way to the top of the ridge on foot. The held horses were caught in a cone of machine–gun fire, and in a space of about fifty square yards many gallant chargers perished. 'B' squadron (Major Wingfield–Digby) in the centre and 'C' squadron (Major Gordon, M.C.) on the right, led by Colonel Sir Randolf Baker, M.P., formed line and galloped the hill, and their horse losses were considerably less than those of the dismounted squadron. The Berks Yeomanry moved to the wadi El Ghor under heavy machine–gun and rifle fire from the village and gardens on the west side, and two squadrons were dismounted and sent into the village to clear it, the remaining squadron riding into the plain on the eastern side of the ridge, where they collected a number of stragglers. Dotted over this plain were many dead Turks who fell under the fire of the Machine–Gun Squadron while attempting to get to Ramleh. The Turkish dead were numerous and their condition showed how thoroughly the sword had done its work. I saw many heads cleft in twain, and Mughar was not a sweet place to look upon and wanted a good deal of clearing up. The yeomanry took 18 officers and 1078 other ranks prisoners, whilst fourteen machine guns and two field guns were captured. But for the tired state of the horses many more prisoners would have been taken, large numbers being seen making their way along the red sand tracks to Ramleh, and an inspection of the route on the morrow told of the pace of the retirement brought about by the shock of contact with cavalry. Machine guns, belts and boxes of ammunition, equipment of all kinds were strewn about the paths, and not a few wounded Turks had given up the effort to escape and had lain down to die.

The casualties in the 6th Mounted Brigade were 1 officer killed and 6 wounded, 15 other ranks killed and 107 wounded and 1 missing, a remarkably small total. Among the mortally wounded was Major de Rothschild, who fell within sight of some of the Jewish colonies which his family had founded. Two hundred and sixty–five horses and two mules were killed and wounded in the action.

Mughar was a great cavalry triumph, and the regiments which took part in it confirmed the good opinions formed of them in this theatre of war. The Dorsets had already made a spirited charge against the Senussi in the Western Desert in 1916,[1] and having suffered from the white arm once those misguided Arabs never gave the cavalry another chance of getting near them. The Bucks and Berks, too, had taken part in that swift and satisfactory campaign. All three regiments on the following day were to make another charge, this time on one of the most famous sites in the battle history of Palestine. The 6th Mounted Brigade moved no farther on the day of Mughar because the 22nd Mounted Brigade,

72

when commencing an attack on Akir, the old Philistine city of Ekron, were counter–attacked on their left. During the night, however, the Turks in Akir probably heard the full story of Mughar, and did not wait long for a similar action against them. The 22nd Mounted Brigade drove them out early next morning, and they went rapidly away across the railway at Naaneh, leaving in our hands the railway guard of seventy men, and seeking the bold crest of Abu Shushe. They moved, as I shall presently tell, out of the frying–pan into the fire.

[Footnote 1: *The Desert Campaigns*: Constable.]

The 155th Infantry which helped to finish up the Mughar business took a gun and fourteen machine guns. Then with the remainder of the 52nd Division it had a few hours of hard–earned rest. The Division had had a severe time, but the men bore their trials with the fortitude of their race and with a spirit which could not be beaten. For several days, when water was holding up the cavalry, the Lowlanders kept ahead of the mounted troops, and one battalion fought and marched sixty–nine miles in seven days. Their training was as complete as any infantry, even the regimental stretcher–bearers being taught the use of Lewis guns, and on more than one occasion the bearers went for the enemy with Mills bombs till a position was captured and they were required to tend the wounded. A Stokes–gun crew found their weapon very useful in open warfare, and at one place where machine guns had got on to a large party of Turks and enclosed them in a box barrage, the Stokes gun searched every corner of the area and finished the whole party. The losses inflicted by the Scots were exceptionally severe. Farther eastwards on the 13th, the 75th Division had also been giving of its best. The objective of this Division was the important Junction Station on the Turks' Jaffa–Jerusalem railway, and a big step forward was made in the early afternoon by the overcoming of a stubborn resistance at Mesmiyeh, troops rushing the village from the south and capturing 292 prisoners and 7 machine guns. The 234th Brigade began an advance on Junction Station during the night, but were strongly counter–attacked and had to halt till the morning, when at dawn they secured the best positions on the rolling downs west of the station, and by 7.30 the station itself was occupied. Two engines and 45 vehicles were found intact; two large guns on trucks and over 100 prisoners were also taken. The enemy shelled the station during the morning, trying in vain to damage his lost rolling stock. This booty was of immense value to us, and to a large extent it solved the transport problem which at this moment was a very anxious one indeed. The line was metre gauge and we had no stock to fit it, though later the Egyptian State Railways brought down some engines and trucks from the

Luxor–Assouan section, but this welcome aid was not available till after the rains had begun and had made lorry traffic temporarily impossible between our standard gauge railhead and our fighting front. Junction Station was no sooner occupied than a light–railway staff under Colonel O'Brien was brought up from Beit Hanun. The whole of the line to Deir Sineid was not in running order, but broken culverts were given minor repairs, attention was bestowed on trucks, and the engines were closely examined while the Turks were shelling the station. The water tanks had been destroyed, as a result of which two men spent hours in filling up the engines by means of a water jug and basin found in the station buildings, and the Turks had the mortification of seeing these engines steam out of the station during the morning to a cutting which was effective cover from their field–gun fire. The light–railway staff were highly delighted at their success, and the trains which they soon had running over their little system were indeed a boon and a blessing to the fighting men and horses.

On this morning of November 14 the infantry were operating with Desert Mounted Corps' troops on both their wings. The Australian Mounted Division was on the right, fighting vigorous actions with the enemy rearguards secreted in the irregular, rocky foothills of the Shephelah which stand as ramparts to the Judean Mountains. It was a difficult task to drive the Turks out of these fastnesses, and while they held on to them it was almost impossible to outflank some of the places like Et Tineh, a railway station and camp of some importance on the line to Beersheba. They had already had some stiff fighting at Tel el Safi, the limestone hill which was the White Guard of the Crusaders. The Division suffered severely from want of water, particularly the 5th Mounted Brigade, and it was necessary to transfer to it the 7th Mounted Brigade and the 2nd Australian Light Horse Brigade. On the left of the infantry the Yeomanry Mounted Division was moving forward from Akir and Mansura, and after the 22nd Mounted Brigade had taken Naaneh they detailed a demolition party to blow up one mile of railway, so that, even if the 75th Division had not taken Junction Station, Jerusalem would have been entirely cut off from railway communication with the Turkish base at Tul Keram, and Haifa and Damascus.

Between Naaneh and Mansura the 6th Mounted Brigade was preparing for another dashing charge. The enemy who had been opposing us for two days consisted of remnants of two divisions of both the Turkish VIIth and VIIIth Armies brought together and hurriedly reorganised. The victory at Mughar had almost, if not quite, split the force in two, that is to say that portion of the line which had been given the duty of holding

How Jerusalem Was Won

Mughar had been so weakened by heavy casualties, and the loss of moral consequent upon the shock of the cavalry charge, that it had fallen back to Ramleh and Ludd and was incapable of further serious resistance. There was still a strong and virile force on the seaside, though that was adequately dealt with, but the centre was very weak, and the enemy's only chance of preventing the mounted troops from working through and round his right centre was to fall back on Abu Shushe and Tel Jezar to cover Latron, with its good water supply and the main metalled road where it enters the hills on the way to Jerusalem. The loss of Tel Jezar meant that we could get to Latron and the Vale of Ajalon, and the action of the 6th Mounted Brigade on the morning of the 14th gave it to us.

The Berks Yeomanry had had outposts on the railway south–east of Naaneh since before dawn. They had seen the position the previous day, and at dawn sent forward a squadron dismounted to engage the machine guns posted in the walled–in house at the north of the village. From the railway to the Abu Shushe ridge is about three miles of up and down country with two or three rises of sufficient height to afford some cover to advancing cavalry. General Godwin arranged that six machine guns should go forward to give covering fire, and, supported by the Berks battery R.H.A. from a good position half a mile west of the railway, the Bucks Hussars were to deliver a mounted attack against the hill, with the assistance on their left of two squadrons of Berks Yeomanry. The Dorset Yeomanry were moved up to the red hill of Melat into support.

At seven o'clock the attack started, the 22nd Mounted Brigade operating on foot on the left. The Bucks Hussars, taking advantage of all the dead ground, galloped about a mile and a half until they came to a dip behind a gently rising mound, when, it being clear that the enemy held the whole ridge in strength, Colonel Cripps signalled to Brigade Headquarters at Melat for support. The Dorset Yeomanry moved out to the right of the Bucks, and the latter then charged the hill a little south of the village and captured it. It was a fine effort. The sides of the hill were steep with shelves of rock, and the crest was a mass of stones and boulders, while from some caves, one or two of them quite big places, the Turks had machine guns in action. When the Bucks were charging there was a good deal of machine–gun fire from the right, but the Dorsets dealt with this very speedily, assisted by the Berks battery which had also moved forward to a near position from which they could command the ridge in flank. A hostile counter–attack developed against the Dorsets, but this was crushed by the Berks battery and some of the 52nd Division's guns. Two squadrons of the Berks Yeomanry in the meantime had charged on the left of

75

the Bucks and secured the hill immediately to the south–east of Abu Shushe village, and at nine o'clock the whole of this strong position was in our hands, the brigade having sustained the extremely slight casualties of three officers and thirty–four other ranks killed and wounded. So small a cost of life was a wonderful tribute to good and dashing leading, and furnished another example of cavalry's power when moving rapidly in extended formation. To the infinite regret of the brigade, indeed of the whole of General Allenby's Army, one of the officers killed that day was the Hon. Neil Primrose, an intrepid leader who, leaving the comfort and safety of a Ministerial appointment, answered the call of duty to be with his squadron of the Bucks Hussars. He was a fine soldier and a favourite among his men, and he died as a good cavalryman would wish, shot through the head when leading his squadron in a glorious charge. His body rests in the garden of the French convent at Ramleh not far from the spot where humbler soldiers take their long repose, and these graves within visual range of the tomb of St. George, our patron saint, will stand as memorials of those Britons who forsook ease to obey the stern call of duty to their race and country.

The overwhelming nature of this victory is illustrated by a comparison of the losses on the two sides. Whereas ours were 37 all told, we counted between 400 and 500 dead Turks on the field, and the enemy left with us 360 prisoners and some material. The extraordinary disparity between the losses can only be accounted for first by the care taken to lead the cavalry along every depression in the ground, and secondly by rapidity of movement. The cavalry were confronted by considerable shell fire, and the volume of machine–gun fire was heavy, though it was kept down a good deal by the covering fire of the 17th Machine Gun Squadron.

I have referred to the importance of Jezar as dominating the approaches to Latron on the north–east and Ramleh on the north–west. Jezar, as we call it on our maps, has been a stronghold since men of all races and creeds, coloured and white, Pagan, Mahomedan, Jew, and Christian, fought in Palestine. It is a spot which many a great leader of legions has coveted, and to its military history our home county yeomen have added another brilliant page. Let me quote the description of Jezar from George Adam Smith's *Historical Geography of the Holy Land*, a book of fascinating interest to all students of the Sacred History which many of the soldiers in General Allenby's Army read with great profit to themselves:

76

How Jerusalem Was Won

'One point in the Northern Shephelah round which these tides of war have swept deserves special notice—Gezer, or Gazar. It is one of the few remarkable bastions which the Shephelah flings out to the west—on a ridge running towards Ramleh, the most prominent object in view of the traveller from Jaffa towards Jerusalem. It is high and isolated, but fertile and well watered—a very strong post and striking landmark. Its name occurs in the Egyptian correspondence of the fourteenth century, where it is described as being taken from the Egyptian vassals by the tribes whose invasion so agitates that correspondence. A city of the Canaanites, under a king of its own—Horam—Gezer is not given as one of Joshua's conquests, though the king is; but the Israelites drave not out the Canaanites who dwelt at Gezer, and in the hands of these it remained till its conquest by Egypt when Pharaoh gave it, with his daughter, to Solomon and Solomon rebuilt it. Judas Maccabeus was strategist enough to gird himself early to the capture of Gezer, and Simon fortified it to cover the way to the harbour of Joppa and caused John his son, the captain of the host, to dwell there. It was virtually, therefore, the key of Judea at a time when Judea's foes came down the coast from the north; and, with Joppa, it formed part of the Syrian demands upon the Jews. But this is by no means the last of it. M. Clermont Ganneau, who a number of years ago discovered the site, has lately identified Gezer with the Mont Gisart of the Crusades. Mont Gisart was a castle and fief in the county of Joppa, with an abbey of St. Katharine of Mont Gisart, "whose prior was one of the five suffragans of the Bishop of Lydda." It was the scene, on the 24th November 1174, seventeen years before the Third Crusade, of a victory won by a small army from Jerusalem under the boy–king, the leper Baldwin IV., against a very much larger army under Saladin himself, and, in 1192, Saladin encamped upon it during his negotiations for a truce with Richard.

'Shade of King Horam, what hosts of men have fallen round that citadel of yours. On what camps and columns has it looked down through the centuries, since first you saw the strange Hebrews burst with the sunrise across the hills, and chase your countrymen down Ajalon—that day when the victors felt the very sun conspiring with them to achieve the unexampled length of battle. Within sight of every Egyptian and every Assyrian invasion of the land, Gezer has also seen Alexander pass by, and the legions of Rome in unusual flight, and the armies of the Cross struggle, waver and give way, and Napoleon come and go. If all could rise who have fallen around its base—Ethiopians, Hebrews, Assyrians, Arabs, Turcomans, Greeks, Romans, Celts, Saxons, Mongols—what a rehearsal of the Judgment Day it would be. Few of the travellers who now rush across the plain realise that the first conspicuous hill they pass in Palestine is also one of the

77

most thickly haunted—even in that narrow land into which history has so crowded itself. But upon the ridge of Gezer no sign of all this now remains, except in the Tel Jezer, and in a sweet hollow to the north, beside a fountain, where lie the scattered Christian stone of Deir Warda, the Convent of the Rose.

'Up none of the other valleys of the Shephelah has history surged as up and down Ajalon and past Gezer, for none arc so open to the north, nor present so easy a passage to Jerusalem.'

CHAPTER XII. LOOKING TOWARDS JERUSALEM

The Anzac Mounted Division had only the 1st Australian Light Horse and the New Zealand Mounted Rifles Brigade operating with it on the 14th. The Australians, by the evening, were in the thick olive groves on the south of Ramleh, and on the ridges about Surafend. On their left the Turks were violently opposing the New Zealanders who were working along the sand–dunes with the port and town of Jaffa as their ultimate objective. There was one very fierce struggle in the course of the day. A force attacked a New Zealand regiment in great strength and for the moment secured the advantage, but the regiment got to grips with the enemy with hand–grenades and bayonets, and so completely repulsed them that they fled in hopeless disorder leaving many dead and wounded behind them. It was unfortunate that there was no mobile reserve available for pursuit, as the Turks were in such a plight that a large number would have been rounded up. General Cox's brigade seized Ramleh on the morning of the 15th, taking ninety prisoners, and then advanced and captured Ludd, being careful that no harm should come to the building which holds the grave of St. George. In Ludd 360 prisoners were taken, and the brigade carried out a good deal of demolition work on the railway running north. The New Zealanders made Jaffa by noon on the 16th, the Turks evacuating the town during the morning without making any attempt to destroy it, though there was one gross piece of vandalism in a Christian cemetery where monuments and tombstones had been thrown down and broken. In the meantime, in order to protect the rear of the infantry, five battalions of the 52nd Division with three batteries were stationed at Yebnah, Mughar, and Akir until they could be relieved by units of the 54th Division advancing from Gaza. To enable the 54th to move, the transport lent to the 52nd and 75th Divisions had to be returned, which did not make the supply of those divisions any easier. The main line of railway was still a long way in the rear, and the landing of stores by the Navy at the mouth of the wadi Sukereir had not yet begun. A little later, and before Jaffa had been made secure enough for the use of ships, many thousands of tons of supplies and ammunition were put ashore at the wadi's mouth, and at a time when heavy rains damaged the newly constructed railway tracks the Sukereir base of supply was an inestimable boon. Yet there were times when the infantry had a bare day's supply with them, though they had their iron rations to fall back upon. It speaks well for the supply branch that in the long forward move of XXIst Corps the infantry were never once put on short rations.

While the 54th were coming up to take over from the 52nd, plans were prepared for the further advance on Jerusalem. The Commander−in−Chief was deeply anxious that there should be no fighting of any description near the Holy Places, and he gave the Turks a chance of being chivalrous and of accepting the inevitable. We had got so far that the ancient routes taken by armies which had captured Jerusalem were just before us. The Turkish forces were disorganised by heavy and repeated defeats, the men demoralised and not in good condition, and there was no hope for them that they could receive sufficient reinforcements to enable them to stave off the ultimate capture of Bethlehem and Jerusalem, though as events proved they could still put up a stout defence. We know from papers taken from the enemy that the Turks believed General Allenby intended to go right up the plain to get to the defile leading to Messudieh and Nablus and thus threaten the Hedjaz railway, in which case the position of the enemy in the Holy City would be hopeless, and the Turks formed an assault group of three infantry divisions in the neighbourhood of Tul Keram to prevent this, and continued to hold on to Jerusalem. General Allenby proposed to strike through the hills to the north−east to try to get across the Jerusalem−Nablus road about Bireh (the ancient Beeroth), and in this operation success would have enabled him to cut off the enemy forces in and about the Holy City, when their only line of retreat would have been through Jericho and the east of the Jordan. The Turks decided to oppose this plan and to make us fight for Jerusalem. That was disappointing, but in the end it could not have suited us better, for it showed to our own people and to the world how after the Turks had declined an opportunity of showing a desire to preserve the Holy Places from attack—an opportunity prompted by our strength, not by any fear that victory could not be won—General Allenby was still able to achieve his great objective without a drop of blood being spilled near any of the Holy Sites, and without so much as a stray rifle bullet searing any of their walls. That indeed was the triumph of military practice, and when Jerusalem fell for the twenty−third time, and thus for the first time passed into the hands of British soldiers, the whole force felt that the sacrifices which had been made on the gaunt forbidding hills to the north–west were worth the price, and that the graves of Englishman, Scot and Colonial, of Gurkha, Punjabi, and Sikh, were monuments to the honour of British arms. The scheme was that the 75th Division would advance along the main Jerusalem road, which cuts into the hills about three miles east of Latron, and occupy Kuryet el Enab, and that the Lowland Division should go through Ludd, strike eastwards and advance to Beit Likia to turn from the north the hills through which the road passes, the Yeomanry Mounted Division on the left flank of the 52nd Division to press on to Bireh, on the Nablus road about a dozen miles north of Jerusalem. A brief survey of the country to be attacked would convince even a civilian of the extreme difficulties of the undertaking. North and east of Latron (which was not yet ours) frown the hills which constitute this important section of the Judean range, the backbone of Palestine. The hills are steep and high, separated one from another by narrow valleys, clothed here and there with fir and olive trees, but elsewhere a mass of rocks and boulders, bare and inhospitable. Practically every hill commands another. There is only one road—the main one—and this about three miles east of Latron passes up a narrow defile with rugged mountains on either side. There is an old Roman road to the north, but, unused for centuries, it is now a road only in name, the very trace of it being lost in many places. In this strong country men fought of old, and the defenders not infrequently held their own against odds. It is pre–eminently suitable for defence, and if the warriors of the past found that flint–tipped shafts of wood would keep the invader at bay, how much more easily could a modern army equipped with rifles of precision and machine guns adapt Nature to its advantage? It will always be a marvel to me how in a country where one machine gun in defence could hold up a battalion, we made such rapid progress, and how having got so deep into the range it was possible for us to feed our front. We had no luck with the weather. In advancing over the plain the troops had suffered from the abnormal heat, and many of the wells had been destroyed or damaged by the retreating enemy. In the hills the troops had to endure heavy rains and piercingly cold winds, with mud a foot deep on the roads and the earth so slippery on the hills that only donkey transport was serviceable. Yet despite all adverse circumstances the infantry and yeomanry pressed on, and if they did not secure all objectives, their dash, resource, and magnificent determination at least paved the way for ultimate triumph.

To the trials of hard fighting and marching on field rations the wet added a severe test of physical endurance. The troops were in enemy country where they scrupulously avoided every native village, and no wall or roof stood to shelter them from wind or water. The heat of the first two weeks of November changed with a most undesirable suddenness, and though the days continued agreeably warm on the plain into December, the nights became chilly and then desperately cold. The single blanket carried in the pack—most of the infantry on the march had no blanket at all—did not give sufficient warmth to men whose blood had been thinned by long months of work under a pitiless Eastern sun, and lucky was the soldier who secured even broken sleep in the early morning hours of that fighting march across the northern part of the Maritime Plain. The Generals, with one eye on the enemy and the other on the weather, must have been dismayed in the third week of November at the gathering storm clouds which in bursting flooded the plain with rains unusually heavy for this period of the year. The surface is a very light cotton soil several feet deep. When baked by summer sun it has a cracked hard crust giving a firm foothold for man and horse, and yielding only slightly to the wheels of light cars; even laden lorries made easy tracks over the country. The lorries generally kept off the ill-made unrolled Turkish road which had been constructed for winter use and, except for slight deviations to avoid wadis and gullies cut by Nature to carry off surplus water, the supply columns could move in almost as direct a course as the flying men. When the heavens opened all this was altered. The first storm turned the top into a slippery, greasy mass. In an hour or two the rain soaked down into the light earth, and any lorry driver pulling out of the line to avoid a skidding vehicle ahead, had the almost certainty of finding his car and load come to a full stop with the wheels held fast axle deep in the soft soil. An hour's hard digging, the fixing of planks beneath the wheels, and a towing cable from another lorry sometimes got the machine on to the pressed-down track again and enabled it to move ahead for a few miles, but many were the supply vehicles that had to wait for a couple of sunny days to dry a path for them.

My own experience of the first of the winter rains was so like that of others in the force who moved on wheels that I may give some idea of the conditions by recounting it. We had taken Ludd and Ramleh, and guided by the ruined tower of the Church of the Forty Martyrs I had followed in the cavalry's wake. I dallied on the way back to see if Akir presented to the latter-day Crusader any signs of its former strength when it stood as the Philistine stronghold of Ekron. Near where the old city had been the ghastly sight of Turks cut down by yeomanry during a hot pursuit offended the senses of sight and smell, and when you saw natives moving towards their village at a rate somewhat in excess of their customary shuffling gait you were almost led to think that their superstitious fears were driving them home before sundown lest darkness should raise the ghosts of the Turkish dead. A few of the Jewish settlers, whose industry has improved the landscape, were leaving the fields and orchards they tended so well, though there was still more than an hour of daylight and their tasks were not yet done. They were weatherwise. They could have been deaf to the rumblings in the south and still have noticed the coming of the storm. I was some forty miles from the spot at which my despatch could be censored and passed over land wire and cable to London, when a vivid lightning flash warned me that the elements were in forbidding mood and that I had misread the obvious signal of the natives' homeward movement.

The map showed a path from Akir through Mansura towards Junction Station, from which the so–called Turkish road ran south. In the gathering gloom my driver picked up wheel tracks through an olive orchard and, crossing a nullah, found the marks of a Ford car's wheels on the other side. The rain fell heavily and soon obliterated all signs of a car's progress, and with darkness coming on there was a prospect of a shivering night with a wet skin in the open. An Australian doctor going up to his regiment at grips with the Turk told me that he had no doubt we were on the right road, for he had been given a line through Mansura, which must be the farmhouse ahead of us. These Australians have a keen nose for country and you have a sense of security in following them. The doctor's horse was slipping in the mud, but my car made even worse going. It skidded to right and left, and only by the skill and coolness of my driver was I saved a ducking in a narrow wadi now full of storm water. After much low–gear work we pulled up a slight rise and saw ahead of us one or two little fires. Under the lee of a dilapidated wall some Scottish infantry were brewing tea and making the most of a slight shelter. It was Mansura, and if we bore to the right and kept the track beaten down by lorries across a field we might, by the favour of fortune, reach Junction Station during the night. The Scots had arranged a bivouac in that field before it became sodden. They knew how bad it had got, and a native instinct to be hospitable prompted an invitation to share the fire for the night. However, London was waiting for news and I decided to press on. The road could not be worse than the sea of mud in which I was floundering, and it might be better. We turned right–handed and after a struggle came up against three lorry drivers hopelessly marooned. They had turned in. Up a greasy bank we came to a stop and slid back. We tried again and failed. I relieved the car of my weight and made an effort to push it from behind, but my feet held fast in the mud and the car cannoned into me when it skidded downhill. 'Better give it up till the morning,' said an M.T. driver whose sleep was disturbed by the running of our engine. 'Can't? Who've you got there? Eh? Oh, very well. Here, Jim, give them a hand or we'll have no sleep to–night'—or words to that effect. Three of the lorry men and the engine got us on the move, and before they took mud back with them to the dry interiors of the lorries they hoped, they said, that we would reach

82

How Jerusalem Was Won

G.H.Q., but declared that it was hopeless to try.

Before getting much farther a light, waved ahead of us, told of some one held up. I walked on and found General Butler, the chief of the Army Veterinary Service with the Force, unable to move an inch. The efforts of two drivers failed to locate the trouble, and everything removable was taken off the General's car and put into ours, and with the heavier load we started off again for Junction Station. This was not difficult to pick up, for there were many flares burning to enable working parties to repair engines, rolling stock, and permanent way. We got on to the road ultimately, carrying more mud on our feet than I imagined human legs could lift. Leaving a driver and all spare gear at the station, we thrashed our way along a road metalled with a soft, friable limestone which had been cut into by the iron–shod wheels of German lorries until the ruts were fully a foot deep, and the soft earth foundation was oozing through to the surface. It was desperately hard to steer a course on this treacherous highway, and a number of lorries we passed had gone temporarily out of action in ditches. The Germans with the Turks had blown up most of the culverts, and the road bridges which had been destroyed had only been lightly repaired with planks and trestles, no safety rails being in position. To negotiate these dangerous paths in the dark the driver had to put on all possible speed and make a dash for it, and he usually got to the other side before a skid became serious. Most of the lorry drivers put out no light because they thought no car would be able to move on such a night, and we had several narrow escapes of finishing our career on a half–sunken supply motor vehicle.

Reinforcements for infantry battalions moved up the road as we came down it. They were going to the front to take the place of casualties, for weather and mud are not considered when bayonets are wanted in the line. So the stolid British infantryman splashed and slipped his way towards the enemy, and he would probably have been sleeping that night if there had not been a risk of his drowning in the mud. The Camel Transport Corps fought the elements with a courage which deserved better luck. The camel dislikes many things and is afraid of some. But if he is capable of thinking at all he regards mud as his greatest enemy. He cannot stand up in it, and if he slips he has not an understanding capable of realising that if all his feet do not go the same way he must spread–eagle and split up. This is what often happens, but if by good luck a camel should go down sideways he seems quite content to stay there, and he is so refractory that he prefers to die rather than help himself to his feet again. On this wild night I had a good opportunity of seeing white officers encourage the Egyptian boys in the Camel Transport Corps. At Julis the roadway passes through the village. There was an ambulance column in difficulties in the village, and while some cars were being extricated a camel supply column came up in the opposite direction. The camels liked neither the headlights nor the running engines, and these had to be made dark and silent before they would pass. The water was running over the roadway several inches deep, carrying with it a mass of garbage and filth which only Arab villagers would tolerate. Officers and Gyppies coaxed and wheedled the stubborn beasts through Julis, but outside the place the animals raised a chorus of protest and went down. They held me up for an hour or more, and though officers and boys did their utmost to get them going again it was a fruitless effort, and the poor beasts were off–loaded where they lay. That night of rain and thunder, wind and cold, was bad alike for man and beast, but beyond a flippant remark of some soldier doing his best and the curious chant of the Gyppies' chorus you heard nothing. Tommy could not trust himself to talk about the weather. It was too bad for words, for even the strongest.

It took our car ten hours to run forty miles, and as the last ten miles was over wet sand and on rabbit wire stretched across the sand where the car could do fifteen miles an hour, we had averaged something under three miles an hour through the mud. Wet through, cold, with a face rendered painful to the touch by driven rain, I reached my tent with a feeling of thankfulness for myself and deep sympathy for the tens of thousands of brave boys enduring intense discomfort and fatigue, coupled with the fear of short rations for the next day or two. The men in the hills which they were just entering had a worse time than those in the waterlogged plain, but no storms could damp their enthusiasm. They were beating your enemies and mine, and they were facing a goal which Britain had never yet won. Jerusalem the Golden was before them, and the honour and glory of winning it from the Turk was a prize to attain which no sacrifice was too great. Those who did not say so behaved in a way to show that they felt it. They were very gallant, perfect knights, these soldiers of the King.

CHAPTER XIII. INTO THE JUDEAN HILLS

When the 52nd Division were moving out of Ludd on the 19th November the 75th Division were fighting hard about Latron, where the Turks held the monastery and its beautiful gardens and the hill about Amwas until late in the morning. Having driven them out, the 75th pushed on to gain the pass into the hills and to begin two days of fighting which earned the unstinted praise of General Bulfin who witnessed it. For nearly three miles from Latron the road passes through a flat valley flanked by hills till it reaches a guardhouse and khan at the foot of the pass which then rises rapidly to Saris, the difference in elevation in less than four miles being 1400 feet. Close to the guardhouse begin the hills which tower above the road. The Turks had constructed defences on these hills and held them with riflemen and machine guns, so that these positions dominated all approaches. Our guns had few positions from which to assist the infantry, but they did sterling service wherever possible. In General Palin the Division had a commander with wide experience of hill fighting on the Indian frontier, and he brought that experience to bear in a way which must have dumb-founded the enemy. Frontal attacks were impossible and suicidal, and each position had to be turned by a wide movement started a long way in rear. All units in the Division did well, the Gurkhas particularly well, and by a continual encircling of their flanks the Turks were compelled to leave their fastnesses and fall back to new hill crests. Thus outwitted and outmatched the enemy retreated to Saris, a high hill with a commanding view of the pass for half a mile. The hill is covered with olive trees and has a village on its eastern slope, and as the road winds at its foot and then takes a left-handed turn to Kuryet el Enab its value for defence was considerable.

The Turks had taken advantage of the cover to place a large body of defenders with machine guns on the hill, but with every condition unfavourable to us the 75th Division had routed out the enemy before three o'clock and were ready to move forward as soon as the guns could get up the pass. Rain was falling heavily, the road surface was clinging and treacherous, and, worse still, the road had been blown up in several places. The guns could not advance to be of service that day, and the infantry had, therefore, to remain where they were for the night. There was a good deal of sniping, but Nature was more unkind than the enemy, who received more than he gave. The troops were wearing light summer clothing, drill shorts and tunics, and the sudden change from the heat and dryness of the plain to bitter cold and wet was a desperate trial, especially to the Indian units, who had little sleep that night. They needed rest to prepare them for the rigour of the succeeding day. A drenching rain turned the whole face of the mountains, where earth covered rock, into a sea of mud. On the positions about Saris being searched a number of prisoners were taken, among them a battalion commander. Men captured in the morning told us there were six Turkish battalions holding Enab, which is something under two miles from Saris.

The road proceeds up a rise from Saris, then falling slightly it passes below the crest of a ridge and again climbs to the foot of a hill on which a red-roofed convent church and buildings stand as a landmark that can be seen from Jaffa. On the opposite side of the road is a substantial house, the summer retreat of the German Consul in Jerusalem, whose staff traded in Jordan Holy Water; and this house, now empty, sheltered a divisional general from the bad weather while the operations for the capture of the Holy City were in preparation. I have a grateful recollection of this building, for in it the military attaches and I stayed before the Official Entry into Jerusalem, and its roof saved us from one inclement night on the blcak hills. On the 20th November the Turks did their best to keep the place under German ownership. The hill on which it stands was well occupied by men under cover of thick stone walls, the convent gardens on the opposite side of the highway was packed with Turkish infantry, and across the deep valley to the west were guns and riflemen on another hill, all of them holding the road under the best possible observation. The enemy's howitzers put down a heavy barrage on all approaches, and on the reverse of the hill covering the village lying in the hollow there were machine guns and many men. Reconnaissances showed the difficulties attending an attack, and it was not until the afternoon that a plan was ready to be put into execution. No weak points in the defences could be discovered, and just as it seemed possible that a daylight attack would be held up, a thick mist rolled up the valley and settled down over Enab. The 2/3rd Gurkhas seized a welcomed opportunity, and as the light was failing the shrill, sharp notes of these gallant hillmen and the deep–throated roar of the 1/5th Somersets told that a weighty bayonet charge had got home, and that the keys of the enemy position had been won. The men of the bold 75th went beyond Enab in the dark, and also out along the old Roman road towards Biddu to deny the Turks a point from which they could see the road as it fell away from the Enab ridge towards the wadi Ikbala. That night many men sought the doubtful shelter of olive groves, and built stone sangars to break the force of a biting wind. A few, as many as could be accommodated, were welcomed by the monks in a monastery in a fold in the hills, whilst some rested and were thankful in a crypt beneath the monks' church, the oldest part of the building, believed to be the work of sixth–century masons. The monks had a tale of woe to tell. They had been proud to have as their guest the Latin Patriarch in Jerusalem, who was a French protege, and this high ecclesiastic remained at the monastery till November 17, when Turkish gendarmerie carried him away. The Spanish Consul in Jerusalem lodged a vigorous protest, and, so the monks were told, he was supported by the German Commandant. But to no purpose, for when General Allenby entered Jerusalem he learned that the Latin Patriarch had been removed to Damascus. For quite a long time the monks did many kindly things for our troops. They gave up the greater part of the monastery and church for use as a hospital, and many a sick man was brought back to health by rest within those ancient walls.

How Jerusalem Was Won

Some, alas, there were whose wounds were mortal, and a number lie in the monks' secluded garden. They have set up wooden crosses over them, and we may be certain that in that quiet sequestered spot their remains will rest in peace and will have the protection of the monks as surely as it has been given to the grave of the Roman centurion which faces those of our brave boys who fell on the same soil fighting the same good fight.

While the 75th Division were making their magnificent effort at Enab the Lowlanders had breasted other and equally difficult hills to the north. General Hill had posted a strong force at Beit Likia, and then moved south−east along the route prepared by Cestius Gallus nearly 1900 years ago to the height of Beit Anan, and thence east again to Beit Dukku. On the 21st the road and ground near it were in exceedingly bad condition, and the difficulty of moving anything on wheels along it could hardly have been greater. Already the 52nd Division had realised it was hopeless to get all their divisional artillery into action, and only three sections of artillery were brought up, the horses of the guns sent back to Ramleh being used to double the teams in the three advanced sections. It was heavy work, too, for infantry who not only had to carry the weight of mud−caked boots, but were handicapped by continual slipping upon the rocky ground. The 75th advancing along the road from Enab to Kustul got an idea of the Turkish lack of attention to the highway, the main road being deep in mud and full of dangerous ruts. They won Kustul about midday, and officers who climbed to the top got their first glimpse of the outskirts of Jerusalem from the ruined walls of a Roman castle that gives its name to the little village perched on the height. They did not, however, see much beyond the Syrian colony behind the main Turkish defences, and the first view of Jerusalem by the troops of the British Army was obtained by General Maclean's brigade when they advanced from Biddu to Nebi Samwil, that crowning height on which many centuries before Richard the Lion Heart buried his face in his casque and exclaimed: 'Lord God, I pray that I may never see Thy Holy City, if so be that I may not rescue it from the hands of Thine enemies.'

What a fight it was for Nebi Samwil! The Turk had made it his advanced work for his main line running from El Jib through Bir Nabala, Beit Iksa to Lifta, as strong a chain of entrenched mountains as any commander could desire. General Maclean's brigade advanced from Biddu along the side of a ridge and up the exposed steep slope of Nebi Samwil, not all of which, in the only direction he could select for an advance, was terraced, as it was on the Turks' side. He was all the time confronted by heavy artillery and rifle fire, and, though supported by guns firing at long range from the neighbourhood

87

of Enab, he could not make Nebi Samwil in daylight. Round the top of the hill the Turk had dug deeply into the stony earth. He knew the value of that hill. From its crest good observation was obtained in all directions, and if, when we had to attack the main Jerusalem defences on December 8, the summit of Nebi Samwil had still been in Turkish hands, not a movement of troops as they issued from the bed of the wadi Surar and climbed the rough face of the western buttresses of Jerusalem would have escaped notice. The brigade won the hill and held it just before midnight, but the battle for the crest ebbed and flowed for days with terrific violence, we never giving up possession of it, though it was stormed again and again by an enemy who, it is fair to admit, displayed fine courage and not a little skill. That hill-top at this period had to submit to a thunderous bombardment, and the Mosque of Nebi Samwil became a battered shell. Here are supposed to lie the remains of the Prophet Samuel. The tradition may or may not be well founded, but at any rate Mahomedans and Christians alike have held the place in veneration for centuries. The Turk paid no regard to the sanctity of the Mosque, and, as it was of military importance to him that we should not hold it, he shelled it daily with all his available guns, utterly destroying it. There may be cases where the Turks will deny that they damaged a Holy Place. They could not hide their guilt on Nebi Samwil. I was at pains to examine the Mosque and the immediate surroundings, and the photographs I took are proof that the wreckage of this church came from artillery fired from the east and north, the direction of the Turkish gun-pits. It is possible we are apt to be a little too sentimental about the destruction in war of a place of worship. If a general has reason to think that a tower or minaret is being used as an observation post, or that a church or mosque is sheltering a body of troops, there are those who hold that he is justified in deliberately planning its destruction, but here was a sacred building with associations held in reverence by all classes and creeds in a land where these things are counted high, and to have set about wrecking it was a crime. The German influence over the Turk asserted itself, as it did in the heavy fighting after we had taken Jerusalem. We had batteries on the Mount of Olives and the Turk searched for them, but they never fired one round at the Kaiserin Augusta Victoria Hospice near by. That had been used as Falkenhayn's headquarters. General Chetwode occupied it as his Corps Headquarters soon after he entered Jerusalem. There was a wireless installation and the Turks could see the coming and going of the Corps' motor cars. I have watched operations from a summer-house in the gardens, and no enemy plane could pass over the building without discovering the purpose to which it was put. And there were spies. But not one shell fell within the precincts of the hospice because it was a German building, containing the statues of the Kaiser and Kaiserin, and (oh, the taste of the Hun!) with effigies of the

Kaiser and his consort painted in the roof of the chapel not far from a picture of the Saviour. Britain is rebuilding what the Turks destroyed, and there will soon arise on Nebi Samwil a new mosque to show Mahomedans that tolerance and freedom abide under our flag.

When the 75th Division were making the attack on Nebi Samwil the 52nd Division put all the men they could spare on to the task of making roads. To be out of the firing line did not mean rest. In fact, as far as physical exertion went, it was easier to be fighting than in reserve. From sunrise till dark and often later the roadmakers were at work with pick, shovel, and crowbar, and the tools were not too many for the job. The gunners joined in the work and managed to take their batteries over the roads long before they were considered suitable for other wheels. The battery commanders sometimes selected firing positions which appeared quite inaccessible to any one save a mountain climber, but the guns got there and earned much credit for their teams.

On the 22nd Nebi Samwil was thrice attacked. British and Indian troops were holding the hill, but the Turks were on the northern slopes. They were, in fact, on strong positions on three sides, and from El Burj, a prominent hill 1200 yards to the south–east, and from the wooded valley of the wadi Hannina, they could advance with plenty of cover. There was much dead ground, stone walls enclosed small patches of cultivation, and when troops halted under the terraces on the slopes no gun or rifle fire could reach them. The enemy could thus get quite close to our positions before we could deal with them, and their attacks were also favoured by an intense volume of artillery fire from 5.9's placed about the Jerusalem–Nablus road and, as some people in Jerusalem afterwards told me, from the Mount of Olives. The attackers possessed the advantage that our guns could not concentrate on them while the attack was preparing, and could only put in a torrent of fire when the enemy infantry were getting near their goal. These three attacks were delivered with the utmost ferocity, and were pressed home each time with determination. But the 75th Division held on with a stubbornness which was beyond praise, and the harder the Turk tried to reach the summit the tighter became the defence. Each attack was repulsed with very heavy losses, and after his third failure the enemy did not put in his infantry again that day.

The 75th Division endeavoured to reach El Jib, a village on the hill a mile and a half to the north of Nebi Samwil. The possession of El Jib by us would have attracted some of the enemy opposing the advance of the Yeomanry Mounted Division on the left, but not only was the position strongly defended in the village and on the high ground on the north and north–west, but our infantry could not break down the opposition behind the sangars and boulders on the northern side of Nebi Samwil. The attack had to be given up, but we made some progress in this mountainous sector, as the 52nd Division had pushed out from Dukku to Beit Izza, between 3000 and 4000 yards from El Jib, and by driving the enemy from this strong village they made it more comfortable for the troops in Biddu and protected the Nebi Samwil flank, the securing of which in those days of bitter fighting was an important factor. It was evident from what was happening on this front, not only where two divisions of infantry had to strain every nerve to hold on to what they had got but where the Yeomanry Mounted Division were battling against enormous odds in the worse country to the north–west, that the Turks were not going to allow us to get to the Nablus road without making a direct attack on the Jerusalem defences. They outnumbered us, had a large preponderance in guns, were near their base, and enjoyed the advantage of prepared positions and a comparatively easy access to supplies and ammunition. Everything was in their favour down to the very state of the weather. But our army struggled on against all the big obstacles. On the 23rd the 75th Division renewed their attack on El Jib, but although the men showed the dash which throughout characterised the Division, it had to be stopped. The garrison of El Jib had been reinforced, and the enemy held the woods, wadi banks, and sangars in greater strength than before, while the artillery fire was extremely heavy. Not only was the 75th Division tired with ceaseless fighting, but the losses they had sustained since they left the Plain of Ajalon had been substantial, and the 52nd Division took over from them that night to prepare for another effort on the following day. The Scots were no more successful. They made simultaneous attacks on the northern and southern ends of Nebi Samwil, and a brigade worked up from Beit Izza to a ridge north–west of El Jib. Two magnificent attempts were made to get into the enemy's positions, but they failed. The officer casualties were heavy; some companies had no officers, and the troops were worn out by great exertions and privations in the bleak hills. The two divisions had been fighting hard for over three weeks, they had marched long distances on hard food, which at the finish was not too plentiful, and the sudden violent change in the weather conditions made it desirable that the men should get to an issue of warmer clothing. General Bulfin realised it would be risking heavy losses to ask his troops to make another immediate effort against a numerically stronger enemy in positions of his own choice, and he therefore applied to General Allenby that the XXth Corps—the 60th Division was already at Latron attached to the XXIst Corps—might take over the line. The Commander–in–Chief that evening ordered the attack on the enemy's positions to be discontinued until the arrival of fresh troops. During the next day or two the enemy's artillery was as active as hitherto, but the punishment he had received in his attacks made him pause, and there were only small half-hearted attempts to reach our line. They were all beaten off by infantry fire, and the reliefs of the various brigades of the XXIst Corps were complete by November 28. It had not been given to the XXIst Corps to obtain the distinction of driving the Turks for ever from Jerusalem, but the work of the Corps in the third and fourth weeks of November had laid the foundation on which victory finally rested. The grand efforts of the 52nd and 75th Divisions in rushing over the foothills of the Shephelah on to the Judean heights, in getting a footing on some of the most prominent hills within three days of leaving the plain, and in holding on with grim tenacity to what they had gained, enabled the Commander-in-Chief to start on a new plan by which to take the Holy City in one stride, so to speak. The 52nd and 75th Divisions and, as will be seen, the Yeomanry Mounted Division as well, share the glory of the capture of Jerusalem with the 53rd, 60th, and 74th Divisions who were in at the finish.

The fighting of the Yeomanry Mounted Division on the left of the 52nd was part and parcel of the XXIst Corps' effort to get to the Nablus road. It was epic fighting, and I have not described it when narrating the infantry's daily work because it is best told in a connected story. If the foot sloggers had a bad time, the conditions were infinitely worse for mounted troops. The ground was as steep, but the hillsides were rougher, the wadis narrower, the patches of open flat fewer than in the districts where infantry operated. So bad indeed was the country that horses were an encumbrance, and most of them were returned to the plain. After a time horse artillery could proceed no farther, and the only guns the yeomanry had with them were those of a section of the Hong Kong and Singapore mountain battery, manned by Sikhs, superb fellows whose service in the Egyptian deserts and in Palestine was worthy of a martial race. But their little guns were outranged by the Turkish artillery, and though they were often right up with the mounted men they could not get near the enemy batteries. The supply of the division in the nooks and crannies where there was not so much as a goat-path was a desperate problem, and could not have been solved without the aid of many hundreds of pack-donkeys which dumped their loads of supplies and ammunition on the hillsides, leaving it to be carried forward by hand. The division were fighting almost continually for a fortnight. They got farther forward than the infantry and met the full force of an opposition which, if not stronger than that about Nebi Samwil, was extremely violent, and they came back to a line which could be supplied with less difficulty when it was apparent that the Turks were not going to accept the opportunity General Allenby gave them to withdraw their army

How Jerusalem Was Won

from Jerusalem. The Division's most bitter struggle was about the Beth–horons, on the very scene where Joshua, on a lengthened day, threw the Canaanites off the Shephelah.

The Yeomanry Mounted Division received orders on the afternoon of November 17 to move across Ajalon into the foothills and to press forward straight on Bireh as rapidly as possible. Their trials they began immediately. One regiment of the 8th Brigade occupied Annabeh, and a regiment of the 22nd Brigade got within a couple of miles of Nalin, where a well–concealed body of the enemy held it up. Soon the report came in that the country was impassable for wheels. By the afternoon of the next day the 8th Brigade were at Beit ur el Foka—Beth–horon the Upper—a height where fig trees and pomegranates flourish. Eastwards the country falls away and there are several ragged narrow valleys between some tree–topped ridges till the eye meets a sheikh's tomb on the Zeitun ridge, standing midway between Foka and Beitunia, which rears a proud and picturesque head to bar the way to Bireh. The wadis cross the valleys wherever torrent water can tear up rock, but the yeomanry found their beds smoother going, filled though they were with boulders, than the hill slopes, which generally rose in steep gradients from the sides of watercourses. During every step of the way across this saw–toothed country one appreciated to the full the defenders' advantage. If dead ground hid you from one hill–top enemy marks–men could get you from another, and it was impossible for the division to proceed unless it got the enemy out of all the hills on its line of advance. The infantry on the right were very helpful, but the brigade on the left flank had many difficulties, which were not lessened when, on the second day of the movement, all Royal Horse Artillery guns and all wheels had to be sent back owing to the bad country. Up to this point the fight against Nature was more arduous than against the enemy. Thenceforward the enemy became more vigilant and active, and the hills and stony hollows more trying. All available men were set to work to make a road for the Hong Kong and Singapore gunners, a battery which would always get as far into the mountains as any in the King's Army. The road parties laboured night and day, but it was only by the greatest exertions that the battery could be got through. The heavy rain of the 19th added to the troubles. The 8th Brigade, having occupied Beit ur et Tahta (Beth–horon the Lower) early on the morning of the 19th, proceeded along the wadi Sunt until a force on the heights held them up, and they had to remain in the wadi while the 6th Mounted Brigade turned the enemy's flank at Foka. The 22nd Mounted Brigade on the north met with the same trouble—every hill had to be won and picqueted—and they could not make Ain Arik that day. As soon as it was light on the following morning the 6th Mounted Brigade brushed away opposition in Foka and entered the village, pushing on thence

92

towards Beitunia. The advance was slow and hazardous; every hill had to be searched, a task difficult of accomplishment by reason of the innumerable caves and boulders capable of sheltering snipers. The Turk had become an adept at sniping, and left parties in the hills to carry on by themselves. When the 6th Brigade got within two miles of the south–west of Beitunia they were opposed by 5000 Turks well screened by woods on the slopes and the wadi. Both sides strove all day without gaining ground. Divisional headquarters were only a short distance behind the 6th, and the 8th Brigade was moved up into the same area to be ready to assist. By two o'clock in the afternoon the 22nd Brigade got into Ain Arik and found a strong force of the enemy holding Beitunia and the hill of Muntar, a few hundred yards to the north of it, thus barring the way to Ramallah and Bireh. Rain fell copiously and the wind was chilly. After a miserable night in bivouac, the 6th Brigade was astir before daylight on the 21st. They were fighting at dawn, and in the half light compelled the enemy to retire to within half a mile of Beitunia. A few prisoners were rounded up, and these told the brigadier that 3000 Turks were holding Beitunia with four batteries of field guns and four heavy camel guns. That estimate was found to be approximately accurate. A regiment of the 8th Brigade sent to reinforce the 6th Brigade on their left got within 800 yards of the hill, when the guns about Bireh and Ramallah opened on them and they were compelled to withdraw, and a Turkish counter–attack forced our forward line back slightly in the afternoon. The enemy had a plentiful supply of ammunition and made a prodigal use of it. While continuing to shell fiercely he put more infantry into his fighting line, and as we had only 1200 rifles and four mountain guns, which the enemy's artillery outranged, it was clear we could not dislodge him from the Beitunia crest. The 22nd Mounted Brigade had made an attempt to get to Ramallah from Ain Arik, but the opposition from Muntar and the high ground to the east was much too severe. Our casualties had not been inconsiderable, and in face of the enemy's superiority in numbers and guns and the strength of his position it would have been dangerous and useless to make a further attack. General Barrow therefore decided to withdraw to Foka during the night. All horses had been sent back in the course of the afternoon, and when the light failed the retirement began. The wounded were first evacuated, and they, poor fellows, had a bad time of it getting back to Foka in the dark over four miles of rock–strewn country. It was not till two o'clock on the following morning that all the convoys of wounded passed through Foka, but by that time the track to Tahta had been made into passable order, and some of these helpless men were out of the hills soon after daylight, journeying in comparative ease in light motor ambulances over the Plain of Ajalon.

How Jerusalem Was Won

The arrangements for the withdrawal worked admirably. The 8th Mounted Brigade, covering the retirement so successfully that the enemy knew nothing about it, held on in front of Beitunia till three o'clock, reaching Foka before dawn, while the 22nd Brigade remained covering the northern flank till almost midnight, when it fell back to Tahta. The Division's casualties during the day were 300 killed and wounded. We still held the Zeitun ridge, observation was kept on Ain Arik from El Hafy by one regiment, and troops were out on many parts north and east of Tahta and Foka.

On the next two days there was nothing beyond enemy shelling and patrol encounters. On the 24th demonstrations were made against Beitunia to support the left of the 52nd Division's attack on El Jib, but the enemy was too strong to permit of the yeomanry proceeding more than two miles east of Foka. The roadmakers had done an enormous amount of navvy work on the track between Foka and Tahta. They had laboured without cessation, breaking up rock, levering out boulders with crowbars, and doing a sort of rough–and–ready levelling, and by the night of the 24th the track was reported passable for guns. The Leicester battery R.H.A. came along it next morning without difficulty. I did not see the road till some time later and its surface had then been considerably improved, but even then one felt the drivers of those gun teams had achieved the almost impossible. The Leicester battery arrived at Foka just in time to unlimber and get into action behind a fig orchard in order to disperse a couple of companies of enemy infantry which were working round the left flank of the Staffordshire Yeomanry at Khurbet Meita, below the Zeitun height. The enemy brought up reinforcements and made an attack in the late afternoon, but this was also broken up. The Berkshire battery reached Tahta the following day and, with the Leicester gunners, answered the Turks' long–range shelling throughout the day and night. On the 27th the enemy made a determined attempt to compel us to withdraw from the Zeitun ridge, which is an isolated hill commanding the valleys on both sides. The 6th Mounted Brigade furnished the garrison of 3 officers and 60 men, who occupied a stone building on the summit. Against them the enemy put 600 infantry with machine guns, and they also brought a heavy artillery fire to bear on the building from Beitunia, 4000 yards away. The garrison put up a most gallant defence. They were compelled to leave the building because the enemy practically destroyed it by gunfire and the infantry almost surrounded the hill, but they obtained cover on the boulder–strewn sides of the hill and held their assailants at bay. At dusk, although the garrison was reduced to 2 officers and 26 men, they refused to give ground. They were instructed to hold on as long as possible, and a reinforcement of 50 men was sent up after dark—all that could be spared, as the division was holding a series of hills ten miles long

94

and every rifle was in the line. This front was being threatened at several points, and the activity of patrols at Deir Ibzia and north of it suggested that the enemy was trying to get into the gap of five miles between the yeomanry and the right of the 54th Division which was now at Shilta. It was an anxious night, and No. 2 Light Armoured Car battery was kept west of Tahta to enfilade the enemy with machine guns should he appear in the neighbourhood of Suffa. The 7th Mounted Brigade was ordered up to reinforce. The fresh troops arrived at dawn on the 28th, and had no sooner got into position at Hellabi, half a mile north–west of Tahta, than their left flank was attacked by 1000 Turks with machine guns. The 155th Brigade of the 52nd Division was on its way through Beit Likia to rest after its hard work in the neighbourhood of Nebi Samwil and El Jib, and it was ordered up to assist. At midday the brigade attacked Suffa but could not take it. The Scots, however, prevented the Turks breaking round the left flank of the yeomanry. The post which had held Zeitun so bravely was brought into Foka under cover of the Leicester and Berkshire batteries' fire, and very heavy fighting continued all day long on the Foka–Tahta–Suffa line, but though the enemy employed 3000 infantry in his attack, and had four batteries of 77's and four heavy camel guns, he was unsuccessful. At dusk the attack on Tahta, which had been under shell–fire all day, was beaten off and the enemy was compelled to withdraw one mile. Suffa was still his, but his advanced troops on the cairn south of that place had suffered heavily during the day at the hands of the 7th Mounted Brigade, who several times drove them off. Some howitzers of the 52nd Division were hauled over the hills in the afternoon and shelled the cairn so heavily that the post sought shelter in Suffa. To the south–east of the line of attack the Turks were doing their utmost to secure Foka. They came again and again, and their attacks were always met and broken with the bayonet by yeomen who were becoming fatigued by continuous fighting, and advancing and retiring in this terrible country. They could have held the place that night, but there was no possibility of sending them reinforcements, and as the enemy had been seen working round to the south of the village with machine guns it might have been impossible to get them out in the morning. General Barrow accordingly withdrew the Foka garrison to a new position on a wooded ridge half–way between that place and Tahta, and the enemy made no attempt to get beyond Foka. Late at night he got so close to Tahta from the north that he threw bombs at our sangars, but he was driven off.

During the evening the Yeomanry Mounted Division received welcome reinforcements. The 4th Australian Light Horse Brigade were placed in support of the 6th Mounted Brigade and a battalion of the 156th Infantry Brigade assisted the 7th Mounted Brigade.

How Jerusalem Was Won

On the 29th the Turks made their biggest effort to break through the important line we held, and all day they persisted with the greatest determination in an attack on our left. At midnight they had again occupied the cairn south of Suffa, and remained there till 8 A.M., when the 268th Brigade Royal Field Artillery crowned the hill with a tremendous burst of fire and drove them off. The machine–gunners of the 7th Mounted Brigade caught the force as it was retiring and inflicted many casualties. The Turks came back again and again, and the cairn repeatedly changed hands, until at last it was unoccupied by either side. Towards dusk the Turks' attacks petered out, though the guns and snipers continued busy, and the Yeomanry Mounted Division was relieved by the 231st Infantry Brigade of the 74th Division and the 157th Infantry Brigade of the 52nd Division, the Australian Mounted Division ultimately taking over the left of the line which XXth Corps troops occupied.

The Yeomanry Mounted Division had made a grand fight against a vastly superior force of the enemy in a country absolutely unfavourable to the movement of mounted troops. They never had more than 1200 rifles holding a far–flung barren and bleak line, and the fine qualities of vigorous and swift attack, unfaltering discipline and heroic stubbornness in defence under all conditions, get their proof in the 499 casualties incurred by the Division in the hill fighting, exclusive of those sustained by the 7th Mounted Brigade which reinforced them. The Division was made up entirely of first–line yeomanry regiments whose members had become efficient soldiers in their spare time, when politicians were prattling about peace and deluding parties into the belief that there was little necessity to prepare for war. Their patriotism and example gave a tone to the drafts sent out to replace casualties and the wastage of war, and were a credit to the stock from which they sprang.

While the Yeomanry Mounted Division had been fighting a great battle alongside the infantry of the XXIst Corps in the hills, the remainder of the troops of the Desert Mounted Corps were employed on the plain and in the coastal sector, hammering the enemy hard and establishing a line from the mouth of the river Auja through some rising ground across the plain. They were busily engaged clearing the enemy out of some of the well–ordered villages east of the sandy belt, several of them German colonies showing signs of prosperity and more regard for cleanliness and sanitation than other of the small centres of population hereabouts. The village of Sarona, north of Jaffa, an almost exclusively German settlement, was better arranged than any others, but Wilhelma was a good second.

The most important move was on November 24, when, with a view to making the enemy believe an attack was intended against his right flank, the New Zealand Mounted Rifles Brigade was sent across the river Auja to seize the villages of Sheikh Muannis near the sea, and Hadrah farther inland, two companies of infantry holding each of the two crossings. The enemy became alarmed and attacked the cavalry in force early next morning, 1000 infantry marching on Muannis. The Hadrah force was driven back across the Auja and the two companies of infantry covering the crossing suffered heavily, having no support from artillery, which had been sent into bivouac. Some of the men had to swim the river. A bridge of boats had been built at Jerisheh mill during the night, and by this means men crossed until Muannis was occupied by the enemy later in the morning. The cavalry crossed the ford at the mouth of the Auja at the gallop. The 1/4th Essex held on to Hadrah until five out of six officers and about fifty per cent. of the men became casualties. There was a good deal of minor fighting on this section of the front, and in a number of patrol encounters the resource of the Australian Light Horse added to their bag of prisoners and to the Army's store of information. Nothing further of importance occurred in this neighbourhood until we seized the crossings of the Auja and the high ground north of the river a week before the end of the year.

CHAPTER XIV. THE DELIVERANCE OF THE HOLY CITY

The impossibility of getting across the road north of Jerusalem by making a wide sweep over the Judean hills caused a new plan to be put into execution. This necessitated a direct attack on the well–prepared system of defences on the hills protecting Jerusalem from the west, but it did not entail any weakening of General Allenby's determination that there should be no fighting by British troops in and about the precincts of the Holy City. That resolve was unshaken and unshakable. When a new scheme was prepared by the XXth Corps, the question was put whether the Turks could be attacked at Lifta, which was part of their system. Now Lifta is a native village on one of the hill–faces to the west of Jerusalem, about a mile from the Holy City's walls, and, as it is not even connected by a road with any of the various colonies forming the suburbs of Jerusalem, could not by any stretch of imagination be described by a Hun propaganda merchant as part of Jerusalem. I happen to know that on the 26th November the Commander–in–Chief sent this communication to General Chetwode: 'I place no restriction upon you in respect of any operation which you may consider necessary against Lifta or the enemy's lines to the south of it, except that on no account is any risk to be run of bringing the City of

How Jerusalem Was Won

Jerusalem or its immediate environs within the area of operations.' The spirit as well as the letter of that order was carried out, and in the very full orders and notes on the operations issued before the victorious attack was made, there is the most elaborate detail regarding the different objectives of divisions and brigades, and scrupulous care was taken that no advance should be made against any resisting enemy within the boundaries not only of the Holy City but of the suburbs. We shall see how thoroughly these instructions were followed.

When it became obvious that Jerusalem could not be secured without the adoption of a deliberate method of attack, there were many matters requiring the anxious consideration of the XXth Corps staff. They took over from XXIst Corps at a time when the enemy was still very active against the line which they had gained under very hard conditions. The XXth Corps, beginning with the advantage of positions which the XXIst Corps had won, had to prepare to meet the enemy with equal gun power and more than equality in rifle strength. We had the men and the guns in the country, but to get them into the line and to keep them supplied was a problem of considerable magnitude. Time was an important factor. The rains had begun. The spells of fine weather were getting shorter, and after each period of rain the sodden state of the country affected all movement. To bring up supplies we could only rely on road traffic from Gaza and Deir Sineid, and the light soil had become hopelessly cut up during the rains. The main line of railway was not to be opened to Mejdel till December 8, and the captured Turkish line between Deir Sineid and Junction Station had a maximum capacity of one hundred tons of ordnance stores a day, and these had to be moved forward again by road. An advance must slow down while communications were improved. The XXth Corps inherited from the XXIst Corps the track between Beit Likia and Biddu which had been prepared with an infinity of trouble and exertion, but this and the main Latron–Jerusalem road were the only highways available.

General Chetwode's Corps relieved General Bulfin's Corps during the day of November 28, and viewed in the most favourable light it appeared that there must be at least one week's work on the roads before it would be possible for heavy and field batteries, in sufficient strength to support an attack, to be got into the mountains. A new road was begun between Latron and Beit Likia, and another from Enab to Kubeibeh, and these, even in a rough state of completion, eased the situation very considerably. An enormous amount of labour was devoted to the main road. The surface was in bad order and was getting worse every hour with the passage of lorry traffic. It became full of holes, and the available metal in the neighbourhood was a friable limestone which, under heavy pressure during rains, was ground into the consistency of a thick cream. Pioneer battalions were reinforced by large parties of Egyptian labour corps, and these worked ceaselessly, clearing off top layers of mud, carrying stones down from the hills and breaking them, putting on a new surface and repairing the decayed walls which held up the road in many places. The roadmakers proved splendid fellows. They put a vast amount of energy into their work, but when the roads were improved rain gravely interfered with traffic, and camels were found to be most unsatisfactory. They slipped and fell and no reliance could be placed on a camel convoy getting to its destination in the hills. Two thousand donkeys were pressed into service, and with them the troops in the distant positions were kept supplied. It would not be possible to exaggerate the value of this donkey transport. In anticipation of the advance the Quartermaster–General's department, with the foresight which characterised that department and all its branches throughout the campaign, searched Egypt for the proper stamp of asses for pack transport in the hills. The Egyptian donkey is a big fellow with a light–grey coat, capable of carrying a substantial load, hardy, generally docile, and less stubborn than most of the species. He is much taller and heavier than the Palestine donkey, and our Army never submitted him to the atrociously heavy loads which crush and break the spirit of the local Arabs' animals. It is, perhaps, too much to hope that the natives will learn something from the British soldier's treatment of animals. It was one of the sights of the campaign to see the donkey trains at work. They carried supplies which, having been brought by the military railway from the Suez Canal to railhead, were conveyed by motor lorries as far as the state of the road permitted self–propelled vehicles to run, were next transhipped into limbers, and, when horse transport could proceed no farther, were stowed on to the backs of camels. The condition of the road presently held up the camels, and then donkey trains took over the loads. Under a white officer you would see a chain of some two hundred donkeys, each roped in file of four, led by an Egyptian who knew all that was worth knowing about the ways of the ass, winding their way up and down hills, getting a foothold on rocks where no other animal but a goat could stand, and surmounting all obstacles with a patient endurance which every soldier admired. They did not like the cold, and the rain made them look deplorably wretched, but they got rations and drinking–water right up to the crags where our infantry were practising mountaineering. Shell–fire did not disturb them much, and they would nibble at any rank stuff growing on the hillsides to supplement the rations which did not always reach their lines at regular intervals. The Gyppy boys were excellent leaders, and to them and the donkeys the front–line fighting men in the hill country owe much. They were saved a good deal of exhausting labour in manhandling stores from the point where camels had to stop, and they could therefore concentrate their attention on the Turk.

By December 2 the fine exertions of the troops on the line of communications had enabled the XXth Corps Commander to make his plans for the capture of Jerusalem, and at a conference at Enab on the following day General Chetwode outlined his scheme, which, put in a nutshell, was to attack with the 60th and 74th Divisions in an easterly direction on the front Ain Karim–Beit Surik and, skirting the western suburbs of Jerusalem, to place these two divisions astride the Jerusalem–Nablus road, while the 53rd Division advanced from Hebron to threaten the enemy from the south and protect the right of the 60th Division. I will not apologise for dealing as fully as possible with the fighting about Jerusalem, because Jerusalem was one of the great victories of the war, and the care taken to observe the sanctity of the place will for all time stand out as one of the brightest examples of the honour of British arms. But before entering upon those details I will put in chronological sequence the course of the fighting on this front from the moment when the XXth Corps took over the command, and show how, despite enemy vigilance and many attacks, the preparations for the outstanding event of the campaign were carried through. It is remarkable that in the short period of ten days the plans could be worked out in detail and carried through to a triumphant issue, notwithstanding the bad weather and the almost overwhelming difficulties of supply. Only the whole–hearted co–operation of all ranks made it possible. On the day after the XXth Corps became responsible for this front General Chetwode had a conference with Generals Barrow, Hill, and Girdwood, and after a full discussion of the situation in the hills decided to abandon the plan of getting on to the Jerusalem–Nablus road from the north in favour of attempting to take Jerusalem from the west and south–west. The commanders of the Yeomanry Mounted Division and the 52nd Division were asked to suggest, from their experience of the fighting of the past ten days, what improvement in the line was necessary to make it certain that the new plan would not be interfered with by an enemy counter–attack. They were in favour of taking the western portion of the Beitunia–Zeitun ridge. Preparations were made immediately to relieve the Yeomanry Mounted Division by the Australian Mounted Division, and when the 10th Division arrived—it was marching up from Gaza—the 52nd Division was to be returned to the XXIst Corps. The hard fighting and the determined attacks of the Turks had made it unavoidable that some portions of the divisions should be mixed, and the reliefs were not completed till the 2nd of December.

How Jerusalem Was Won

The Yeomanry Mounted Division troops gave over the Tahta defences to the 157th Infantry Brigade on the night of November 29–30, and the enemy made an attack on the new defenders at dawn, but were swiftly beaten off. A local effort against Nebi Samwil was easily repulsed, but the 60th Division reported that the enemy had in the past few days continued his shelling of the Mosque, and had added to his destruction of that sacred place by demolishing the minaret by gunfire. The 231st Infantry Brigade with one battalion in the front line took over from the 8th Mounted Brigade from Beit Dukku to Jufna, and while the reliefs were in progress there was continual fighting in the Et Tireh–Foka area. The former place was won and lost several times, and finally the infantry consolidated on the high ground west of those villages. Early on the 30th a detachment of the 231st Brigade took Foka, capturing eight officers and 298 men, but as it was not possible to hold the village the infantry retired to our original line. On December 1 the 10th Division relieved the 52nd in the sector wadi Zait–Tahta–Kh. Faaush, but on that day the 155th Brigade had had another hard brush with the Turks. A regiment of the 3rd Australian Light Horse on a hill north of El Burj in front of them was heavily attacked at half–past one in the morning by a specially prepared sturmtruppen battalion of the Turkish 19th Division, and a footing was gained in our position, but with the aid of a detachment of the Gloucester Yeomanry and the 1/4th Royal Scots Fusiliers the enemy was driven out at daybreak and six officers and 106 unwounded and 60 wounded Turks, wearing steel hats and equipped like German storming troops, were taken prisoners. The attack was pressed with the greatest determination, and the enemy, using hand grenades, got within thirty yards of our line. During the latter part of their advance the Turks were exposed to a heavy cross fire from machine guns and rifles of the 9th Light Horse Regiment, and this fire and the guns of the 268th Brigade Royal Field Artillery and the Hong Kong and Singapore battery prevented the retirement of the enemy. The capture of the prisoners was effected by an encircling movement round both flanks. Our casualties were 9 killed and 47 wounded. That storming battalion left over 100 dead about our trenches. At the same time a violent attack was made on the Tahta defences held by the 157th Brigade; the enemy, rushing forward in considerable strength and with great impetus, captured a ridge overlooking Tahta—a success which, if they had succeeded in holding the position till daylight, would have rendered that village untenable, and would have forced our line back some distance at an important point. It proved to be a last desperate effort of the enemy at this vital centre. No sooner were the Scots driven off the ridge than they re–formed and prepared to retake it. Reinforced, they attacked with magnificent courage in face of heavy machine–gun fire, but it was not until after a rather prolonged period of bayonet work that the Lowland troops got the upper hand, the Turks trying again and again to force them out. At half-past four they gave up the attempt, and from that hour Tahta and the rocks about it were objects of terror to them.

Nor did the Turks permit Nebi Samwil to remain in our possession undisputed. The Londoners holding it were thrice attacked with extreme violence, but the defenders never flinched, and the heavy losses of the enemy may be measured by the fact that when we took Jerusalem and an unwonted silence hung over Nebi Samwil, our burying parties interred more than 500 Turkish dead about the summit of that lofty hill. Their graves are mostly on the eastern, northern, and southern slopes. Ours lie on the west, where Scot, Londoner, West Countryman, and Indian, all equally heroic sons of the Empire, sleep, as they fought, side by side.

The last heavy piece of fighting on the XXth Corps' front before the attack on Jerusalem was on December 3, when a regiment of yeomanry, which like a number of other yeomanry regiments had been dismounted to form the 74th Division, covered itself with glory. The 16th (Royal Devon Yeomanry) battalion of the Devon Regiment belonging to the 229th Brigade was ordered to make an attack on Beit ur el Foka in the dark hours of the morning. All the officers had made reconnaissances and had learned the extreme difficulties of the ground. At 1 A.M. these yeomen worked their way up the wadi Zeit to the head of that narrow watercourse at the base of the south-western edge of the hill on which the village stands. The attack was launched from this position, the company on the right having the steepest face to climb. Here the villagers, to get the most out of the soil and to prevent the winter rains washing it off the rocks into the wadi, had built a series of terraces, and the retaining walls, often crumbling to the touch, offered some cover from the Turkish defenders' fire. With the advantage of this shelter the troops on the right reached the southern end of the village soon after 2 o'clock, but the company on the left met with much opposition on the easier slope, and had to call in aid the support of a machine-gun section posted in the woods on a ridge north-west of the village. By 3 o'clock the whole battalion was in the village, using rifle and bayonet in the road scarcely more than a couple of yards wide, and bombing the enemy out of native mud and stone houses and caves. Two officers and fifteen unwounded men were taken prisoners with three machine guns, but before any consolidation could be done the Turks began a series of counter-attacks which lasted all day. As we had previously found, Foka was very hard to defend. It is overlooked on the north, north-east, and east by ridges a few hundred yards away, and by a high hill north of Ain Jeruit, 1200 yards to the north, by another hill

How Jerusalem Was Won

1000 yards to the east, and by the famous Zeitun ridge about 1500 yards beyond it, and attacks from these directions could be covered very effectively by overhead machine–gun fire. To enlarge the perimeter of defence would be to increase the difficulties and require a much larger force than was available, and there was no intention of going beyond Foka before the main operation against Jerusalem was started. To hold Foka securely a force must be in possession of the heights on the north and east, and to keep these Beitunia itself must be gained. Before daylight arrived some work on defences was begun, but it was interfered with by snipers and not much could be done. Immediately the sun rose from behind the Judean hills there was a violent outburst of fire from machine guns and rifles on three sides, increasing in volume as the light improved. The enemy counter–attacked with a determination fully equal to that which he had displayed during the past fortnight's battle in the hills. He had the advantage of cover and was supported by artillery and a hurricane of machine–gun fire, but although he climbed the hill and got into the small gardens outside the very houses, he was repulsed with bomb and bayonet. At one moment there was little rifle fire, and the two sides fought it out with bombs. The Turks retired with heavy losses, but they soon came back again and fought with the same determination, though equally unsuccessfully. The Devons called for artillery, and three batteries supported them splendidly, though the gunners were under a great disadvantage in that the ground did not permit the effect of gunfire to be observed and it was difficult to follow the attackers. The supplies of bombs and small–arms ammunition were getting low, and to replenish them men had to expose themselves to a torrent of fire, so fierce indeed that in bringing up two boxes of rifle ammunition which four men could carry twelve casualties were incurred. A head shown in the village instantly drew a hail of bullets from three sides. Reinforcements were on the way up, and the Fife and Forfar Yeomanry battalion of the Royal Highlanders were prepared to make a flank attack from their outpost line three–quarters of a mile south–east of Foka to relieve the Devons, but this would have endangered the safety of the outpost line without reducing the fire from the heights, and as the Fife and Forfar men would have had to cross two deep wadis under enfilade fire on their way to Foka their adventure would have been a perilous one. By this time three out of four of the Devons' company commanders were wounded and the casualties were increasing. The officer commanding the battalion therefore decided, after seven hours of terrific fighting, that the village of Foka was no longer tenable, and authority was given him to withdraw. In their last attack the enemy put 1000 men against the village, and it was not until the O.C. Devons had seen this strength that he proposed the place should be evacuated. His men had put up a great fight. The battalion went into action 762 strong; it came out 488. Three officers were killed and nine wounded, and 49 other ranks killed and 132 wounded. Thirteen were wounded and missing and 78 missing. In Foka to-day you will see most of the battered houses repaired, but progress through the streets is partially barred by the graves of Devon yeomen who were buried where they fell. It was not possible to hew a grave in rock, therefore earth and stone were piled up round the bodies, so that in at least two spots you find several graves serving as buttresses to rude dwellings. On one of these graves, beside the identification tablet of two strong sons of Devon, you will find, on a piece of paper inserted in a slit cut into wood torn from an ammunition box, the words 'Grave of unknown Turk.' Friend and foe share a common resting–place. The natives of this village are more than usually friendly, and those graves seem safe in their keeping.

Between the 4th and 7th December there was a reshuffling of the troops holding the line to enable a concentration of the divisions entrusted with the attack on the defences covering Jerusalem. The 10th Division relieved the 229th and 230th Brigades of the 74th Division and extended its line to cover Beit Dukku, a point near and west of Et Tireh, to Tahta, and when the enemy retired from the immediate front of the 10th Division's left, Hellabi and Suffa were occupied. The Australian Mounted Division also slightly advanced its line. On the night of December 5 the 231st Brigade relieved the 60th Division in the Beit Izza and Nebi Samwil positions, and on December 6 the line held by the 74th was extended to a point about a mile and a half north of Kulonieh. The 53rd Division had passed through Hebron, and its advance was timed to reach the Bethlehem–Beit Jala district on December 7. The information gained by the XXth Corps led the staff to estimate the strength of the enemy opposite them to be 13,300 rifles and 2700 sabres, disposed as follows: east of Jerusalem the 7th cavalry regiment, 500 sabres; the 27th Division covering Jerusalem and extending to the Junction Station–Jerusalem railway at Bitter Station, 1200 rifles; thence to the Latron–Jerusalem road with strong points at Ain Karim and Deir Yesin, the 53rd Turkish Division, 2000 rifles; from the road to Nebi Samwil (Beit Iksa being very strongly held) the 26th Turkish Division, 1800 rifles; Nebi Samwil to Beit ur el Foka, 19th Turkish Division with the 2/61st regiment and the 158th regiment attached, 4000 rifles; Beit ur el Foka to about Suffa, the 24th Division, 1600 rifles; thence to the extreme left of the XXth Corps the 3rd Cavalry Division, 1500 sabres. The 54th Turkish Division was in reserve at Bireh with 2700 rifles. The enemy held a line covering Bethlehem across the Hebron road to Balua, then to the hill Kibryan south–west of Beit Jala, whence the line proceeded due north to Ain Karim and Deir Yesin, both of which were strongly entrenched, on to the hill overlooking the Jerusalem road above Lifta. From this point the line crossed the road to the high ground west of Beit Iksa—entrenchments were cut deep into the face of this hill to cover the road from Kulonieh—thence northward again to the east of Nebi Samwil, west of El Jib, Dreihemeh (one mile north–east of Beit Dukku) to Foka, Kh. Aberjan, and beyond Suffa.

During the attack the Australian Mounted Division was to protect the left flank of the 10th Division, which with one brigade of the 74th Division was to hold the whole of the line in the hills from Tahta through Foka, Dukku, Beit Izza to Nebi Samwil, leaving the attack to be conducted by two brigade groups of the 74th Division, the whole of the 60th Division, and two brigade groups of the 53rd Division, with the 10th regiment of Australian Light Horse watching the right flank of the 60th Division until the left of the 53rd could join up with it. One brigade of the 53rd Division was to advance from the Bethlehem–Beit Jala area with its left on the line drawn from Sherafat through Malhah to protect the 60th Division's flank, the other brigade marching direct on Jerusalem, and to move by roads south of the town to a position covering Jerusalem from the east and north–east, but—and these were instructions specially impressed on this brigade—'the City of Jerusalem will not be entered, and all movements by troops and vehicles will be restricted to roads passing outside the City.' The objective of the 60th and 74th Divisions was a general line from Ras et Tawil, a hill east of the Nablus road about four miles north of Jerusalem, to Nebi Samwil, one brigade of the 74th Division holding Nebi Samwil and Beit Izza defences and to form the pivot of the attack. The dividing line between the 60th and 74th Divisions was the Enab–Jerusalem road as far as Lifta and from that place to the wadi Beit Hannina. The form of the attack was uncertain until it was known how the enemy would meet the advance of the 53rd Division, which, on the 3rd December, was in a position north of Hebron within two ten–mile marches of the point at which it would co–operate on the right of the 60th. If the enemy increased his strength south of Jerusalem to oppose the advance of the 53rd Division, General Chetwode proposed that the 60th and 74th Divisions should force straight through to the Jerusalem–Nablus road, the 60th throwing out a flank to the south–east, so as to cut off the Turks opposing the 53rd from either the Nablus or the Jericho road. It was not considered probable that the enemy would risk the capture of a large body of troops south of Jerusalem. On the other hand, should the Turks withdraw from in front of the Welsh Division, the alternative plan provided that the latter attack should take the form of making a direct advance on Jerusalem and a wheel by the 60th and 74th Divisions, pivoting on the Beit Izza and Nebi Sainwil defences, so as to drive the enemy northwards. The operations were to be divided into four phases. The first phase fell to the 60th and 74th Divisions, and consisted in the capture of the whole of the south–western and western defences of Jerusalem.

These ran from a point near the railway south–west of Malhah round to the west of Ain Karim, then on to the hill of Khurbet Subr, down a cleft in the hills and up on to the high Deir Yesin ridge, thence round the top of two other hills dominating the old and new roads to Jerusalem from Jaffa as they pass by the village of Kulonieh. North of the new road the enemy's line ran round the southern face of a bold hill overlooking the village of Beit Iksa and along the tortuous course of the wadi El Abbeideh. In the second phase the 60th Division was to move over the Jaffa–Jerusalem road with its right almost up to the scattered houses on the north–western fringe of Jerusalem's suburbs, and its left was to pass the village of Lifta on the slope of the hill rising from the wadi Beit Hannina. The objective of the 60th Division in the third phase was the capture of a line of a track leaving the Jerusalem–Nablus road well forward of the northern suburb and running down to the wadi Hannina, the 74th Division advancing down the spur running south–east from Nebi Samwil to a point about 1000 yards south–west of Beit Hannina, the latter a prominent height with a slope amply clothed with olive trees. The fourth phase was an advance astride the road to Ras et Tawil. As will be seen hereafter all these objectives were not obtained, but the first, and chief of them, was, and the inevitable followed—Jerusalem became ours.

Let us now picture some of the country the troops had to cross and the defences they had to capture before the Turks could be forced out of Jerusalem. We will first look at it from Enab, the ancient Kir–jath–jearim, which the Somersets, Wilts, and Gurkhas had taken at the point of the bayonet. From the top of Enab the Jaffa–Jerusalem road winds down a deep valley, plentifully planted with olive and fig trees and watered by the wadi Ikbala. A splendid supply of water had been developed by Royal Engineers near the ruins of a Crusader fortress which, if native tradition may be relied on, housed Richard of the Lion Heart. From the wadi rises a hill on which is Kustul, a village covering the site of an old Roman castle from which, doubtless, its name is derived. Kustul stands out the next boldest feature to Nebi Samwil, and from it, when the atmosphere is clear, the red–tiled roofs of houses in the suburbs of Jerusalem are plainly visible. A dozen villages clinging like limpets to steep hillsides are before you, and away on your right front the tall spires of Christian churches at Ain Karim tell you you are approaching the Holy Sites. Looking east the road falls, with many short zigzags in its length, to Kulonieh, crosses the wadi Surar by a substantial bridge (which the Turks blew up), and then creeps up the hills in heavy gradients till it is lost to view about Lifta. The wadi Surar winds round the foot of the hill which Kustul crowns, and on the other side of the watercourse there rises the series of hills on which the Turks intended to hold our hands off Jerusalem. The descent from Kustul is very rapid and the rise on the other side is almost as precipitous. On both sides of the wadi olive trees are thickly planted, and on the terraced slopes vines yield a plentiful harvest. Big spurs run down to the wadi, the sides are rough even in dry weather, but when the winter rains are falling it is difficult to keep a foothold. South−west of Kustul is Soba, a village on another high hill, and below it and west of Ain Karim, on lower ground, is Setaf, both having orchards and vineyards in which the inhabitants practise the arts of husbandry by the same methods as their remote forefathers. An aerial reconnaissance nearly a year before we took Jerusalem showed the Turks busily making trenches on the hills east of the wadi Surar. An inspection of the defences proved the work to have been long and arduous, though like many things the Turk began he did not finish them. What he did do was done elaborately. He employed masons to chisel the stone used for revetting, and in places the stones fit well and truly one upon the other, while an enormous amount of rock must have been blasted to excavate the trenches. The system adopted was to have three fire trenches near the top of the hills, one above the other, so that were the first two lines taken the third would still offer a difficult obstacle, and, if the defenders were armed with bombs, it would be hard for attackers to retain the trenches in front of them. There was much dead ground below the entrenchments, but the defences were so arranged that cross fire from one system swept the dead ground on the next spur, and, if the hills were properly held, an advance up them would have been a stupendous task. The Turk had put all his eggs into one basket. Perhaps he considered his positions impregnable—they would have been practically impregnable in British hands—and he made no attempt to cut support trenches behind the crest. There was one system only, and his failure to provide defences in depth cost him dear.

Looking eastwards from Kustul, the Turkish positions south of the Jaffa−Jerusalem road, each of them on a hill, were called by us the 'Liver Redoubt' (near Lifta), the 'Heart Redoubt,' 'Deir Yesin,' and 'Khurbet Subr,' with the village of Ain Karim in a fold of the hills and a line of trenches south−west of it running down to the railway. Against the 74th Division's front the nature of the country was equally difficult. From Beit Surik down to the Kulonieh road the hills fell sharply with the ground strewn with boulders. Our men had to advance across ravines and beds of watercourses covered with large stones, and up the wooded slopes of hills where stone walls constituted ready−made sangars easily capable of defence. The hardest position they had to tackle was the hill covering Beit

How Jerusalem Was Won

Iksa, due north of the road as it issued from Kulonieh, where long semicircular trenches had been cut to command at least half a mile of the main road. In front of the 53rd Division was an ideal rearguard country where enterprising cavalry could have delayed an advance by infantry for a lengthened period. To the south of Bethlehem, around Beit Jala and near Urtas, covering the Pools of Solomon, an invaluable water supply, there were prepared defences, but though the Division was much delayed by heavy rain and dense mist, the fog was used to their advantage, for the whole of the Division's horses were watered at Solomon's Pools one afternoon without opposition from the Urtas garrison.

December 8 was the date fixed for the attack. On December 7 rain fell unceasingly. The roads, which had been drying, became a mass of slippery mud to the west of Jerusalem, and on the Hebron side the Welsh troops had to trudge ankle deep through a soft limy surface. It was soon a most difficult task to move transport on the roads. Lorries skidded, and double teams of horses could only make slow progress with limbers. Off the road it became almost impossible to move. The ground was a quagmire. On the sodden hills the troops bivouacked without a stick to shelter them. The wind was strong and drove walls of water before it, and there was not a man in the attacking force with a dry skin. Sleep on those perishing heights was quite out of the question, and on the day when it was hoped the men would get rest to prepare them for the morrow's fatigue the whole Army was shivering and awake. So bad were the conditions that the question was considered as to whether it would not be advisable to postpone the attack, but General Chetwode, than whom no general had a greater sympathy for his men, decided that as the 53rd Division were within striking distance by the enemy the attack must go forward on the date fixed. That night was calculated to make the stoutest hearts faint. Men whose blood had been thinned by summer heat in the desert were now called upon to endure long hours of piercing cold, with their clothes wet through and water oozing out of their boots as they stood, with equipment made doubly heavy by rain, caked with mud from steel helmet to heel, and the toughened skin of old campaigners rendered sore by rain driven against it with the force of a gale. Groups of men huddled together in the effort to keep warm: a vain hope. And all welcomed the order to fall in preparatory to moving off in the darkness and mist to a battle which, perhaps more than any other in this war, stirred the emotions of countless millions in the Old and New Worlds. Yet their spirits remained the same. Nearly frozen, very tired, 'fed up' with the weather, as all of them were, they were always cheerful, and the man who missed his footing and floundered in the mud regarded the incident as light-heartedly as his fellows. An Army which could face the trials of such a night with cheerfulness was unbeatable. One section of the force did regard the prospects with rueful countenances. This was the Divisional artillery. Tractors, those wonderfully ugly but efficient engines which triumphed over most obstacles, had got the heavies into position. The 96th Heavy Group, consisting of three 6–inch howitzer batteries, one complete 60–pounder battery, and a section of another 60–pounder battery, and the Hong Kong and Singapore Mountain Battery, were attached to and up with the 74th Division. The 10 and B 9 Mountain Batteries were with the 60th Division waiting to try their luck down the hills, and the 91st Heavy Battery (60–pounders) was being hauled forward with the 53rd. The heavies could get in long–range fire from Kustul, but what thought the 18–pounder batteries? With the country in such a deplorable state it looked hopeless for them to expect to be in the show, and the prospect of remaining out of the big thing had more effect upon the gunners than the weather. As a matter of fact but few field batteries managed to get into action. Those which succeeded in opening fire during the afternoon of December 8 did most gallant work for hours, with enemy riflemen shooting at them from close range, and their work formed a worthy part in the victory. The other field gunners could console themselves with the fact that the difficulties which were too great for them—and really field–gun fire on the steep slopes could not be very effective—prevented even the mountain batteries, which can go almost anywhere, from fully co–operating with the infantry.

The preliminary moves for the attack were made during the night. The 179th Infantry Brigade group consisting of 2/13th London, 2/14th London, 2/15th London, and 2/16th London with the 2/23rd London attached, the 10th Mountain Battery and B 9 Mountain Battery, a section of the 521st Field Coy. R.E., C company of Loyal North Lancashire Pioneers, and the 2/4th Field Ambulance specially equipped on an all–mule scale, moved to the wadi Surar in two columns. The right column was preceded by an advance guard of the Kensington battalion, the Loyal North Lancashire Pioneers, and the section of R.E., which left the brigade bivouacs behind Soba at five o'clock on the afternoon of the 7th to enable the pioneers and engineers to improve a track marked on the map. For the greater part of the way the track had evidently been unused for many years, and all traces of it had disappeared, but in three hours' time a way had been made down the hill to the wadi, and the brigade got over the watercourse just north of Setaf a little after midnight. As a preliminary to the attack on the first objective it was necessary to secure the high ground south of Ain Karim and the trenches covering that bright and picturesque little town. At two o'clock, when rain and mist made it so dark it was not possible to see a wall a couple of yards ahead, the Kensingtons advanced to gain the heights south of Ain Karim in order to enable the 179th Brigade to be deployed. A scrambling climb brought the Kensingtons to the top of the hill, and, after a weird fight of an hour and a half in such blackness of night that it was hard to distinguish between friend and foe, they captured it and beat off several persistent counter–attacks. The 179th Brigade thus had the ground secured for preparing to attack their section of the main defences. The 180th Infantry Brigade, whose brigadier, Brig.–General Watson, had the honour of being the first general in Jerusalem, the first across the Jordan, and the first to get through the Turkish line in September 1918 when General Allenby sprang forward through the Turks and made the mighty march to Aleppo, was composed of the 2/17th London, 2/18th London, 2/19th London, and 2/20th London, 519th Coy. R.E., two platoons of pioneers, and the 2/5th Field Ambulance. It reached its position of assembly without serious opposition, though a detachment which went through the village of Kulonieh met some enemy posts. These, to use the brigadier's phrase, were 'silently dealt with.'

It was a fine feat to get the two brigades of Londoners into their positions of deployment well up to time. The infantry had to get from Kustul down a precipitous slope of nearly a thousand feet into a wadi, now a rushing torrent, and up a rocky and almost as steep hill on the other side. Nobody could see where he was going, but direction was kept perfectly and silence was well maintained, the loosened stones falling into mud. The assault was launched at a quarter–past five, and in ten minutes under two hours the two brigades (the 181st Brigade being in reserve just south of Kustul) had penetrated the whole of the front line of the defences. The Queen's Westminsters on the left of the Kensingtons had cleared the Turks out of Ain Karim and then climbed up a steep spur to attack the formidable Khurbet Subr defences. They took the garrison completely by surprise, and those who did not flee were either killed or taken prisoners. The Queen's Westminsters were exposed to a heavy flanking fire at a range of about a thousand yards from a tumulus south–east of Ain Karim, above the road from the village to the western suburbs of Jerusalem. Turkish riflemen were firmly dug in on this spot, and their two machine guns poured in an annoying fire on the 179th Brigade troops which threatened to hold up the attack. Indeed preparations were being made to send a company to take the tumulus hill in flank, but two gallant London Scots settled the activity of the enemy and captured the position by themselves. Corporal C.W. Train and Corporal F.S. Thornhill stalked the garrison. Corporal Train fired a rifle grenade at one machine gun, which he hit and put out of action, and then shot the whole of the gun team. Thornhill was attacking the other gun, and he, with the assistance of Train, accounted for that crew as well. The two guns were captured and Tumulus Hill gave no more trouble. Both these Scots were rewarded, and

How Jerusalem Was Won

Train has the unique honour of wearing the only V.C. awarded during the capture of Jerusalem.

At about the same time there was another very gallant piece of work being done by two men of the Queen's Westminsters above the Khurbet Subr ridge. When the battalion got to the first objective an enemy battery of 77's was found in action on the reverse slope of the hill. The guns were firing from a hollow near the Ain Karim–Jerusalem track, some 600 yards behind the forward trenches on Subr, and were showing an uncomfortable activity. A company was pushed forward to engage the battery. The movement was exposed to a good deal of sniping fire, and it was not a simple matter for riflemen to work ahead on to a knoll on the east of the Subr position to deal with the guns. To two men may be given the credit for capturing the battery. Lance–Corporal W.H. Whines of the Westminsters got along quickly and brought his Lewis gun to bear on the battery and, with an admirably directed fire, caused many casualties. Two gun teams were wiped out, either killed or wounded, by the corporal. At the same time Rifleman C.D. Smith, who had followed his comrade, rushed in on another team and bombed it. Smith's rifle had been smashed and was useless, but with his bombs he laid low all except one man. His supply was then exhausted, but before the Turk could use his weapons Smith got to grips and a rare wrestling bout followed. The Turk would not surrender, and Smith gave him a stranglehold and broke his neck. The enemy managed to get one of the four guns away. The battery horses were near at hand, but while this one gun was escaping at the gallop the Westminsters' fire brought down one horse and two drivers, and I saw their bodies on the road as evidence of how the Westminsters had developed the art of shooting at a rapidly moving target. The two incidents I have described in detail merely as examples of the fighting prowess, not only of one but of all three divisions alike in the capture of Jerusalem. Perhaps it would be fairer to say that they were examples of the spirit of General Allenby's whole force, for English, Scottish, Irish, Welsh, Australians, New Zealanders, Indians, cavalry, infantry, and artillery, had all, during the six weeks of the campaign, shown the same high qualities in irresistible attack and stubborn defence.

The position of the 179th Brigade at this time was about one mile east of Ain Karim, where it was exposed to heavy enfilade fire from its right and, as it was obvious that the advance of the 53rd Division had been delayed owing to the fog and rain, the brigadier decided not to go further during the early part of the day but to wait till he could be supported by the mountain batteries, which the appalling state of the ground had prevented from keeping up with him.

How Jerusalem Was Won

Now as to the advance of the 180th Infantry Brigade. Their principal objective was the Deir Yesin position, the hill next on the northern side of Subr, from which it was separated by a deep though narrow valley. The trenches cut on both sides of this gorge supported Subr as well as Deir Yesin, and the Subr defences were also arranged to be helpful to the Deir Yesin garrison by taking attackers in flank. The 180th Brigade's advance was a direct frontal attack on the hill, the jumping–off place being a narrow width of flat ground thickly planted with olive trees on the banks of the wadi Surar. The 2/19th Londons, the right battalion of the 180th Brigade, had not got far when it became the target of concentrated machine–gun fire and was unable to move, with the result that a considerable gap existed between it and the 179th Brigade. The stoppage was only temporary, for, with the advance of the centre and right, the 19th battalion pushed forward in series of rushes and, with the other battalions, carried the crest of Deir Yesin at the point of the bayonet, so that the whole system of entrenchments was in their hands by seven o'clock. The brigade at once set about reorganising for the attack on the second objective, which, as will be remembered, was a wheel to the left and, passing well on the outside of the western suburbs of Jerusalem, an advance to the rocky ground to the north–west of the city down to the wadi Beit Hannina. The commander of the 2/18th Londons in his preparations had pushed out a platoon in advance of his left, and these men at half–past nine saw 200 of the enemy with pack mules retiring down a wadi north–east of Kulonieh. The platoon held its fire until the Turks were within close range, and then engaged them with rifles and machine guns, completely surprising them and taking prisoners the whole of the survivors, 5 officers and 50 men. The Turks now began to develop a serious opposition to the 180th Brigade from a quarry behind Deir Yesin and from a group of houses forming part of what is known as the Syrian colony, nearly a mile from the Deir Yesin system. There were some Germans and a number of machine guns in these houses, and by noon they held up the advance.

The brigade was seriously handicapped by the difficulty in moving guns. The road during the morning had got into a desperate state. It was next to impossible to haul field guns anywhere off the road, and as the Turks had paid no attention to the highway for some time—or where they had done something it was merely to dump down large stones to fill a particularly bad hole—it had become deeply rutted and covered with a mass of adhesive mud. The guns had to pass down from Kustul by a series of zigzags with hairpin bends in full view of enemy observers, and it was only by the greatest exertion and devotion to duty that the gunners got their teams into the neighbourhood of the wadi. The bridge over the Surar at Kulonieh having been wholly destroyed, they had to negotiate the wadi, which was now in torrent and carrying away the waters which had washed the face of the hills over a wide area. The artillery made a track through a garden on the right of the village just before the road reached the broken bridge, and two batteries, the 301st and 302nd, got their guns and limbers across. They went up the old track leading from Kulonieh to Jerusalem, when first one section and then another came into action at a spot between Deir Yesin and Heart Redoubt, where both batteries were subjected to a close−range rifle fire.

For several hours the artillery fought their guns with superb courage, and remained in action until the fire from the houses was silenced by a brilliant infantry attack. At half−past one General Watson decided he would attack the enemy on a ridge in front of the houses of the Syrian colony with the 18th and 19th battalions. With them were units of other battalions of the Brigade. Soon after three o'clock they advanced under heavy fire from guns, machine guns, and rifles, and at a quarter to four a glorious bayonet charge, during which the London boys went through Germans and Turks in one overwhelming stride, sealed the fate of the Turk in Jerusalem. That bayonet charge was within sight of the Corps Commander, who was with General Shea at his look−out on Kustul, and when he saw the flash of steel driven home with unerring certainty by his magnificent men, General Chetwode may well have felt thankful that he had been given such troops with which to deliver Jerusalem from the Turks. The 74th Division, having taken the whole of its first objectives early in the morning and having throughout the day supported the left of the London Division, was ready to commence operations against the second objective. The dismounted yeomanry, whose condition through the wet and mud was precisely similar to that of the 60th Division troops, for they, too, had found the hills barren of shelter and equally cold, did extremely well in forcing the enemy from his stronghold on the hill covering Beit Iksa and the Kulonieh−Jerusalem road, from which, had he not been ejected, he could have harassed the Londoners' left. The Beit Iksa defences were carried by a most determined rush. A gallant attempt was also made to get the El Burj ridge which runs south−east from Nebi Samwil, but owing to strong enfilade fire from the right they could not get on.

There was no doubt in any minds that Jerusalem would be ours, but the difficulties the 53rd Division were contending with had slowed down their advance. Thus the right flank of the 60th Division was exposed and a considerable body of Turks was known to be south of Jerusalem. Late in the afternoon the advance was ordered to be stopped, and the positions gained to be held. With a view to continuing the advance next day the 181st

Brigade (2/21st London, 2/22nd London, 2/23rd London, and 2/24th London) was ordered to get into a position of readiness to pass through the 179th Brigade and resume the attack on the right of the 180th Brigade. On the evening of December 8 the position of the attacking force was this. The 53rd Division (I will deal presently with the advance of this Division) was across the Bethlehem–Hebron road from El Keiseraniyeh, two miles south of Bethlehem, to Ras el Balua in an east and west direction, then north–west to the hill of Haud Kibriyan with its flank thrown south to cover Kh. el Kuseir. The 10th Australian Light Horse were at Malhah. The 179th and 180th Brigades of the 60th Division occupied positions extending from Malhah through a line more than a mile east of the captured defences west of Jerusalem to Lifta, with the 181st Brigade in divisional reserve near Kustul. The 229th and 230th Brigades of the 74th Division held a due north and south line from the Jaffa–Jerusalem road about midway between Kulonieh and Lifta through Beit Iksa to Nebi Samwil. The 53rd Division had not reached their line without enormous trouble. But for the two days' rain and fog it is quite possible that the whole of the four objectives planned by the XXth Corps would have been gained, and whether any substantial body of Turks could have left the vicinity of Jerusalem by either the Nablus or Jericho roads is doubtful. The weather proved to be the Turks' ally. The 53rd Division battled against it. Until fog came down to prevent reconnaissance in an extremely bad bit of country they were well up to their march table, and in the few clear moments of the afternoon of the 7th, General Mott, from the top of Ras esh Sherifeh, a hill 3237 feet high, the most prominent feature south of Jerusalem, caught a glimpse of Bethlehem and the Holy City. It was only a temporary break in the weather, and the fog came down again so thick that neither the positions of the Bethlehem defences nor those of Beit Jala could be reconnoitred.

The Division, after withstanding the repeated shocks of enemy attacks at Khuweilfeh immediately following the taking of Beersheba, had had a comparatively light time watching the Hebron road. They constructed a track over the mountains to get the Division to Dharahiyeh when it should be ordered to take part in the attack on the Jerusalem defences, and while they were waiting at Dilbeih they did much to improve the main road. The famous zigzag on the steep ridge between Dharahiyeh and Dilbeih was in good condition, and you saw German thoroughness in the gradients, in the well–banked bends, and in the masonry walls which held up the road where it had been cut in the side of a hill. It was the most difficult part of the road, and the Germans had taken as much care of it as they would of a road in the Fatherland—because it was the way by which they hoped to get to the Suez Canal. Other portions of the road required renewing, and the labour which the Welshmen devoted to the work helped the feeding of the Division not only during the march to Jerusalem but for several weeks after it had passed through it to the hills on the east and north–east. The rations and stores for this Division were carried by the main railway through Shellal to Karm, were thence transported by limber to a point on the Turks' line to Beersheba, which had been repaired but was without engines, were next hauled in trucks by mules on the railway track, and finally placed in lorries at Beersheba for carriage up the Hebron road. At this time the capacity of the Latron–Jerusalem road was taxed to the utmost, and every bit of the Welshmen's spadework was repaid a hundredfold. The 159th Brigade got into Hebron on the night of the 5th of December, but instead of going north of it—if they had done so an enemy cavalry patrol would have seen them—they set to work to repair the road through the old Biblical town, for the enemy had blown holes in the highway. Next day the infantry had a ten–miles' march and made the wadi Arab, a brigade being left in Hebron to watch that area, the natives of which were reported as not being wholly favourable to us. There were many rifles in the place, and a number of unarmed Turks were believed to be in the rough country between the town and the Dead Sea ready to return to take up arms. Armoured cars also remained in Hebron. The infantry and field artillery occupied the roads during the day, and the heavy guns came along at night and joined the infantry as the latter were about to set off again.

On the night of the 6th the Division got to a strong line unopposed and saw enemy cavalry on the southern end of Sherifeh, on which the Turks had constructed a powerful system of defences, the traverses and breastworks of which were excellently made. In front of the hill the road took a bend to the west, and the whole of the highway from this point was exposed to the ground in enemy hands south of Bethlehem, and it was necessary to make good the hills to the east before we could control this road. Next morning the 7th Cheshires, supported by the 4th Welsh, deployed and advanced direct on Sherifeh and gained the summit soon after dawn in time to see small parties of enemy cavalry moving off; then the fog and rain enveloped everything. The 4th Welsh held the hill during the night in pouring rain with no rations—pack mules could not get up the height—and the men having no greatcoats were perished with the cold. Colonel Pemberton, their C.O., came down to report the men all right, and asked for no relief till the morning when they could be brought back to their transport. The General went beyond Solomon's Pools and was within rifle fire from the Turkish trenches in his efforts to reconnoitre, but it was impossible to see ahead, and instead of being able to begin his attack in the Beit Jala–Bethlehem area on the morning of the 8th, that morning arrived

115

before any reconnaissance could be made. He decided to attack on the high ground of Beit Jala (two miles north–west of Bethlehem) from the south, to send his divisional cavalry, the Westminster Dragoons, on the infantry's left to threaten Beit Jala from the west and to refuse Bethlehem.

Before developing this attack it was essential to drive the enemy off the observation post looking down upon the main road along which the guns and troops had to pass. The fog enabled the guns to pass up the road, although the Turks had seven mountain guns in the gardens of a big house south of Bethlehem and had registered the road to a yard. They also had a heavy gun outside the town. The weather cleared at intervals about noon, but about two o'clock a dense fog came down again and once more the advance was held up. Late in the afternoon the Welsh Division troops reached the high ground west and south–west of Beit Jala, but the defences of Bethlehem on the south had still to be taken. Advance guards were sent into Bethlehem and Beit Jala during the night, and by early morning of the 9th it was found that the enemy had left, and the leading brigade pressed on, reaching Mar Elias, midway between Bethlehem and Jerusalem, by eleven o'clock, and the southern outskirts of Jerusalem an hour later.

Meanwhile the 60th and 74th Divisions had actively patrolled their fronts during the night, and the Turks having tasted the quality of British bayonets made no attempt to recover any of the lost positions. We had outposts well up the road above Lifta, and at half–past eight they saw a white flag approaching. The nearest officer was a commander of the 302nd Brigade Royal Field Artillery, to whom the Mayor, the head of the Husseiny family, descendants of the Prophet and hereditary mayors of Jerusalem, signified his desire to surrender the City. The Mayor was accompanied by the Chief of Police and two of the gendarmerie, and while communications were passing between General Shea, General Chetwode and General Headquarters, General Watson rode as far as the Jaffa Gate of the Holy City to learn what was happening in the town. I believe Major Montagu Cooke, one of the officers of the 302nd Artillery Brigade, was the first officer actually in the town, and I understand that whilst he and his orderly were in the Post Office a substantial body of Turks turned the corner outside the building and passed down the Jericho road quite unconscious of the near presence of a British officer. General Shea was deputed by the Commander–in–Chief to enter Jerusalem in order to accept the surrender of the City. It was a simple little ceremony, lasting but a minute or two, free from any display of strength, and a fitting prelude to General Allenby's official entry. At half–past twelve General Shea, with his aide–de–camp and a guard of honour furnished by the

How Jerusalem Was Won

2/17th Londons, met the Mayor, who formally surrendered the City. To the Chief of Police General Shea gave instructions for the maintenance of order, and guards were placed over the public buildings. Then the commander of the 60th Division left to continue the direction of his troops who were making the Holy City secure from Turkish attacks. I believe the official report ran: 'Thus at 12.30 the Holy City was surrendered for the twenty–third time, and for the first time to British arms, and on this occasion without bloodshed among the inhabitants or damage to the buildings in the City itself.'

Simple as was the surrender of Jerusalem, there were scenes in the streets during the short half–hour of General Shea's visit which reflected the feeling of half the civilised world on receiving the news. It was a world event. This deliverance of Jerusalem from Turkish misgovernment was bound to stir the emotions of Christian, Jewish, and Moslem communities in the two hemispheres. In a war in which the moral effect of victories was only slightly less important than a big strategical triumph, Jerusalem was one of the strongest possible positions for the Allies to win, and it is not making too great a claim to say that the capture of the Holy City by British arms gave more satisfaction to countless millions of people than did the winning back for France of any big town on the Western Front. The latter might be more important from a military standpoint, but among the people, especially neutrals, it would be regarded merely as a passing incident in the ebb and flow of the tide of war. Bagdad had an important influence on the Eastern mind; Jerusalem affected Christian, Jew, and Moslem alike the world over. The War Cabinet regarded the taking of Jerusalem by British Imperial troops in so important a light that orders were given to hold up correspondents' messages and any telegrams the military attaches might write until the announcement of the victory had been made to the world by a Minister in the House of Commons. This instruction was officially communicated to me before we took Jerusalem, and I believe it was the case that the world received the first news when the mouthpiece of the Government gave it to the chosen representatives of the British people in the Mother of Parliaments.

The end of Ottoman dominion over the cradle of Christianity, a place held in reverence by the vast majority of the peoples of the Old and New World, made a deep and abiding impression, and as long as people hold dearly to their faiths, sentiment will make General Allenby's victory one of the greatest triumphs of the war. The relief of the people of Jerusalem, as well as their confidence that we were there to stay, manifested itself when General Shea drove into the City. The news had gone abroad that the General was to arrive about noon, and all Jerusalem came into the streets to welcome him. They clapped their hands and raised shrill cries of delight in a babel of tongues. Women threw flowers into the car and spread palm leaves on the road. Scarcely had the Turks left, probably before they had all gone and while the guns were still banging outside the entrances to Jerusalem, stray pieces of bunting which had done duty on many another day were hung out to signify the popular pleasure at the end of an old, hard, extortionate regime and the beginning of an era of happiness and freedom.

After leaving Jerusalem the enemy took up a strong position on the hills north and north–east of the City from which he had to be driven before Jerusalem was secure from counter–attack. During the morning General Chetwode gave orders for a general advance to the line laid down in his original plan of attack, which may be described as the preliminary line for the defence of Jerusalem. The 180th and 181st Brigades were already on the move, and some of the 53rd Division had marched by the main road outside the Holy City's walls to positions from which they were to attempt to drive the enemy off the Mount of Olives. The 180th Brigade, fresh and strong but still wet and muddy, went forward rapidly over the boulders on the hills east of the wadi Beit Hannina and occupied the rugged height of Shafat at half–past one. Shafat is about two miles north of Jerusalem. In another half–hour they had driven the Turks from the conical top of Tel el Ful, that sugar–loaf hill which dominates the Nablus road, and which before the end of the year was to be the scene of an epic struggle between Londoner and Turk. The 181st Brigade, on debouching from the suburbs of Jerusalem north–east of Lifta, was faced with heavy machine–gun and rifle fire on the ridge running from the western edge of the Mount of Olives across the Nablus road through Kh. es Salah. On the left the 180th Brigade lent support, and at four o'clock the 2/21st and 2/24th Londons rushed the ridge with the bayonet and drove off the Turks, who left seventy dead behind them. The London Division that night established itself on the line from a point a thousand yards north of Jerusalem and east of the Nablus road through Ras Meshari to Tel el Ful, thence westwards to the wadi behind the olive orchards south of Beit Hannina. The 74th Division reached its objective without violent opposition, and its line ran from north of Nebi Samwil to the height of Beit Hannina and out towards Tel el Ful. The 53rd Division was strongly opposed when it got round the south–east of Jerusalem on to the Jericho road in the direction of Aziriyeh (Bethany), and it was necessary to clear the Turks from the Mount of Olives. Troops of the Welsh Division moved round the Holy City and drove the enemy off the Mount, following them down the eastern spurs, and thus denied them any direct observation over Jerusalem. The next day they pushed the enemy still farther eastwards, and by the night of the 10th held the line from the well at Azad, 4000 yards

118

south–east of Jerusalem, the hill 1500 yards south of Aziriyeh, Aziriyeh itself, to the Mount of Olives, whence our positions continued to Ras et Tawil, north of Tel el Ful across the Nablus road to Nebi Samwil. This was our first line of positions for the defence of Jerusalem, and we continued to hold these strong points for some time. They were gradually extended on the east and north–east by the Welsh Division in order to prevent an attack from the direction of Jericho, where we knew the Turks had received reinforcements. Indeed, during our attack on the Jerusalem position the Turks had withdrawn a portion of their force on the Hedjaz railway. A regiment had passed through Jericho from the Hedjaz line at Amman and was marching up the road to assist in Jerusalem's defence, but was 'Too late.' The regiment was turned back when we had captured Jerusalem. Our casualties from November 28 to December 10—these figures include the heavy fighting about Tahta, Foka, and Nebi Samwil prior to the XXth Corps' attack on the Jerusalem defences—were: officers, 21 killed, 64 wounded, 3 missing; other ranks, 247 killed, 1163 wounded, 169 missing, a total of 1667. The casualties of the 60th Division during the attack on and advance north of Jerusalem on December 8–9 are interesting, because they were so extremely light considering the strength of the defences captured and the difficulties of the ground, namely: 8 officers killed and 24 wounded, 98 other ranks killed, 420 wounded and 3 missing, a total of 553. The total for the whole of the XXth Corps on these days was 12 officers killed, 35 wounded, and 137 other ranks killed, 636 wounded and 7 missing—in all 47 officers and 780 other ranks. The prisoners taken from November 28 to December 10 were: 76 officers, 1717 other ranks—total, 1793. On December 8 and 9, 68 officers and 918 other ranks—986 in all—were captured. The booty included two 4–2 Krupp howitzers, three 77–mm. field guns and carriages, nine heavy and three light machine guns, 137 boxes of small–arms ammunition, and 103,000 loose rounds.

CHAPTER XV. GENERAL ALLENBY'S OFFICIAL ENTRY

Jerusalem became supremely happy.

It had passed through the trials, if not the perils, of war. It had been the headquarters and base of a Turkish Army. Great bodies of troops were never quartered there, but staffs and depots were established in the City, and being in complete control, the military paid little regard to the needs of the population. Unfortunately a not inconsiderable section of Jerusalem's inhabitants is content to live, not by its own handiwork, but on the gifts of charitable religious people of all creeds. When war virtually shut off Jerusalem from the outer world the lot of the poor became precarious. The food of the country, just about sufficient for self–support, was to a large extent commandeered for the troops, and while prices rose the poor could not buy, and either their appeals did not reach the benevolent or funds were intercepted. Deaths from starvation were numbered by the thousand, Jews, Christians, and Moslems alike suffering, and there were few civilians in the Holy City who were not hungry for months at a time.

When I reached Jerusalem the people were at the height of their excitement over the coming of the British and they put the best face on their condition, but the freely expressed feeling of relief that the days of hunger torture were nearly past did not remove the signs of want and misery, of infinite suffering by father, mother, and child, brought about by a long period of starvation. That a people, pale, thin, bent, whose movements had become listless under the lash of hunger, could have been stirred into enthusiasm by the appearance of a khaki coat, that they could throw off the lethargy which comes of acute want, was only to be accounted for by the existence of a profound belief that we had been sent to deliver them. Some hours before the Official Entry I was walking in David Street when a Jewish woman, seeing that I was English, stopped me and said: 'We have prayed for this day. To–day I shall sing "God Save our Gracious King, Long Live our Noble King." We have been starving, but what does that matter? Now we are liberated and free.' She clasped her hands across her breasts and exclaimed several times, 'Oh how thankful we are.' An elderly man in a black robe, whose pinched pale face told of a long period of want, caught me by the hand and said: 'God has delivered us. Oh how happy we are.' An American worker in a Red Crescent hospital, who had lived in Jerusalem for upwards of ten years and knew the people well, assured me there was not one person in the Holy City who in his heart was not devoutly thankful for our victory. He told me that on the day we captured Nebi Samwil three wounded Arab officers were brought to the hospital. One of them spoke English—it was astonishing how many people could speak our mother tongue—and while he was having his wounds dressed he exclaimed: 'I can shout Hip–hip–hurrah for England now.' The officer was advised to be careful, as there were many Turkish wounded in the hospital, but he replied he did not care, and in unrestrained joy cried out, 'Hurrah for England.'

The deplorable lot of the people had been made harder by profiteering officers. Those who had money had to part with it for Turkish paper. The Turkish note was depreciated to about one–fifth of its face value. German officers traded in the notes for gold, sent the notes to Germany where, by a financial arrangement concluded between Constantinople and Berlin, they were accepted at face value. The German officer and soldier got richer the more they forced Turkish paper down. Turkish officers bought considerable supplies of wheat and flour from military depots, the cost being debited against their pay which was paid in paper. They then sold the goods for gold. That accounted for the high prices of foodstuffs, the price in gold being taken for the market valuation.

In the middle of November when there was a prospect of the Turks evacuating Jerusalem, the officers sold out their stocks of provisions and prices became less prohibitive, but they rose again quickly when it was decided to defend the City, and the cost of food mounted to almost famine prices. The Turks by selling for gold that which was bought for paper, rechanging gold for paper at their own prices, made huge profits and caused a heavy depreciation of the note at the expense of the population. Grain was brought from the district east of the Dead Sea, but none of it found its way to civilian mouths except through the extortionate channel provided by officers. Yet when we got into Jerusalem there were people with small stocks of flour who were willing to make flat loaves of unleavened bread for sale to our troops. The soldiers had been living for weeks on hard biscuit and bully beef, and many were willing to pay a shilling for a small cake of bread. They did not know that the stock of flour in the town was desperately low and that by buying this bread they were almost taking it out of the mouths of the poor. Some traders were so keen on getting good money, not paper, that they tried to do business on this footing, looking to the British Army to come to the aid of the people. The Army soon put a stop to this trade and the troops were prohibited from buying bread in Jerusalem and Bethlehem. As it was, the Quarter–master–General's branch had to send a large quantity of foodstuffs into the towns, and this was done at a time when it was a most anxious task to provision the troops. Those were very trying days for the supply and transport departments, and one wonders whether the civilian population ever realised the extent of the humanitarian efforts of our Army staff.

During the period when no attempt was made to alleviate the lot of the people the Turks gave them a number of lessons in frightfulness. There were public executions to show the severity of military law. Gallows were erected outside the Jaffa Gate and the victims were left hanging for hours as a warning to the population. I have seen a photograph of six natives who suffered the penalty, with their executioners standing at the swinging feet of their victims. Before the first battle of Gaza the Turks brought the rich Mufti of Gaza and his son to Jerusalem, and the Mufti was hanged in the presence of a throng compulsorily assembled to witness the execution. The son was shot. Their only crime was that they were believed to have expressed approval of Britain's policy in dealing with Moslem races. Thus were the people terrorised. They knew the Turkish ideas of justice, and dared not talk of events happening in the town even in the seclusion of their homes. The evils of war, as war is practised by the Turk, left a mark on Jerusalem's population which will be indelible for this generation, despite the wondrous change our Army has wrought in the people.

When General Allenby had broken through the Gaza line the Turks in Jerusalem despaired of saving the City. That all the army papers were brought from Hebron on November 10, shows that even at that date von Kress still imagined we would come up the Hebron road, though he had learnt to his cost that a mighty column was moving through the coastal sector and that our cavalry were cutting across the country to join it. The notorious Enver reached Jerusalem from the north on November 12 and went down to Hebron. On his return it was reported that the Turks would leave Jerusalem, the immediate sale of officers' stocks of foodstuffs giving colour to the rumour. Undoubtedly some preparations were made to evacuate the place, but the temptation to hold on was too great. One can see the influence of the German mind in the Turkish councils of war. At a moment when they were flashing the wireless news throughout the world that their Caporetto victory meant the driving of Italy out of the war they did not want the icy blast of Jerusalem's fall to tell of disaster to their hopes in the East. Accordingly on the 16th November a new decision was taken and Jerusalem was to be defended to the last. German officers came hurrying south, lorries were rushed down with stores until there were six hundred German lorry drivers and mechanics in Jerusalem. Reinforcements arrived and the houses of the German Colony were turned into nests of machine guns. The pains the Germans were at to see their plans carried out were reflected in the fighting when we tried to get across the Jerusalem–Nablus road and to avoid fighting in the neighbourhood of the Holy City. But all this effort availed them nought. Our dispositions compelled the enemy to distribute his forces, and when the attack was launched the Turk lacked sufficient men to man his defences adequately. And German pretensions in the Holy Land, founded upon years of scheming and the formation of settlements for German colonists approved and supported by the Kaiser himself, were shattered beyond hope of recovery, as similar pretensions had been shattered at Bagdad by General Maude. The Turks had made their headquarters at the Hospice of Notre Dame in Jerusalem, and, taking their cue from the Hun, carried away all the furniture belonging to that French religious institution. They had also deported some of the heads of religious bodies.

How Jerusalem Was Won

Falkenhayn wished that all Americans should be removed from Jerusalem, issuing an order to that effect a fortnight before we entered. Some members of the American colony had been running the Red Crescent hospital, and Turkish doctors who appreciated their good work insisted that the Americans should remain. Their protest prevailed in most cases, but just as we arrived several Americans were carried off.

I have asked many men who were engaged in the fight for Jerusalem what their feelings were on getting their first glimpse of the central spot of Christendom. Some people imagine that the hard brutalities of war erase the softer elements of men's natures; that killing and the rough life of campaigning, where one is familiarised with the tragedies of life every hour of every day, where ease and comfort are forgotten things, remove from the mind those earlier lessons of peace on earth and goodwill toward men. That is a fallacy. Every man or officer I spoke to declared that he was seized with emotion when, looking from the shell−torn summit of Nebi Samwil, he saw the spires on the Mount of Olives; or when reconnoitring from Kustul he got a peep of the red roofs of the newer houses which surround the old City. Possibly only a small percentage of the Army believed they were taking part in a great mission, not a great proportion would claim to be really devout men, but they all behaved like Christian gentlemen. One Londoner told me he had thought the scenes of war had made him callous and that the ruthless destruction of those things fashioned by men's hands in prosecuting the arts of peace had prompted the feeling that there was little in civilisation after all, if civilisation could result in so bitter a thing as this awful fighting. Man seemed as barbaric as in the days before the Saviour came to redeem the world, and whether we won or lost the war all hopes of a happier state of things were futile. So this Cockney imagined that his condition showed no improvement on that of the savage warrior of two thousand years ago, except in that civilisation had developed finer weapons to kill with and be killed by. The finer instincts had been blunted by the naked and unashamed horrors of war. But the lessons taught him before war scourged the world came back to him on getting his first view of the Holy City. He felt that sense of emotion which makes one wish to be alone and think alone. He was on the ground where Sacred History was made, perhaps stood on the rock the Saviour's foot had trod. In the deep stirring of his emotions the rougher edges of his nature became rounded by feelings of sympathy and a belief that good would come out of the evil of this strife. That view of Jerusalem, and the knowledge of what the Holy Sites stand for, made him a better man and a better fighting man, and he had no doubt the first distant glimpse of the Holy City had similarly affected the bulk of the Army. That bad language is used by almost all troops in the field is notorious, but in Jerusalem one seldom heard an oath or an indecent word. When Jerusalem was won and small parties of our soldiers were allowed to see the Holy City, their politeness to the inhabitants, patriarch or priest, trader or beggar, man or woman, rebuked the thought that the age of chivalry was past, while the reverent attitude involuntarily adopted by every man when seeing the Sacred Places suggested that no Crusader Army or band of pilgrims ever came to the Holy Land under a more pious influence. Many times have I watched the troops of General Allenby in the streets of Jerusalem. They bore themselves as soldiers and gentlemen, and if they had been selected to go there simply to impress the people they could not have more worthily upheld the good fame of their nation. These soldier missionaries of the Empire left behind them a record which will be remembered for generations.

If it had been possible to consult the British people as to the details to be observed at the ceremony of the Official Entry into Jerusalem, the vast majority would surely have approved General Allenby's programme. Americans tell us the British as a nation do not know how to advertise. Our part in the war generally proves the accuracy of that statement, but the Official Entry into Jerusalem will stand out as one great exception. By omitting to make a great parade of his victory—one may count elaborate ceremonial as advertisement—General Allenby gave Britain her best advertisement. The simple, dignified, and, one may also justly say, humble order of ceremony was the creation of a truly British mind. To impress the inhabitant of the East things must be done on a lavish ostentatious scale, for gold and glitter and tinsel go a long way to form a native's estimate of power. But there are times when the native is shrewd enough to realise that pomp and circumstance do not always indicate strength, and that dignity is more powerful than display. Contrast the German Emperor's visit to Jerusalem with General Allenby's Official Entry. The Kaiser brought a retinue clothed in white and red, and blue and gold, with richly caparisoned horses, and, like a true showman, he himself affected some articles of Arab dress. He rode into the Holy City—where One before had walked—and a wide breach was even made in those ancient walls for a German progress. All this to advertise the might and power of Germany.

In parenthesis I may state we are going to restore those walls to the condition they were in before German hands defiled them. The General who by capturing Jerusalem helped us so powerfully to bring Germany to her knees and humble her before the world, entered on foot by an ancient way, the Jaffa Gate, called by the native 'Bab–el–Khalil,' or the Friend. In this hallowed spot there was no great pageantry of arms, no pomp and panoply, no display of the mighty strength of a victorious army, no thunderous salutes to acclaim a world-resounding victory destined to take its place in the chronicles of all time. There was no enemy flag to haul down and no flags were hoisted. There were no soldier shouts of triumph over a defeated foe, no bells in ancient belfrys rang, no Te Deums were sung, and no preacher mounted the rostrum to eulogise the victors or to point the moral to the multitude. A small, almost meagre procession, consisting of the Commander-in-Chief and his Staff, with a guard of honour, less than 150 all told, passed through the gate unheralded by a single trumpet note; a purely military act with a minimum of military display told the people that the old order had changed, yielding place to new. The native mind, keen, discerning, receptive, understood the meaning and depth of this simplicity, and from the moment of high noon on December 11, 1917, when General Allenby went into the Mount Zion quarter of the Holy City, the British name rested on a foundation as certain and sure as the rock on which the Holy City stands. Right down in the hearts of a people who cling to Jerusalem with the deepest reverence and piety there was unfeigned delight. They realised that four centuries of Ottoman dominion over the Holy City of Christians and Jews, and 'the sanctuary' of Mahomedans, had ended, and that Jerusalem the Golden, the central Site of Sacred History, was liberated for all creeds from the blighting influence of the Turk. And while war had wrought this beneficent change the population saw in this epoch-marking victory a merciful guiding Hand, for it had been achieved without so much as a stone of the City being scratched or a particle of its ancient dust disturbed. The Sacred Monuments and everything connected with the Great Life and its teaching were passed on untouched by our Army. Rightly did the people rejoice.

When General Allenby went into Jerusalem all fears had passed away. The Official Entry was made while there was considerable fighting on the north and east of the City, where our lines were nowhere more than 7000 yards off. The guns were firing, the sounds of bursts of musketry were carried down on the wind, whilst droning aeroplane engines in the deep-blue vault overhead told of our flying men denying a passage to enemy machines. The stern voices of war were there in all their harsh discordancy, but the people knew they were safe in the keeping of British soldiers and came out to make holiday. General Allenby motored into the suburbs of Jerusalem by the road from Latron which the pioneers had got into some sort of order. The business of war was going on, and the General's car took its place on the highway on even terms with the lorry, which at that time when supplying the front was the most urgent task and had priority on the roads. The people had put on gala raiment. From the outer fringe of Jerusalem the Jaffa road was blocked not merely with the inhabitants of the City but with people who had followed in the Army's wake from Bethlehem. It was a picturesque throng. There were sombre–clad Jews of all nationalities, Armenians, Greeks, Russians, and all the peoples who make Jerusalem the most cosmopolitan of cities. To the many styles of European dress the brighter robes of the East gave vivid colour, and it was obvious from the remarkable free and spontaneous expression of joy of these people, who at the end of three years of war had such strong faith in our fight for freedom, that they recognised freedom was permanently won to all races and creeds by the victory at Jerusalem. The most significant of all the signs was the attitude of Moslems. The Turks had preached the Holy War, but they knew the hollowness of the cry, and the natives, abandoning their natural reserve, joined in loud expression of welcome. From flat–topped roofs, balconies, and streets there were cries of 'Bravo!' and 'Hurrah!' uttered by men and women who probably never spoke the words before, and quite close to the Jaffa Gate I saw three old Mahomedans clap their hands while tears of joy coursed down their cheeks. Their hearts were too full to utter a word. There could be no doubt of the sincerity of this enthusiasm. The crowd was more demonstrative than is usual with popular assemblies in the East, but the note struck was not one of jubilation so much as of thankfulness at the relief from an insufferable bondage of bad government. Outside the Jaffa Gate was an Imperial guard of honour drawn from men who had fought stoutly for the victory. In the British Guard of fifty of all ranks were English, Scottish, Irish, and Welsh troops, steel–helmeted and carrying the kit they had an hour or two earlier brought with them from the front line. Opposite them were fifty dismounted men of the Australian Light Horse and New Zealand Mounted Rifles, the Australians, under the command of Captain Throssel, V.C., being drawn from the 10th Light Horse regiment, which had been employed in the capture of Jerusalem on the right of the London Division. These Colonial troops had earned their place, for they had done the work of the vanguard in the Sinai Desert, and their victories over the Turks on many a hard–won field in the torrid heat of summer had paved the way for this greater triumph. A French and an Italian guard of honour was posted inside the Jaffa Gate. As I have previously said, the Italians had held a portion of the line in front of Gaza with a composite brigade, but the French troops had not yet been in action in Palestine, though their Navy had assisted with a battleship in the Gaza bombardment. We welcomed the participation of the representatives of our Allies in the Official Entry, as it showed to those of their nationality in Jerusalem that we were fighting the battle of freedom for them all. Outside the Jaffa Gate the Commander–in–Chief was received by Major–General Borton, who had been appointed Military Governor of the City, and a procession being formed, General Allenby passed

126

between the iron gates to within the City walls. Preceded by two aides–de–camp the Commander–in–Chief advanced with the commander of the French Palestine detachment on his right and the commander of the Italian Palestine detachment on his left. Four Staff officers followed. Then came Brigadier–General Clayton, Political Officer; M. Picot, head of the French Mission; and the French, Italian, and United States Military Attaches. The Chief of the General Staff (Major–General Sir L.J. Bols) and the Brigadier–General General Staff (Brigadier–General G. Dawnay) marched slightly ahead of Lieutenant–General Sir Philip W. Chetwode, the XXth Corps Commander, and Brigadier–General Bartholomew, who was General Chetwode's B.G.G.S. The guard closed in behind. That was all.

The procession came to a halt at the steps of El Kala, the Citadel, which visitors to Jerusalem will better remember as the entrance to David's Tower. Here the Commander–in–Chief and his Staff formed up on the steps with the notables of the City behind them, to listen to the reading of the Proclamation in several languages. That Proclamation, telling the people they could pursue their lawful business without interruption and promising that every sacred building, monument, holy spot, shrine, traditional site, endowment, pious bequest, or customary place of prayer of whatsoever form of three of the great religions of mankind would be maintained and protected according to existing customs and beliefs to those to whose faiths they are sacred, made a deep impression on the populace. So you could judge from the expressions on faces and the frequent murmurs of approval, and it was interesting to note how, when the procession was being re–formed, many Christians, Jews, and Moslems broke away from the crowd to run and spread the good news in their respective quarters. How faithfully and with what scrupulous care our promises have been kept the religious communities of Jerusalem can tell.

The procession next moved into the old Turkish barrack square less than a hundred yards away, where General Allenby received the notables of the City and the heads of religious communities. The Mayor of Jerusalem, who unfortunately died of pneumonia a fortnight later, and the Mufti, who, like the Mayor, was a member of a Mahomedan family which traces its descent back through many centuries, were presented, as were also the sheikhs in charge of the Mosque of Omar, 'the Tomb of the Rock,' and the Mosque of El Aksa, and Moslems belonging to the Khaldieh and Alamieh families. The Patriarchs of the Latin, Greek Orthodox, and Armenian Churches and the Coptic bishop had been removed from the Holy City by the Turks, but their representatives were introduced to the

127

How Jerusalem Was Won

Commander–in–Chief, and so too were the heads of Jewish communities, the Syriac Church, the Greek Catholic Church, the Abyssinian bishop, and the representative of the Anglican Church. A notable presentation was the Spanish Consul, who had been in charge of the interests of almost all countries at war, and whom General Allenby congratulated upon being so busy a man. The presentations over, the Commander–in–Chief returned to the Jaffa Gate and left for advanced General Headquarters, having been in the Holy City not more than a quarter of an hour.

For succinctness it would be difficult to improve upon the Commander–in–Chief's own description of his Official Entry into Jerusalem. Cabling to London within two hours of that event, General Allenby thus narrated the events of the day:

(1) At noon to–day I officially entered this City with a few of my Staff, the commanders of the French and Italian detachments, the heads of the Picot Mission, and the Military Attaches of France, Italy, and the United States of America.

The procession was all on foot.

I was received by Guards representing England, Scotland, Ireland, Wales, Australia, India, New Zealand, France, and Italy at the Jaffa Gate.

(2) I was well received by the population.

(3) The Holy Places have had Guards placed over them.

(4) My Military Governor is in touch with the Acting Custos of Latins, and the Greek representative has been detailed to supervise Christian Holy Places.

(5) The Mosque of Omar and the area round it has been placed under Moslem control and a military cordon composed of Indian Mahomedan officers and soldiers has been established round the Mosque. Orders have been issued that without permission of the Military Governor and the Moslem in charge of the Mosque no non–Moslem is to pass this cordon.

(6) The Proclamation has been posted on the walls, and from the steps of the Citadel was read in my presence to the population in Arabic, Hebrew, English, French, Italian, Greek,

and Russian.

(7) Guardians have been established at Bethlehem and on Rachel's Tomb. The Tomb of Hebron has been placed under exclusive Moslem control.

(8) The hereditary custodians of the Wakfs at the Gates of the Holy Sepulchre have been requested to take up their accustomed duties in remembrance of the magnanimous act of the Caliph Omar who protected that Church.

As a matter of historical interest I give in the Appendix the orders issued on the occasion of the Official Entry into Jerusalem, the order of General Allenby's procession into the Holy City for the reading of the Proclamation, together with the text of that historic document, and the special orders of the day issued by the Commander–in–Chief to his troops after the capture of Jerusalem.[1]

[Footnote 1: See Appendix VII.]

CHAPTER XVI. MAKING JERUSALEM SECURE

General Allenby within two days of capturing Jerusalem had secured a line of high ground which formed an excellent defensive system, but his XXth Corps Staff was busy with plans to extend the defences to give the Holy City safety from attack. Nothing could have had so damaging an influence on our prestige in the East, which was growing stronger every day as the direct result of the immense success of the operations in Palestine, as the recapture of Jerusalem by the Turks. We thought the wire–pulling of the German High Command would have its effect in the war councils of Turkey, and seeing that the regaining of the prize would have such far–reaching effect on public opinion no one was surprised that the Germans prevailed upon their ally to make the attempt. It was a hopeless failure. The attack came at a moment when we were ready to launch a scheme to secure a second and a third line of defences for Jerusalem, and gallantly as the Turks fought—they delivered thirteen powerful attacks against our line on the morning of December 27—the venture had a disastrous ending, and instead of reaching Jerusalem the enemy had to yield to British arms seven miles of most valuable country and gave us, in place of one line, four strong lines for the defence of the Holy City. By supreme judgment, when the Turks had committed themselves to the attack on Tel el Ful, without which they could not move a yard on the Nablus road, General Chetwode started his operations on the left of his line with the 10th and 74th Divisions, using his plan as it had been prepared for some days to seize successive lines of hills, and compelled the enemy, in order to meet this attack, to divert the fresh division held in waiting at Bireh to throw forward into Jerusalem the moment the storming troops should pierce our line. With the precision of clockwork the Irish and dismounted yeomanry divisions secured their objectives, and on the second day of the fighting we regained the initiative and compelled the Turks to conform to our dispositions. On the fourth day we were on the Ramallah–Bireh line and secured for Jerusalem an impregnable defence. Prisoners told us that they had been promised, as a reward for their hoped–for success, a day in Jerusalem to do as they liked. We can imagine what the situation in the Holy City would have been had our line been less true. The Londoners who had won the City saved it. Probably only a few of the inhabitants had any knowledge of the danger the City was in on December 27. Their confidence in the British troops had grown and could scarcely be stronger, but some of them were alarmed, and throughout the early morning and day they knelt on housetops earnestly praying that our soldiers would have strength to withstand the Turkish onslaughts. From that day onward the sound of the guns was less violent, and as our artillery advanced northwards the people's misgivings vanished and they reproached themselves for their fears.

It will be remembered how the troops of the XXth Corps were disposed. The 53rd Division held the line south–east and east of Jerusalem from Bir Asad through Abu Dis, Bethany, to north of the Mount of Olives, whence the 60th Division took it up from Meshari, east of Shafat to Tel el Ful and to Beit Hannina across the Jerusalem–Nablus road. The 74th Division carried on to Nebi Samwil, Beit Izza to Beit Dukku, with the 10th Division on their left through Foka, Tahta to Suffa, the gap between the XXth Corps to the right of the XXIst Corps being held by the 3rd Australian Light Horse Brigade of the Australian Mounted Division. Against us were the 27th Turkish Division and the 7th and 27th cavalry regiments south of the Jericho road, with the 26th, 53rd, 19th, and 24th Divisions on the north of that road and to the west of the Jerusalem–Nablus road, one division being in reserve at Bireh, the latter a new division fresh from the Caucasus. The 6th and 8th Turkish cavalry regiments were facing our extreme left, the estimated strength of the enemy in the line being 14,700 rifles and 2300 sabres. Just as it was getting dark on December 11 a party of the enemy attacked the 179th Brigade at Tel el Ful but were repulsed. There was not much activity the following day, but the 53rd Division began a series of minor operations by which they secured some features of tactical importance. On the 13th the 181st Brigade made a dashing attack on Ras el Kharrabeh and secured it, taking 43 prisoners and two machine guns, with 31 casualties to themselves.

It was about this time the Corps Commander framed plans for the advance of our front north of Jerusalem. There had been a few days of fine weather, and a great deal had been done to improve the condition of the roads and communications. An army of Egyptian labourers had set to work on the Enab–Jerusalem road and from the villages had come strong reinforcements of natives, women as well as men (and the women did quite as much work as the men), attracted by the unusual wage payable in cash. In Jerusalem, too, the natives were sent to labour on the roads and to clean up some of the filth that the Turks had allowed to accumulate for years, if not for generations, inside the Holy City. The Army not merely provided work for idle hands but enabled starving bodies to be vitalised. Food was brought into Jerusalem, and with the cash wages old and young labourers could get more than a sufficiency. The native in the hills proved to be a good road repairer, and the boys and women showed an eagerness to earn their daily rates of pay; the men generally looked on and gave directions. It was some time before steam rollers crushed in the surface, but even rammed–in stones were better than mud, and the lorry drivers' tasks became lighter.

General Chetwode's plan was to secure a line from Obeid, 9000 yards east of Bethlehem, the hill of Zamby covering the Jericho road three miles from Jerusalem, Anata, Hismeh, Jeba, Burkah, Beitun, El Balua, Kh. el Burj, Deir Ibzia to Shilta. The scheme was to strike with the 53rd and 60th Divisions astride the Jerusalem–Nablus road, and at the same time to push the 10th Division and a part of the 74th Division eastwards from the neighbourhood of Tahta and Foka. The weather again became bad on December 14 and the troops suffered great discomfort from heavy rains and violent, cold winds, so that only light operations were undertaken. On the 17th the West Kent and Sussex battalions of the 160th Brigade stalked the high ground east of Abu Dis at dawn, and at the cost of only 26 casualties took the ridge with 5 officers and 121 other ranks prisoners, and buried 46 enemy dead. One battalion went up the hill on one side, while the Sussex crept up the opposite side, the Turks being caught between two fires. The 53rd Division also improved their position on the 21st December. As one leaves Bethany and proceeds down the Jericho road one passes along a steep zigzag with several hairpin bends until one reaches a guardhouse near a well about a mile east of Bethany. The road still falls smartly, following a straighter line close to a wadi bed, but hills rise very steeply from the highway, and for its whole length until it reaches the Jordan valley the road is always covered by high bare mountains. Soon after leaving the zigzag there is a series of three hills to the north of the road. It was important to obtain possession of two of these hills, the first called Zamby and the second named by the Welsh troops 'Whitehill,' from the bright limestone outcrop at the crest. The 159th Brigade attacked and gained Zamby and then turned nearer the Jericho road to capture Whitehill. The Turks resisted very stoutly, and there was heavy fighting about the trenches just below the top of the hill. By noon the brigade had driven the enemy off, but three determined counter–attacks were delivered that day and the next and the brigade lost 180 killed and wounded. The Turks suffered heavily in the counter–attacks and left over 50 dead behind them; also a few prisoners. At a later date there was further strong fighting around this hill, and at one period it became impossible for either side to hold it.

By the 21st there was a readjustment of the line on the assumption that the XXth Corps would attack the Turks on Christmas Day, the 53rd Division taking over the line as far north as the wadi Anata, the 60th Division extending its left to include Nebi Samwil, and the 74th going as far west as Tahta. As a preliminary to the big movement the 180th Brigade was directed to move on Kh. Adaseh, a hill between Tel el Ful and Tawil, in the early hours of December 23, and the 181st Brigade was to seize a height about half a mile north of Beit Hannina. The latter attack succeeded, but despite the most gallant and repeated efforts the 180th Brigade was unable to gain the summit of Adaseh, though they got well up the hill. The weather became bad once more, and meteorological reports indicated no improvement in the conditions for at least twenty–four hours, and as the moving forward of artillery and supplies was impossible in the rain, General Chetwode with the concurrence of G.H.Q. decided that the attack should not be made on Christmas Day. The 60th Division thereupon did not further prosecute their attack on Adaseh. On the 24th December, while General Chetwode was conferring with his divisional commanders, information was brought in that the Turks were making preparations to recapture Jerusalem by an attack on the 60th Division, and the Corps Commander decided that the moment the enemy was found to be fully committed to this attack the 10th Division and one brigade of the 74th Division would fall on the enemy's right and advance over the Zeitun, Kereina, and Ibzia ridges. How well this plan worked out was shown before the beginning of the New Year, by which time we had secured a great depth of ground at a cost infinitely smaller than could have been expected if the Turks had remained on the defensive, while the Turkish losses, at a moment when they required to preserve every fighting man, were much greater than we could have hoped to inflict if they had not come into the open. There was never a fear that the enemy would break through. We had commanding positions everywhere, and the more one studied our line on the chain of far—flung hills the more clearly one realised the prevision and military skill of General Chetwode and the staff of the XXth Corps in preparing the plans for its capture before the advance on Jerusalem was started. The 'fourth objective' of December 8–9 well and truly laid the foundations for Jerusalem's security, and relieved the inhabitants from the accumulated burdens of more than three years of war. We had nibbled at pieces of ground to flatten out the line here and there, but in the main the line the Turks assaulted was that fourth objective. The Turks put all their hopes on their last card. It was trumped; and when we had won the trick there was not a soldier in General Allenby's Army nor a civilian in the Holy City who had not a profound belief in the coming downfall of the Turkish Empire.

Troops in the line and in bivouac spent the most cheerless Christmas Day within their memories. Not only in the storm—swept hills but on the Plain the day was bitterly cold, and the gale carried with it heavy rain clouds which passed over the tops of mountains and rolled up the valleys in ceaseless succession, discharging hail and rain in copious quantities. The wadis became roaring, tearing torrents fed by hundreds of tributaries, and men who had sought shelter on the lee side of rocks often found water pouring over them in cascades. The whole country became a sea of mud, and the trials of many months of desert sand were grateful and comforting memories. Transport columns had an unhappy time: the Hebron road was showing many signs of wear, and it was a long journey for lorries from Beersheba when the retaining walls were giving way and a foot—deep layer of mud invited a skid every yard. The Latron—Jerusalem road was better going, but the soft metal laid down seemed to melt under the unceasing traffic in the wet, and in peace time this highway would have been voted unfit for traffic. The worst piece of road, however, was also the most important. The Nablus road where it leaves Jerusalem was wanted to supply a vital point on our front. It could not be used during the day because it was under observation, and anything moving along it was liberally dosed with shells. Nor could its deplorable condition be improved by working parties. The ground was so soft on either side of it that no gun, ammunition, or supply limber could leave the track, and whatever was required for man, or beast, or artillery had to be carried across the road in the pitch—black hours of night. Supplies were only got up to the troops after infinite labour, yet no one went hungry. Boxing Day was brighter, and there were hopes of a period of better weather. During the morning there were indications that an enemy offensive was not far off, and these were confirmed about noon by information that the front north of Jerusalem would be attacked in the night. General Chetwode thereupon ordered General Longley to start his offensive on the left of the XXth Corps line at dawn next morning. Shortly before midnight the Turks began their operations against the line held by the 60th Division across the Nablus road precisely where it had been expected. They attacked in considerable strength at Ras et Tawil and about the quarries held by our outposts north of that hill, and the outposts were driven in. About the same time the 24th Welsh Regiment—dismounted yeomanry—made the enemy realise that we were on the alert, for they assaulted and captured a hill quite close to Et Tireh, just forestalling an attack by a Turkish storming battalion, and beat off several determined counter–attacks, as a result of which the enemy left seventy killed with the bayonet and also some machine guns on the hill slopes.

The night was dark and misty, and by half–past one the Turks had developed a big attack against the whole of the 60th Division's front, the strongest effort being delivered on the line in front of Tel el Ful, though there was also very violent fighting on the west of the wadi Ed Dunn, north of Beit Hannina. The Turks fought with desperate bravery. They had had no food for two days, and the commander of one regiment told his men: 'There are no English in front of you. I have been watching the enemy lines for a long time; they are held by Egyptians, and I tell you there are no English there. You have only to capture two hills and you can go straight into Jerusalem and get food. It is our last chance of getting Jerusalem, and if we fail we shall have to go back.' This officer gave emphatic orders that British wounded were not to be mutilated. Between half–past one and eight A.M. the Turks attacked in front of Tel el Ful eight times, each attack being stronger than the last. Tel el Ful is a conical hill covered with huge boulders, and on the top is a mass of rough stones and ruined masonry. The Turks had registered well and severely shelled our position before making an assault, and they covered the advance with machine guns. In one attack made just after daybreak the enemy succeeded in getting into a short length of line, but men of the 2/15th Londons promptly organised a counter–attack and, advancing with fine gallantry, though their ranks were thinned by a tremendous enfilade fire from artillery and machine guns, they regained the sangars. For several hours after eight o'clock this portion of the line was quieter, but the Turk was reorganising for a last effort. A very brilliant defence had been made during the night of Beit Hannina by the 2/24th Londons, which battalion was commanded by a captain, the colonel and the majors being on the sick list. The two companies in the line were attacked four times by superior numbers, the last assault being delivered by more than five hundred men, but the defenders stood like rocks, and though they had fifty per cent, of their number killed or

134

wounded, and the Turks got close to the trenches, the enemy were crushingly defeated.

The morning lull was welcome. Our troops got some rest though their vigilance was unrelaxed, and few imagined that the Turks had yet given up the attempt to reach Jerusalem. We were ready to meet a fresh effort, but the strength with which it was delivered surprised everybody. The Turk, it seemed, was prepared to stake everything on his last throw. He knew quite early on that morning that his Caucasus Division could not carry out the role assigned to it. General Chetwode had countered him by smashing in with his left with a beautiful weighty stroke precisely at the moment when the Turk had compromised himself elsewhere, and instead of being able to put in his reserves to support his main attack the enemy had to divert them to stave off an advance which, if unhindered, would threaten the vital communications of the attackers north of Jerusalem.

It was a remarkable situation, but all the finesse in the art of war was on one side. Every message the Turkish Commander received from his right must have reported progress against him. Each signal from the Jerusalem front must have been equally bitter, summing up want of progress and heavy losses. With us, Time was a secondary factor; with the Turk, Time was the whole essence of the business, so he pledged his all on one tremendous final effort. It was almost one o'clock when it started, and it was made against the whole front of our XXth Corps. It was certainly made in unexpected strength and with a courage beyond praise. The Turk threw himself forward to the assault with the violence of despair, and his impetuous onrush enabled him to get into some small elements of our front line; but counter–attacks immediately organised drove him out. Over the greater portion of the front the advance was stopped dead, but in some places the enemy tried a whirlwind rush and used bomb against bomb. He had met his match.

The 60th Division which bore the brunt of the onslaught, as it was bound to do from its position astride the main road, was absolutely unbreakable, and at Tel el Ful there lay a dead Turk for every yard of its front. The enemy drew off, but to save the remnants of his storming troops kept our positions from near Ras et Tawil, Tel el Ful to the wadi Beit Hannina under heavy gunfire for the rest of the day. The Turk was hopelessly beaten, his defeat irretrievable. He had delivered thirteen costly attacks, and his sole gains were the exposed outpost positions at the Tawil and the quarries. All his reserves had been vigorously engaged, while at two o'clock in the afternoon General Chetwode had in reserve nineteen battalions less one company still unused, and the care exercised in keeping this large body of troops fresh for following up the Turkish defeat undoubtedly contributed to the great success of the advances on the next three days. Simultaneously with their attack on the 60th Division positions the Turks put in a weighty effort to oust the 53rd Division from the positions they held north and south of the Jericho road. Whether in their wildest dreams they imagined they could enter Jerusalem by this route is doubtful, but if they had succeeded in driving in our line on the north they would have put the 53rd Division in a perilous position on the east with only one avenue of escape. The Turks concentrated their efforts on Whitehill and Zamby. A great fight raged round the former height and we were driven off it, but the divisional artillery so sprinkled the crest with shell that the Turk could not occupy it, and it became No Man's Land until the early evening when the 7th Royal Welsh Fusiliers recaptured and held it. The contest for Zamby lasted all day, and for a long time it was a battle of bombs and machine guns, so closely together were the fighting men, but the Turks never got up to our sangars and were finally driven off with heavy loss, over 100 dead being left on the hill. The Turkish ambulances were seen hard at work on the Jericho road throughout the day. There was a stout defence of a detached post at Ibn Obeid. A company of the 2/10th Middlesex Regiment had been sent on to Obeid, about five miles east of Bethlehem, to watch for the enemy moving about the rough tracks in that bare and broken country which falls away in jagged hills and sinuous valleys to the Dead Sea. The little garrison, whose sole shelter was a ruined monastic building on the hill, were attacked at dawn by 700 Turkish cavalry supported by mountain guns. The garrison stood fast all day though practically surrounded, and every attack was beaten off. The Turks tried again and again to secure the hill, which commands a track to Bethlehem, but, although they fired 400 shells at the position, they could not enter it, and a battalion sent up to relieve the Middlesex men next morning found that the company had driven the enemy off, its casualties having amounted to only 2 killed and 17 wounded. Thus did the 'Die Hards' live up to the traditions of the regiment.

Having dealt with the failure of the Turkish attacks against the 60th and 53rd Divisions in front of Jerusalem, let us change our view point and focus attention on the left sector of XXth Corps, where the enemy was feeling the full power of the Corps at a time when he most wished to avoid it. General Longley had organised his attacking columns in three groups. On the right the 229th Brigade of the 74th Division was set the task of moving from the wadi Imeish to secure the high ground of Bir esh Shafa overlooking Beitunia; the 31st Brigade, starting from near Tahta, attacked north of the wadi Sunt, to drive the enemy from a line from Jeriut through Hafy to the west of the olive orchards near Ain Arik; while the left group, composed of the 29th and 30th Brigades, aimed at getting

How Jerusalem Was Won

Shabuny across the wadi Sad, and Sheikh Abdallah where they would have the Australian Mounted Division on their left. The advance started from the left of the line. The 29th Brigade leading, with the 30th Brigade in support, left their positions of deployment at six o'clock, by which time the Turk had had more than he had bargained for north and east of Jerusalem. The 1st Leinsters and 5th Connaught Rangers found the enemy in a stubborn mood west of Deir Ibzia, but they broke down the opposition in the proper Irish style and rapidly reached their objectives. The centre group started one hour after the left and got their line without much difficulty. The right group was hotly opposed. Beginning their advance at eight o'clock the 229th Brigade had reached the western edge of the famous Zeitun ridge in an hour, but from this time onwards they were exposed to incessant artillery and machine–gun fire, and the forward movement became very slow. In five hours small parties had worked along the ridge for about half its length, fighting every yard, and it was not until the approach of dusk that we once more got control of the whole ridge. It was appropriate that dismounted yeomen should gain this important tactical point which several weeks previously had been won and lost by their comrades of the Yeomanry Mounted Division. Descending from the ridge the brigade gave the Turk little chance to stand, and with a bayonet charge they reached the day's objective in the dark. At two o'clock, when the Turks' final effort against Jerusalem had just failed, the 60th and 74th Divisions both sent in the good news that the Turkish commander was moving his reserve division from Bireh westwards to meet the attack from our left. Airmen confirmed this immediately, and it was now obvious that General Chetwode's tactics had compelled the enemy to conform to his movements and that we had regained the initiative. At about ten o'clock the 24th Royal Welsh Fusiliers of the 231st Brigade captured Kh. ed Dreihemeh on the old Roman road a mile east of Tireh, and at eleven o'clock advanced to the assault of hill 2450, a little farther eastward. They gained the crest, but the enemy had a big force in the neighbourhood and counter–attacked, forcing the Welshmen to withdraw some distance down the western slope. They held this ground till 4.30 when our guns heavily bombarded the summit, under cover of which fire the infantry made another attack. This was also unsuccessful owing to the intense volume of fire from machine guns. The hill was won, however, next morning.

The night of December 27–28 was without incident. The Turk had staked and lost, and he spent the night in making new dispositions to meet what he must have realised was being prepared for him on the following day.

How Jerusalem Was Won

It is doubtful whether there was a more successful day for our Army in the Palestine campaign than December 27. The portion of our line which was on the defensive had stood an absolutely unmovable wall, against which the enemy had battered himself to pieces. Our left, or attacking sector, had gained all their objectives against strong opposition in a most difficult country, and had drawn against them the very troops held in reserve for the main attack on Jerusalem. The physical powers of some of our attacking troops were tried highly. One position captured by the 229th Brigade was a particularly bad hill. The slope up which the infantry had to advance was a series of almost perpendicular terraces, and the riflemen could only make the ascent by climbing up each others' backs. When dismounted yeomen secured another hill some men carrying up supplies took two hours to walk from the base of the hill to the summit. The trials of the infantry were shared by the artillery. What surprises every one who has been over the route taken by the 10th and 74th Divisions is that any guns except those with the mountain batteries were able to get into action. The road work of engineers and the 5th Royal Irish Regiment (Pioneers) was magnificent, and they made a way where none seemed possible; but though these roadmakers put their backs into their tasks, it was only by the untiring energies of the gunners and drivers that artillery was got up to support the infantry. The guns were brought into action well ahead of the roads, and were man–hauled for considerable distances. Two howitzers and one field gun were kept up with the infantry on the first day of the advance where no horses could get a foothold, and the manner in which the gunners hauled the guns through deep ravines and up seemingly unclimbable hills constituted a wonderful physical achievement. The artillery were called upon to continue their arduous work on the 28th and 29th under conditions of ground which were even more appalling than those met with on the 27th. The whole country was devoid of any road better than a goat track, and the ravines became deeper and the hills more precipitous. In some places, particularly on the 10th Division front, the infantry went forward at a remarkable pace; but guns moved up with them, and by keeping down the fire of machine guns dotted about on every hill, performed services which earned the riflemen's warm praise. The 9th and 10th Mountain Batteries were attached to the 10th Division, but field and howitzer batteries were also well up. On the 28th the 53rd Division bit farther into the enemy's line in order to cover the right of the 60th Division, which was to continue its advance up the Nablus road towards Bireh. The 158th Brigade captured Anata, and after fighting all day the 1/7th Royal Welsh Fusiliers secured Ras Urkub es Suffa, a forbidding–looking height towering above the storm–rent sides of the wadi Ruabeh. The 1/1st Herefords after dark took Kh. Almit.

138

How Jerusalem Was Won

In front of the 60th Division the Turks were still holding some strong positions from which they should have been able seriously to delay the Londoners' advance had it not been for the threat to their communications by the pressure by the 10th and 74th Divisions. The Londoners had previously tested the strength of Adaseh, and had found it an extremely troublesome hill. They went for it again—the 179th Brigade this time—and after a several hours' struggle took it at dusk. Meanwhile the 181st Brigade had taken the lofty villages of Bir Nebala and El Jib, and after Adaseh became ours the Division went ahead in the dark and got to the line across the Nablus road from Er Ram to Rafat, capturing some prisoners. The 74th Division also made splendid progress. In the early hours the Division, with the 24th Royal Welsh Fusiliers and the 24th Welsh Regiment attached, secured Jufeir and resumed their main advance in the afternoon, the 230th and 231st Brigades cooperating with the 229th Brigade which was under the orders of the 10th Division. Before dark they had advanced their line from the left of the 60th Division in Rafat past the east of Beitunia to the hill east of Abu el Ainein, and this strong line of hills once secured, everybody was satisfied that the Turks' possession of Ramallah and Bireh was only a question of hours. Part of this line had been won by the 10th Division, which began its advance before noon in the same battle formation as on the 27th. Soon after the three groups started the heavy artillery put down a fierce fire on the final objectives, and before three o'clock the Turks were seen to be evacuating Kefr Skyan, Ainein, and Rubin. The enemy put up a stout fight at Beitunia and on a hill several hundred yards north–west of the village, but the 229th Brigade had good artillery and machine–gun assistance, and got both places before four o'clock, capturing seventy prisoners, including the commander of the garrison, and a number of machine guns. The left group was hotly opposed from a hill a mile west of Rubin and from a high position south–west of Ainein. The nature of the ground was entirely favourable to defence and for a time the Turk took full advantage of it, but our artillery soon made him lose his stomach for fighting, and doubtless the sound of many shell–bursts beyond Ramallah made him think that his rock sangars and the deep ravines in front of him were not protection against a foe who fought Nature with as much determination as he fought the Turkish soldier. Six–inch howitzers of the 378th Siege Battery had been brought up to Foka in the early hours, and all the afternoon and evening they were plastering the road from Ramallah along which the enemy were retreating. The left group defied the nests of machine guns hidden among the rocks and broke down the defence. The centre group had been delayed by the opposition encountered by the left, but they took Skyan at six o'clock and all of the objectives for one day were in our hands by the early evening. An advance along the whole front was ordered to begin at six o'clock on December 29. On his right

139

flank the enemy was willing to concede ground, and the 159th Brigade occupied Hismeh, Jeba, and the ridges to the north–west to protect the flank of the 60th Division. The 53rd Division buried 271 enemy dead on their front as the result of three days' fighting. The 181st Brigade made a rapid advance up the Nablus road until they were close to Bireh and Tahunah, a high rocky hill just to the north–west of the village. The Turks had many machine guns and a strong force of riflemen in these places, and it was impossible for infantry to advance against them over exposed ground without artillery support. The 303rd Field Artillery Brigade was supporting the brigade, and they were to move up a track from Kullundia while the foot–sloggers used the high road, but the track was found impassable for wheels and the guns had to be brought to the road. The attack was postponed till the guns were in position. The gunners came into action at half–past two, and infantry moved to the left to get on to the Ramallah–Bireh metalled road which runs at right angles to the trunk road between Nablus and Jerusalem. The 2/22nd and the 2/23rd Londons, working across the road, reached the Tahunah ridge, and after a heavy bombardment dashed into the Turkish positions, which were defended most stubbornly to the end, and thus won the last remaining hill which commanded our advance up the Nablus road as far as Bireh. On the eastern side of the main highway the 180th Brigade had once more done sterling service. There is a bold eminence called Shab Saleh, a mile due south of Bireh. It rises almost sheer from a piece of comparatively flat ground, and the enemy held it in strength. The 2/19th and the 2/20th Londons attacked this feature, and displaying great gallantry in face of much machine–gun fire seized it at half–past three. Once again the gunners supported the infantry admirably. The 2/17th and 2/18th Londons pushed past Saleh in a north–easterly direction and, leaving Bireh on their left, got into extremely bad country and took the Turks by surprise on a wooded ridge at Sheikh Sheiban. The two brigades rested and refreshed for a couple of hours and then advanced once more, and by midnight they had routed the Turks out of another series of hills and were in firm possession of the line from Beitin, across the Nablus road north of the Balua Lake, to the ridge of El Burj, having carried through everything which had been planned for the Division.

Ramallah had been taken at nine o'clock in the morning without opposition by the 230th and 229th Brigades, and at night the 74th Division held a strong line north of the picturesque village as far as Et Tireh. The 10th Division also occupied the Tireh ridge quite early in the day, and one of their field batteries and both mountain batteries got within long range of the Nablus road, and not only assisted in shelling the enemy in Bireh but harassed with a hot fire any bodies of men or transport seen retreating northwards.

How Jerusalem Was Won

The Flying Corps, too, caused the Turks many losses on the road. The airmen bombed the enemy from a low altitude and also machine–gunned them, and moreover by their timely information gave great assistance during the operations. By the 30th December all organised resistance to our advance had ceased and the XXth Corps consolidated its line, the 60th Division going forward slightly to improve its position and the other divisions rearranging their own. The consolidation of the line was not an easy matter. It had to be very thoroughly and rapidly done. The supply difficulty compelled the holding of the line with as few troops as possible, and when it had been won it was necessary to put it in a proper order in a minimum of time, and to bring back a considerable number of the troops who had been engaged in the fighting to hold the grand defensive chain which made Jerusalem absolutely safe. The standard gauge railway was still a long way from Ramleh, and the railway construction parties had to fight against bad weather and washouts. The Turkish line from Ramleh to Jerusalem was in bad order; a number of bridges were down, so that it was not likely the railway could be working for several weeks. Lorries could supply the troops in the neighbourhood of the Nablus road, though the highway was getting into bad condition, but in the right centre of the line the difficulties of terrain were appalling. The enemy had had a painful experience of it and was not likely to wish to fight in that country again; consequently it was decided to hold this part of the line with light forces.

In this description of the operations I have made little mention of the work of the Australian Mounted Division which covered the gap between XXth and XXIst Corps. These Australian horsemen and yeomanry guarded an extended front in inaccessible country, and every man in the Division will long remember the troubles of supply in the hills. They had some stiff fighting against a wily enemy, and not for a minute could they relax their vigilance. When, with the Turks' fatal effort to retake Jerusalem, the 10th Division changed their front and attacked in a north–easterly direction, the Australian Mounted Division moved with it, and they found the country as they progressed become more rugged and bleak and extremely difficult for mounted troops. The Division was in the fighting line for the whole month of December, and when they handed over the new positions they had reached to the infantry on the last day of the year, their horses fully needed the lengthened period of rest allotted to them.

141

CHAPTER XVII. A GREAT FEAT OF WAR

From the story of how Jerusalem was made secure (for we may hope the clamour of war has echoed for the last time about her Holy Shrines and venerable walls) we may turn back to the coastal sector and see how the XXIst Corps improved a rather dangerous situation and laid the foundations for the biggest break–through of the world struggle. For it was the preparations in this area which made possible General Allenby's tremendous gallop through Northern Palestine and Syria, and gave the Allies Haifa, Beyrout, and Tripoli on the seaboard, and Nazareth, Damascus, and Aleppo in the interior. The foundations were soundly laid when the XXIst Corps crossed the Auja before Christmas 1917, and the superstructure of the victory which put Turkey as well as Bulgaria and Austria out of the war was built up with many difficulties from the sure base provided by the XXIst Corps line. The crossing of the Auja was a great feat of war, and this is the first time I am able to mention the names of those to whom the credit of the operation is due. It was one of the strange regulations of the Army Council in connection with the censorship that no names of the commanders of army corps, divisions, brigades, or battalions should be mentioned by correspondents. Nor indeed was I permitted to identify in my despatches any particular division, yet the divisions concerned—the 52nd, 53rd, 54th, 60th, and so on—had often been mentioned in official despatches; the enemy not only knew they were in Palestine but were fully aware of their positions in the line; their commanders and brigadiers were known by name to the Turks. On the other hand, in describing a certain battle I was allowed to speak of divisions of Lowland troops, Welshmen and Londoners, allusions which would convey (if there were anything to give away) precisely as much information to the dull old Turk and his sharper Hun companion in arms as though the 52nd, 53rd, and 60th Divisions had been explicitly designated. This practice seemed in effect to be designed more with the object of keeping our people at home in the dark, of forbidding them glory in the deeds of their children and brothers, than of preventing information reaching the enemy. Some gentleman enthroned in the authority of an official armchair said 'No,' and there was an end of it. You could not get beyond him. His decision was final, complete—and silly—and the correspondent was bound hand and foot by it. Doubtless he would have liked one to plead on the knee for some little relaxation of his decision. Then he would have answered 'No' in a louder tone. Let me give one example from a number entered in my notebooks of how officers at home exercised their authority. In January 1917 the military railway from the Suez Canal had been constructed across the Sinai Desert and the first train was run into El Arish, about ninety miles from the Canal. I was asked by General Headquarters to send a cablegram to London announcing the fact that railhead was at El Arish, the town having been captured a fortnight previously after a fine night march. That message was never published, and I knew it was a waste of time to ask the reason. I happened to be in London for a few days in the following August and my duties took me to the War Office. A Colonel in the Intelligence Branch heard I was there and sent for me to tell me I had sent home information of value to the enemy. I reminded him there was a G.H.Q. censorship in Egypt which dealt with my cablegrams, and asked the nature of the valuable information which should have been concealed. 'You sent a telegram that the railway had reached El Arish when the Turks did not know it was beyond Bir el Abd.' Abd is fifty miles nearer the Suez Canal than El Arish. What did this officer care about a request made by G.H.Q. to transmit information to the British public? He knew better than G.H.Q. what the British public should know, and he was certain the enemy thought we were hauling supplies through those fifty miles of sand to our troops at El Arish, an absolutely physical impossibility, for there were not enough camels in the East to do it. But he did not know, and he should have known, being an Intelligence officer, that the Turks were so far aware of where our railhead was that they were frequently bombing it from the air. I had been in these bombing raids and knew how accurately the German airmen dropped their eggs, and had this Intelligence officer taken the trouble to inquire he would have found that between thirty and forty casualties were inflicted by one bomb at El Arish itself when railhead was being constructed. This critic imagined that the Turk knew only what the English papers told him. If the Turks' knowledge had been confined to what the War Office Intelligence Branch gave him credit for he would have been in a parlous state. While this ruling of the authorities at home prevailed it was impossible for me to give the names of officers or to mention divisions or units which were doing exceptionally meritorious work. Unfortunately the bureaucratic interdict continued till within a few days of the end of the campaign, when I was told that, 'having frequently referred to the work of the Australians, which was deserved,' the mention of British and Indian units would be welcomed. We had to wait until within a month of the end of the world war before the War Office would unbend and realise the value of the best kind of propaganda. No wonder our American friends consider us the worst national advertisers in the world.

The officer who was mainly responsible for the success of the Auja crossing was Major–General J. Hill, D.S.O., A.D.C., commanding the 52nd Division. His plan was agreed to by General Bulfin, although the Corps Commander had doubts about the possibility of its success, and had his own scheme ready to be put into instant operation if General Hill's failed. In the state of the weather General Hill's own brigadiers were not sanguine, and they were the most loyal and devoted officers a divisional commander ever had. But despite the most unfavourable conditions, calling for heroic measures on the part of officers and men alike to gain their objectives through mud and water and over ground that was as bad as it could be, the movements of the troops worked to the clock. One brigade's movements synchronised with those of another, and the river was crossed, commanding positions were seized, and bridges were built with an astoundingly small loss to ourselves. The Lowland Scots worked as if at sport, and they could not have worked longer or stronger if the whole honour of Scotland had depended upon their efforts. At a later date, when digging at Arsuf, these Scots came across some marble columns which had graced a hall when Apollonia was in its heyday. The glory of Apollonia has long vanished, but if in that age of warriors there had been a belief that those marble columns would some day be raised as monuments to commemorate a great operation of war the ancients would have had a special veneration for them. Three of the columns marked the spots where the Scots spanned the river, and it is a pity they cannot tell the full story to succeeding generations.

The river Auja is a perennial stream emptying itself into the blue Mediterranean waters four miles north of Jaffa. Its average width is forty yards and its depth ten feet, with a current running at about three miles an hour. Till we crossed it the river was the boundary between the British and Turkish armies in this sector, and all the advantage of observation was on the northern bank. From it the town of Jaffa and its port were in danger, and the main road between Jaffa and Ramleh was observed and under fire. The village of Sheikh Muannis, about two miles inland, stood on a high mound commanding the ground south of the river, and from Hadrah you could keep the river in sight in its whole winding course to the sea. All this high ground concealed an entrenched enemy; on the southern side of the river the Turks were on Bald Hill, and held a line of trenches covering the Jewish colony of Mulebbis and Fejja. A bridge and a mill dam having been destroyed during winter the only means of crossing was by a ford three feet deep at the mouth, an uncertain passage because the sand bar over which one could walk shifted after heavy rain when the stream was swollen with flood water. Reconnaissances at the river mouth were carried out with great daring. As I said, all the southern approaches to the river were commanded by the Turks on the northern bank, who were always alert, and the movement of one man in the Auja valley was generally the signal for artillery activity. So often did the Turkish gunners salute the appearance of a single British soldier that the

How Jerusalem Was Won

Scots talked of the enemy 'sniping' with guns. To reconnoitre the enemy's positions by daylight was hazardous work, and the Scots had to obtain their first-hand knowledge of the river and the approaches to it in the dark hours.

An officers' patrol swam the river one night, saw what the enemy was doing, and returned unobserved. A few nights afterwards two officers swam out to sea across the river mouth and crept up the right bank of the stream within the enemy's lines to ascertain the locality of the ford and its exact width and depth. They also learnt that there were no obstacles placed across the ford, which was three feet deep in normal times and five feet under water after rains. It was obvious that bridges would be required, and it was decided to force the passage of the river in the dark hours by putting covering troops across to the northern bank, and by capturing the enemy's positions to form a bridgehead while pontoon bridges were being constructed for the use of guns and the remainder of the Division.

Time was all-important. December and January are the wettest months of the season at Jaffa, and after heavy rains the Auja valley becomes little better than a marsh, so that a small amount of traffic will cut up the boggy land into an almost impassable condition.

The XXIst Corps' plan was as follows: At dawn on December 21 a heavy bombardment was to open on all the enemy's trenches covering the crossings, the fire of heavy guns to be concentrated on enemy batteries and strong positions in the rear, while ships of the Royal Navy bombarded two strong artillery positions at Tel el Rekket and El Jelil, near the coast. When darkness fell covering troops were to be ferried across the river, and then light bridges would be constructed for the passage of larger units charged with the task of getting the Turks out of their line from Hadrah, through El Mukras to Tel el Rekket. After these positions had been gained the engineers were to build pontoon bridges to carry the remainder of the Division and guns on the night of the 22nd–23rd December, in time to advance at daylight on the 23rd to secure a defensive line from Tel el Mukhmar through Sheikh el Ballatar to Jelil. On the right of the 52nd Division the 54th Division was to attack Bald Hill on the night of 21st–22nd December, and on the following morning assault the trench system covering Mulebbis and Fejja; then later in the day to advance to Rantieh, while the 75th Division farther east was to attack Bireh and Beida. This plan was given to divisional commanders at a conference in Jaffa on December 12. Two days later General Hill submitted another scheme which provided for a surprise attack by night with no naval or land artillery bombardment, such a demonstration being likely to attract

145

attention. General Hill submitted his proposals in detail. General Bulfin gave the plan most careful consideration, but decided that to base so important an operation on the success of a surprise attack was too hazardous, and he adhered to his scheme of a deliberate operation to be carried through systematically. He, however, gave General Hill permission to carry out his surprise attack on the night of December 20, but insisted that the bombardment should begin according to programme at daylight on the 21st unless the surprise scheme was successful.

A brigade of the 54th Division and the 1st Australian Light Horse Brigade relieved the Scots in the trenches for three nights before the attempt. Every man in the Lowland Division entered upon the work of preparation with whole-hearted enthusiasm. There was much to be done and materials were none too plentiful. Pontoons were wired for and reached Jaffa on the 16th. There was little wood available, and some old houses in Jaffa were pulled down to supply the Army's needs. The material was collected in the orange groves around the German colony at Sarona, a northern suburb of Jaffa, and every man who could use a tool was set to work to build a framework of rectangular boats to a standard design, and on this framework of wood tarpaulins and canvas were stretched. These boats were light in structure, and were so designed that working parties would be capable of transferring them from their place of manufacture to the river bank. Each boat was to carry twenty men fully armed and equipped over the river. They became so heavy with rain that they in fact only carried sixteen men. The boat builders worked where enemy airmen could not see them, and when the craft were completed the troops were practised at night in embarking and ferrying across a waterway—for this purpose the craft were put on a big pond—and in cutting a path through thick cactus hedges in the dark. During these preparations the artillery was also active. They took their guns up to forward positions during the night, and before the date of the attack there was a bombardment group of eight 6-inch howitzers and a counter battery group of ten 60-pounders and one 6-inch Mark VII. gun in concealed positions, and the artillery dumps had been filled with 400 rounds for each heavy gun and 700 rounds for each field piece. The weather on the 18th, 19th, and 20th December was most unfavourable. Rain was continuous and the valley of the Auja became a morass. The luck of the weather was almost always against General Allenby's Army, and the troops had become accustomed to fighting the elements as well as the Turks, but here was a situation where rain might have made all the difference between success and failure. General Bulfin saw General Hill and his brigadiers on the afternoon of the 20th. The brigadiers were depressed owing to the floods and the state of the ground, because it was then clear that causeways would have to be made through the mud to the river banks. General Hill remained enthusiastic and hopeful and, the Corps Commander supporting him, it was decided to proceed with the operation. For several nights, with the object of giving the enemy the impression of a nightly strafe, there had been artillery and machine—gun demonstrations occurring about the same time and lasting as long as those planned for the night of the crossing. After dusk on December 20 there was a big movement behind our lines. The ferrying and bridging parties got on the move, each by their particular road, and though the wind was searchingly cold and every officer and man became thoroughly drenched, there was not a sick heart in the force. The 157th Brigade proceeded to the ford at the mouth of the Auja, the 156th Brigade advanced towards the river just below Muannis, and the 155th Brigade moved up to the mill and dam at Jerisheh, where it was to secure the crossing and then swing to the right to capture Hadrah. The advance was slow, but that the Scots were able to move at all is the highest tribute to their determination. The rain—soaked canvas of the boats had so greatly added to their weight that the parties detailed to carry them from the Sarona orange orchards found the task almost beyond their powers. The bridge rafts for one of the crossings could not be got up to the river bank because the men were continually slipping in the mud under the heavy load, and the attacking battalion at this spot was ferried over in coracles. On another route a section carrying a raft lost one of its number, who was afterwards found sunk in mud up to his outstretched arms. The tracks were almost impassable, and a Lancashire pioneer battalion was called up to assist in improving them. The men became caked with mud from steel helmet to boots, and the field guns which had to be hauled by double teams were so bespattered that there was no need for camouflage. In those strenuous hours of darkness the weather continued vile, and the storm wind flung the frequent heavy showers with cutting force against the struggling men. The covering party which was to cross at the ford found the bar had shifted under the pressure of flood water and that the marks put down to direct the column had been washed away. The commanding officer reconnoitred, getting up to his neck in water, and found the ford considerably out of position and deeper than he had hoped, but he brought his men together in fours and, ordering each section to link arms to prevent the swirling waters carrying them out to sea, led them across without a casualty. In the other places the covering parties of brigades began to be ferried over at eight o'clock. The first raft—loads were paddled across with muffled oars. A line was towed behind the boats, and this being made fast on either side of the river the rafts crossed and recrossed by haulage on the rope, in order that no disturbance on the surface by oars on even such a wild night should cause an alarm. As soon as the covering parties were over, light bridges to carry infantry in file were constructed by lashing the rafts together and placing planks on them. One of these bridges was burst by the strength of the current, but the delay thus caused mattered little as the surprise was complete. When the bridges of rafts had been swung and anchored, blankets and carpets were laid upon them to deaden the fall of marching feet, and during that silent tramp across the rolling bridges many a keen–witted Scot found it difficult to restrain a laugh as he trod on carpets richer by far than any that had lain in his best parlour at home. He could not see the patterns, but rightly guessed that they were picked out in the bright colours of the East, and the muddy marks of war–travelled men were left on them without regret, for the carpets had come from German houses in Sarona. How perfectly the operation was conducted—noiselessly, swiftly, absolutely according to time–table—may be gathered from the fact that two officers and sixteen Turks were awakened in their trench dug–outs at the ford by the river mouth two hours after we had taken the trenches. The officers resisted and had to be killed. Two miles behind the river the Lowlanders captured the whole garrison of a post near the sea, none of whom had the slightest idea that the river had been crossed. An officer commanding a battalion at Muannis was taken in his bed, whilst another commanding officer had the surprise of his life on being invited to put his hands up in his own house. He looked as if he had just awakened from a nightmare. In one place some Turks on being attacked with the bayonet shouted an alarm and one of the crossings was shelled, but its position was immediately changed and the passage of the river continued without interruption. The whole of the Turkish system covering the river, trenches well concealed in the river banks and in patches of cultivated land, were rushed in silence and captured. Muannis was taken at the point of the bayonet, the strong position at Hadrah was also carried in absolute silence, and at daylight the whole line the Scots had set out to gain was won and the assailants were digging themselves in. And the price of their victory? The Scots had 8 officers and 93 other ranks casualties. They buried over 100 Turkish dead and took 11 officers and 296 other ranks prisoners, besides capturing ten machine guns.

The forcing of the passage of the Auja was a magnificent achievement, planned with great ability by General Hill and carried out with that skill and energy which the brigadiers, staff, and all ranks of the Division showed throughout the campaign. One significant fact serves to illustrate the Scots' discipline. Orders were that not a shot was to be fired except by the guns and machine guns making their nightly strafe. Death was to be dealt out with the bayonet, and though the Lowlanders were engaged in a life and death struggle with the Turks, not a single round of rifle ammunition was used by them till daylight came, when, as a keen marksman said, they had some grand running–man practice. During the day some batteries got to the north bank by way of the ford, and two heavy pontoon bridges were constructed and a barrel bridge, which had been put together in a wadi flowing into the Auja, was floated down and placed in position. There was a good deal of shelling by the Turks, but they fired at our new positions and interfered but little with the bridge construction.

On the night of the 21st–22nd December the 54th Division assaulted Bald Hill, a prominent mound south of the Auja from which a magnificent view of the country was gained. Stiff fighting resulted, but the enemy was driven off with a loss of 4 officers and 48 other ranks killed, and 3 officers and 41 men taken prisoners. At dawn the Division reported that the enemy was retiring from Mulebbis and Fejja, and those places were soon in our hands. H.M.S. *Grafton*, with Admiral T. Jackson, the monitors M29, M31, and M32, and the destroyers *Lapwing* and *Lizard*, arrived off the coast and shelled Jelil and Arsuf, and the 52nd Division, advancing on a broad front, occupied the whole of their objectives by five o'clock in the afternoon. The 157th Brigade got all the high ground about Arsuf, and thus prevented the enemy from obtaining a long–range view of Jaffa. A few rounds of shell fired by a naval gun at a range of nearly twenty miles fell in Jaffa some months afterwards, but with this exception Jaffa was quite free from the enemy's attentions. The brilliant operation on the Auja had saved the town and its people many anxious days. By the end of the year there were three strong bridges across the river, and three others substantial enough to bear the weight of tractors and their loads were under construction. The troops received their winter clothing; bivouac shelters and tents were beginning to arrive. Baths and laundries were in operation, and the rigours of the campaign began to be eased. But the XXIst Corps could congratulate itself that, notwithstanding two months of open warfare, often fifty to sixty miles from railhead, men's rations had never been reduced. Horses and mules had had short allowances, but they could pick up a little in the country. The men were in good health, despite the hardships in the hills and rapid change from summer to winter, and their spirit could not be surpassed.

CHAPTER XVIII. BY THE BANKS OF THE JORDAN

We have seen how impregnable the defences of Jerusalem had become as the result of the big advance northwards at the end of December. As far as any military forecast could be made we were now in an impenetrable position whatever force the Turk, with his poor communications, could employ against us either from the direction of Nablus or from the east of the Jordan. There seemed to be no risk whatever, so long as we chose to hold the line XXth Corps had won, of the Turks again approaching Jerusalem, but the Commander-in-Chief determined to make the situation absolutely safe by advancing eastwards to capture Jericho and the crossings of the Jordan. This was not solely a measure of precaution. It certainly did provide a means for preventing the foe from operating in the stern, forbidding, desolate, and awe-inspiring region which has been known as the Wilderness since Biblical days, and doubtless before. In that rough country it would be extremely difficult to stop small bands of enterprising troops getting through a line and creating diversions which, while of small military consequence, would have been troublesome, and might have had the effect of unsettling the natives. A foothold in the Jordan valley would have the great advantage of enabling us to threaten the Hedjaz railway, the Turks' sole means of communication with Medina, where their garrison was holding out staunchly against the troops of the King of the Hedjaz, and any assistance we could give the King's army would have a far-reaching effect on neutral Arabs. It would also stop the grain trade on the Dead Sea, on which the enemy set store, and would divert traffic in foodstuffs to natives in Lower Palestine, who at this time were to a considerable extent dependent on supplies furnished by our Army. The Quartermaster-General carried many responsibilities on his shoulders. Time was not the important factor, and as General Allenby was anxious to avoid an operation which might involve heavy losses, it was at first proposed that the enemy should be forced to leave Jericho by the gradually closing in on the town from north and south. The Turks had got an immensely strong position about Talat ed Dumm, the 'Mound of Blood,' where stands a ruined castle of the Crusaders, the Chastel Rouge. One can see it with the naked eye from the Mount of Olives, and weeks before the operation started I stood in the garden of the Kaiserin Augusta Victoria hospice and, looking over one of the most inhospitable regions of the world, could easily make out the Turks walking on the road near the Khan, which has been called the Good Samaritan Inn. The country has indeed been rightly named. Gaunt, bare mountains of limestone with scarcely a patch of green to relieve the nakedness of the land make a wilderness indeed, and one sees a drop of some four thousand feet in a distance of about fifteen miles. The hills rise in continuous succession, great ramparts of the Judean range, and instead of valleys between them there are huge clefts in the rock, hundreds of feet deep, which carry away the winter torrents to the Jordan and Dead Sea. Over beyond the edge of hills are the green wooded banks of the Sacred River, then a patch or two of stunted trees, and finally the dark walls of the mountains of Moab shutting out the view of the land which still holds fascinating remains of Greek

150

civilisation.

But there was no promise of an early peep at such historic sights, and the problem of getting at the nearer land was hard enough for present deliberation. It was at first proposed that the whole of the XXth Corps and a force of cavalry should carry out operations simultaneously on the north and east of the Corps front which should give us possession of the roads from Mar Saba and Muntar, and also from Taiyibeh and the old Roman road to Jericho, thus allowing two cavalry forces supported by infantry columns to converge on Jericho from the north and south. However, by the second week of February there had been bad weather, and the difficulties of supplying a line forty miles from the railway on roads which, notwithstanding a vast amount of labour, were still far from good, were practically insuperable, and it was apparent that a northerly and easterly advance at the same time would involve a delay of three weeks.

New circumstances came to light after the advance was first arranged, and these demanded that the enemy should be driven across the Jordan as soon as possible. General Allenby decided that the operations should be carried out in two phases. The first was an easterly advance to thrust the enemy from his position covering Jericho, to force him across the Jordan, and to obtain control of the country west of the river. The northerly advance to secure the line of the wadi Aujah was to follow. This river Aujah which flows into the Jordan must not be confused with the Auja on the coast already described.

The period of wet weather was prolonged, and the accumulation of supplies of rations and ammunition did not permit of operations commencing before February 19. That they started so early is an eloquent tribute to the hard work of the Army, for the weather by the date of the attack had improved but little, and the task of getting up stores could only be completed by extraordinary exertions. General Chetwode ordered a brigade of the 60th Division to capture Mukhmas as a preliminary to a concentration at that place. On the 19th the Division occupied a front of about fourteen miles from near Muntar, close to which the ancient road from Bethlehem to Jericho passes, through Ras Umm Deisis, across the Jerusalem–Jericho road to Arak Ibrahim, over the great chasm of the wadi Farah which has cliff–like sides hundreds of feet deep, to the brown knob of Ras et Tawil. The line was not gained without fighting. The Turks did not oppose us at Muntar—the spot where the Jews released the Scapegoat—but there was a short contest for Ibrahim, and a longer fight lasting till the afternoon for an entrenched position a mile north of it; Ras et Tawil was ours by nine in the morning. Tawil overlooks a track which has been trodden from time immemorial. It leads from the Jordan valley north–west of Jericho, and passes beneath the frowning height of Jebel Kuruntul with its bare face relieved by a monastery built into the rock about half–way up, and a walled garden on top to mark the Mount of Temptation, as the pious monks believe it to be. The track then proceeds westwards, winding in and out of the tremendous slits in rock, to Mukhmas, and it was probably along this rough line that the Israelites marched from their camp at Gilgal to overthrow the Philistines. On the right of the Londoners were two brigades of the Anzac Mounted Division, working through the most desolate hills and wadis down to the Dead Sea with a view to pushing up by Nebi Musa, which tradition has ascribed as the burial place of Moses, and thence into the Jordan valley. Northward of the 60th Division the 53rd was extending its flank eastwards to command the Taiyibeh–Jericho road, and the Welsh troops occupied Rummon, a huge mount of chalk giving a good view of the Wilderness. This was the position on the night of 19th February.

At dawn on the 20th the Londoners were to attack the Turks in three columns. The right column was to march from El Muntar to Ekteif, the centre column to proceed along the Jerusalem–Jericho road between the highway and the wadi Farah, and the left column was to go forward by the Tawil–Jebel Kuruntul track. The 1st Australian Light Horse Brigade and the New Zealand Mounted Rifles Brigade were, if possible, to make Nebi Musa.

The infantry attack was as fine as anything done in the campaign. I had the advantage of witnessing the centre column carry out the whole of its task and of seeing the right column complete as gallant an effort as any troops could make, and as one saw them scale frowning heights and clamber up and down the roughest of torrent beds, one realised that more than three months' fighting had not removed the 'bloom' from these Cockney warriors, and that their physique and courage were proof against long and heavy trials of campaigning. The chief objective of the centre column was Talat ed Dumm which, lying on the Jericho road just before the junction of the old and the new road to the Jordan valley, was the key to Jericho. It is hard to imagine a better defensive position. To the north of the road is the wadi Farah, a great crack in the rocks which can only be crossed in a few places, and which a few riflemen could cover. Likewise a platoon distributed behind rocks on the many hills could command the approaches from all directions, while the hill of Talat ed Dumm, by the Good Samaritan Inn, and the height whereon the Crusader ruins stand, dominated a broad flat across which our troops must move. This position the 180th Brigade attacked at dawn. The guns opened before the sun appeared above the black crest line of the mountains of Moab, and well before long shadows were cast across the Jordan valley the batteries were tearing to pieces the stone walls and rocky eyries sheltering machine–gunners and infantry. This preliminary bombardment, if short, was wonderfully effective. From where I stood I saw the heavies pouring an unerring fire on to the Crusader Castle, huge spurts of black smoke, and the dislocation of big stones which had withstood the disintegrating effect of many centuries of sun power, telling the Forward Observing Officer that his gunners were well on the target and that to live in that havoc the Turks must seek the shelter of vaults cut deep down in the rock by masons of old. No enemy could delay our progress from that shell–torn spot. Lighter guns searched other positions and whiffs of shrapnel kept Turks from their business. There are green patches on the western side of Talat ed Dumm in the early months of the year before the sun has burned up the country. Over these the infantry advanced as laid down in the book. The whirring rap–rap of machine guns at present unlocated did not stop them, and as our machine–gun sections, ever on the alert to keep down rival automatic guns, found out and sprayed the nests, the enemy was seen to be anxious about his line of retreat. One large party, harried by shrapnel and machine–gun fire, left its positions and rushed towards a defile, but rallied and came back, though when it reoccupied its former line the Londoners had reached a point to enfilade it, and it suffered heavily. We soon got this position, and then our troops, ascending some spurs, poured a destructive fire into the defile and so harassed the Turks re–forming for a counterattack as to render feeble their efforts to regain what they had lost.

By eight o'clock we had taken the whole of the Talat ed Dumm position, and long–range sniping throughout the day did not disturb our secure possession of it. Immediately the heights were occupied the guns went ahead to new points, and armoured cars left the road to try to find a way to the south–east to protect the flank of the right column. They had a troublesome journey. Some of the crews walked well ahead of the cars to reconnoitre the tracks, and it speaks well for the efficiency of the cars as well as for the pluck and cleverness of the drivers that in crossing a mile or two of that terribly broken mountainous country no car was overturned and all got back to the road without mishap.

Throughout the night and during the greater part of the day of February 20 the right column were fighting under many difficulties. In their march from the hill of Muntar they had to travel over ground so cracked and strewn with boulders that in many parts the brigade could only proceed in single file. In some places the track chosen had a huge cleft in the mountain on one side and a cliff face on the other. It was a continual succession of

153

watercourses and mountains, of uphill and downhill travel over the most uneven surface in the blackness of night, and it took nearly eight hours to march three miles. The nature of the country was a very serious obstacle and the column was late in deploying for attack. But bad as was the route the men had followed during the night, it was easy as compared with the position they had set out to carry. This was Jebel Ekteif, the southern end of the range of hills of which Talat ed Dumm was the northern. Ekteif presented to this column a face as precipitous as Gibraltar and perhaps half as high. There was a ledge running round it about three-quarters of the way from the top, and for hours one could see the Turks lying flat on this rude path trying to pick off the intrepid climbers attempting a precarious ascent. Some mountain guns suddenly ranged on the enemy on this ledge, and, picking up the range with remarkable rapidity, forced the Turks into more comfortable positions. The enemy, too, had some well-served guns, and they plastered the spurs leading to the crest from the west, but our infantry's audacity never faltered, and after we had got into the first lines on the hill our men proceeded methodically to rout out the machine guns from their nooks and crannies. This was a somewhat lengthy process, but small parties working in support of each other gradually crushed opposition, and the huge rocky rampart was ours by three o'clock in the afternoon. Meanwhile two brigades of the Anzac Mounted Division were moving eastwards from Muntar over the hills and wadis down to the Dead Sea, whence turning northwards they marched towards Nebi Musa to try to get on to the Jordan valley flats to threaten the Turks in rear. The terrain was appallingly bad and horses had to be led, the troops frequently proceeding in Indian file. No guns could be got over the hills to support the Anzacs, and when they tried to pass through a narrow defile south of Nebi Musa it was found that the enemy covered the approach with machine guns, and progress was stopped dead until, during the early hours of the following morning, some of the Londoners' artillery managed by a superhuman effort to get a few guns over the mountains to support the cavalry. By this time the Turks had had enough of it, and while it was dark they were busy trekking through Jericho towards the Ghoraniyeh bridge over the river, covered by a force on the Jebel Kuruntul track which prevented the left column from reaching the cliffs overlooking the Jordan valley. By dawn on the 21st Nebi Musa was made good, the 1st Australian Light Horse Brigade and the New Zealand Brigade were in Jericho by eight o'clock and had cleared the Jordan valley as far north as the river Aujah, the Londoners holding the line of cliffs which absolutely prevented any possibility of the enemy ever again threatening Jerusalem or Bethlehem from the east. This successful operation also put an end to the Turks' Dead Sea grain traffic. They had given up hope of keeping their landing place on the northern shores of the Dead Sea when we took Talat ed Dumm, and one hour after our infantry had planted themselves on the Hill of Blood we saw the enemy burning his boats, wharves, and storehouses at Rujm el Bahr, where he had expended a good deal of labour to put up buildings to store grain wanted for his army. Subsequently we had some naval men operating motor boats from this point, and these sailors achieved a record on that melancholy waterway at a level far below that at which any submarine, British or German, ever rested.

CHAPTER XIX. THE TOUCH OF THE CIVILISING HAND

It is doubtful whether the population of any city within the zones of war profited so much at the hands of the conqueror as Jerusalem. In a little more than half a year a wondrous change was effected in the condition of the people, and if it had been possible to search the Oriental mind and to get a free and frank expression of opinion, one would probably have found a universal thankfulness for General Allenby's deliverance of the Holy City from the hands of the Turks. And with good reason. The scourge of war so far as the British Army was concerned left Jerusalem the Golden untouched. For the 50,000 people in the City the skilfully applied military pressure which put an end to Turkish misgovernment was the beginning of an era of happiness and contentment of which they had hitherto had no conception. Justice was administered in accordance with British ideals, every man enjoyed the profits of his industry, traders no longer ran the gauntlet of extortionate officials, the old time corruption was a thing of the past, public health was organised as far as it could be on Western lines, and though in matters of sanitation and personal cleanliness the inhabitants still had much to learn, the appearance of the Holy City and its population vastly improved under the touch of a civilising hand. Sights that offended more than one of the senses on the day when General Allenby made his official entry had disappeared, and peace and order reigned where previously had been but misery, poverty, disease, and squalor.

One of the biggest blots upon the Turkish government of the City was the total failure to provide an adequate water supply. What they could not, or would not, do in their rule of four hundred years His Majesty's Royal Engineers accomplished in a little more than two months, and now for the first time in history every civilian in Jerusalem can obtain as much pure mountain spring water as he wishes, and for this water, as fresh and bright as any bubbling out of Welsh hills, not a penny is charged. The picturesque, though usually unclean, water carrier is passing into the limbo of forgotten things, and his energies are being diverted into other channels. The germs that swarmed in his leathern water bags will no longer endanger the lives of the citizens, and the deadly perils of stagnant cistern water have been to a large extent removed.

For its water Jerusalem used to rely mainly upon the winter rainfall to fill its cisterns. Practically every house has its underground reservoir, and it is estimated that if all were full they would contain about 360,000,000 gallons. But many had fallen into disrepair and most, if not the whole of them, required thorough cleansing. One which was inspected by our sanitary department had not been emptied for nineteen years. To supplement the cistern supply the Mosque of Omar reservoir halved with Bethlehem the water which flowed from near Solomon's Pools down an aqueduct constructed by Roman engineers under Herod before the Saviour was born. This was not nearly sufficient, nor was it so constant a supply as that provided by our Army engineers. They went farther afield. They found a group of spring–heads in an absolutely clean gathering ground on the hills yielding some 14,000 gallons an hour, and this water which was running to waste is lifted to the top of a hill from which it flows by gravity through a long pipe–line to Jerusalem, where a reservoir has been built on a high point on the outskirts of the city. Supplies of this beautiful water run direct to the hospitals, and at standpipes all over the city the inhabitants take as much as they desire. The water consumption of the people became ten times what it was in the previous year, and this fact alone told how the boon was appreciated.

The scheme did not stop at putting up standpipes for those who fetched the water. A portion of the contents of the cisterns was taken for watering troop horses in the spring—troops were not allowed to drink it. The water level of these cisterns became very low, and as they got emptied the authorities arranged for refilling them on the one condition that they were first thoroughly cleansed and put in order. The British administration would not be parties to the perpetuation of a system which permitted the fouling of good crystal water. A householder had merely to apply to the Military Governor for water, and a sanitary officer inspected the cistern, ordered it to be cleansed, and saw that this was done; then the Department of Public Health gave its certificate, and the engineers ran a pipe to the cistern and filled it, no matter what its capacity. Two cisterns were replenished with between 60,000 and 70,000 gallons of sparkling water from the hills in place of water heavily charged with the accumulation of summer dust on roofs, and the dust of Jerusalem roads, as we had sampled it, is not as clean as desert sand.

How Jerusalem Was Won

The installation of the supply was a triumph for the Royal Engineers. In peace times the work would have taken from one to two years to complete. A preliminary investigation and survey of the ground was made on February 14, and a scheme was submitted four days later. Owing to the shortage of transport and abnormally bad weather work could not be commenced till April 12. Many miles of pipe line had to be laid and a powerful pumping plant erected, but water was being delivered to the people of Jerusalem on the 18th of June. Other military works have done much for the common good in Palestine, but none of them were of greater utility than this. Mahomedans seeing bright water flow into Jerusalem regarded it as one of the wonders of all time. It is interesting to note that the American Red Cross Society, which sent a large and capable staff to the Holy Land after America came into the war, knew of the lack of an adequate water supply for Jerusalem, and with that foresight which Americans show, forwarded to Egypt for transportation to Jerusalem some thousand tons of water mains to provide a water service. When the American Red Cross workers reached the Holy City they found the Army's plans almost completed, and they were the first to pay a tribute to what they described as the 'civilising march of the British Army.'

Those who watched the ceaseless activities of the Public Health Administration were not surprised at the remarkable improvement in the sick and death rates, not only of Jerusalem but of all the towns and districts. The new water supply will unquestionably help to lower the figures still further. A medical authority recently told me that the health of the community was wonderfully good and there was no suspicion of cholera, outbreaks of which were frequent under the Turkish regime. Government hospitals were established in all large centres. In this country where small-pox takes a heavy toll the 'conscientious objector' was unknown, and many thousands of natives in a few months came forward of their own free will to be vaccinated. Typhus and relapsing fever, both lice-borne diseases, used to claim many victims, but the figures fell very rapidly, due largely, no doubt, to the full use to which disinfecting plants were put in all areas of the occupied territory. The virtues of bodily cleanliness were taught, and the people were given that personal attention which was entirely lacking under Turkish rule. It is not easy to overcome the prejudices and cure the habits of thousands of years, but progress is being made surely if slowly, and already there is a gratifying improvement in the condition of the people which is patent to any observer.

In Jerusalem an infants' welfare bureau was instituted, where mothers were seen before and after childbirth, infants' clinics were established, a body of health was formed, and a

157

kitchen was opened to provide food for babies and the poor. The nurses were mainly local subjects who had to undergo an adequate training, and there was no one who did not confidently predict a rapid fall in the infant mortality rate which, to the shame of the Turkish administration, was fully a dozen times that of the highest of English towns. The spadework was all done by the medical staff of the Occupied Enemy Territory Administration. The call was urgent, and though labouring under war–time difficulties they got things going quickly and smoothly. Some voluntary societies were assisting, and the enthusiasm of the American Red Cross units enabled all to carry on a great and beneficent work.

CHAPTER XX. OUR CONQUERING AIRMEN

The airmen who were the eyes of the Army in Sinai and Palestine can look back on their record as a great achievement. Enormous difficulties were faced with stout hearts, and the Royal Flying Corps spirit surmounted them. It was one long test of courage, endurance, and efficiency, and so triumphantly did the airmen come through the ordeal that General Allenby's Army may truthfully be said to have secured as complete a mastery of the air as it did of the plains and hills of Southern Palestine. Those of us who watched the airmen 'carrying on,' from the time when their aeroplanes were inferior to those of the Germans in speed, climbing capacity, and other qualities which go to make up first–class fighting machines, till the position during the great advance when few enemy aviators dared cross our lines, can well testify to the wonderful work our airmen performed.

With comparatively few opportunities for combat because the enemy knew his inferiority and declined to fight unless forced, the pilots and observers from the moment our attack was about to start were always aggressive, and though the number of their victims may seem small compared with aerial victories on the Western Front they were substantial and important. In the month of January 1917 the flying men accounted for eleven aeroplanes, five of these falling victims to one pilot. The last of these victories I myself witnessed. In a single–seater the pilot engaged two two–seater aeroplanes of a late type, driving down one machine within our line, the pilot killed by eleven bullets and the observer wounded. He then chased the other plane, whose pilot soon lost his taste for fighting, dropped into a heavy cloud bank, and got away. No odds were too great for our airmen. I have seen one aeroplane swoop down out of the blue to attack a formation of six enemy machines, sending one crashing to earth and dispersing the remainder. In one brief fight another pilot drove down three German planes. The airman does not talk of his work, and we knew that what we saw and heard of were but fragments in the silent records of great things done. Much that was accomplished was far behind our visual range, high up over the bleak hills of Judea, above even the rain clouds driven across the heights by the fury of a winter gale, or skimming over the dull surface of the Dead Sea, flying some hundreds of feet below sea level to interrupt the passage of foodstuffs of which the Turk stood in need.

All through the Army's rapid march northwards from the crushed Gaza–Beersheba line the airmen's untiring work was of infinite value. When the Turkish retreat began the enemy was bombed and machine–gunned for a full week, the railway, aerodromes, troops on the march, artillery, and transport being hit time and again, and five smashed aeroplanes and a large quantity of aircraft stores of every description were found at Menshiye alone. The raid on that aerodrome was so successful that at night the Germans burnt the whole of the equipment not destroyed by bombs. Three machines were also destroyed by us at Et Tineh, five at Ramleh and one at Ludd, and the country was covered with the debris of a well–bombed and beaten army. After Jerusalem came under the safe protection of our arms airmen harassed the retiring enemy with bombs and machine guns. The wind was strong, but defying treacherous eddies, the pilots came through the valleys between steep–sloped hills and caught the Turks on the Nablus road, emptying their bomb racks at a height of a few hundred feet, and giving the scattered troops machine–gun fire on the return journey.

A glance at the list of honours bestowed on officers and other ranks of the R.F.C. serving with the Egyptian Expeditionary Force in 1917 is sufficient to give an idea of the efficiency of the service of our airmen. It must be remembered that the Palestine Wing was small, if thoroughly representative of the Flying Corps; its numbers were few but the quality was there. Indeed I heard the Australian squadron of flying men which formed part of the Wing described by the highest possible authority as probably the finest squadron in the whole of the British service. This following list of honours is, perhaps, the most eloquent testimony to the airmen's work in Palestine:

Victoria Cross 1
Distinguished Service Order . . . 4
Military Cross 34
Croix de Guerre 2

159

How Jerusalem Was Won

The sum total of the R.F.C. work was not to be calculated merely from death and damage caused to the enemy from the air. Strategical and tactical reconnaissances formed a large part of the daily round, and the reports brought in always added to our Army's store of information. In Palestine, possibly to a greater extent than in any other theatre of war, our map–makers had to rely on aerial photographs to supply them with the details required for military maps. The best maps we had of Palestine were those prepared by Lieutenant H.H. Kitchener, R.E., and Lieutenant Conder in 1881 for the Palestine Exploration Fund. They were still remarkably accurate so far as they went, but 'roads,' to give the tracks a description to which they were not entitled, had altered, and villages had disappeared, and newer and additional information had to be supplied. The Royal Flying Corps—it had not yet become the Royal Air Force—furnished it, and all important details of hundreds of square miles of country which survey parties could not reach were registered with wonderful accuracy by aerial photographers.

The work began for the battle of Rafa, and the enemy positions on the Magruntein hill were all set out before General Chetwode when the Desert Column attacked and scored an important victory. Then when 12,000 Turks were fortifying the Weli Sheikh Nuran country covering the wadi Ghuzze and the Shellal springs, not a redoubt or trench but was recorded with absolute fidelity on photographic prints, and long before the Turks abandoned the place and gave us a fine supply of water we had excellent maps of the position. In time the whole Gaza–Beersheba line was completely photographed and maps were continually revised, and if any portion of the Turkish system of defences was changed or added to the commander in the district concerned was notified at once. To such perfection did the R.F.C. photographic branch attain, that maps showing full details of new or altered trenches were in the hands of generals within four hours of the taking of the photographs. Later on the work of the branch increased enormously, and the results fully repaid the infinite care and labour bestowed upon it.

The R.F.C. made long flights in this theatre of war, and some of them were exceptionally difficult and dangerous. A French battleship when bombarding a Turkish port of military importance had two of our machines to spot the effect of her gunfire. To be with the ship when the action opened the airmen had to fly in darkness for an hour and a half from a distant aerodrome, and they both reached the rendezvous within five minutes of the appointed time. The Turks on their lines of communication with the Hedjaz have an unpleasant recollection of being bombed at Maan. That was a noteworthy expedition. Three machines set out from an aerodrome over 150 miles away in a straight line, the pilots having to steer a course above country with no prominent landmarks. They went over a waterless desert so rough that it would have been impossible to come down without seriously damaging a plane, and if a pilot had been forced to land his chance of getting back to our country would have been almost nil. Water bottles and rations were carried in the machines, but they were not needed, for the three pilots came home together after hitting the station buildings at Maan and destroying considerable material and supplies.

The aeroplane has been put to many uses in war and, it may be, there are instances on other fronts of it being used, in emergencies, as an ambulance. When a little mobile force rounded up the Turkish post at Hassana, on the eastern side of the Sinai Peninsula, one of our men received so severe a wound that an immediate operation was necessary. An airman at once volunteered to carry the wounded man to the nearest hospital, forty-four miles away across the desert, and by his action a life was saved.

APPENDICES

I

The following telegram was sent by Enver Pasha to Field-Marshal von Hindenburg, at Supreme Army Command Headquarters, from Constantinople on August 23, 1917:

The news of the despatch of strong enemy forces to Egypt,
together with the nomination of General Allenby as Commander-in-Chief
on our Syrian Front, indicates that the
British contemplate an offensive on the Syrian Front, and
very probably before the middle of November.

The preservation of the Sinai Front is a primary condition
to the success of the Yilderim undertaking.

How Jerusalem Was Won

After a further conversation with the Commander of
the IVth Army (Jemal Pasha) I consider it necessary to
strengthen this front by one of the infantry divisions intended
for Yilderim, and to despatch this division immediately
from Aleppo.

With this reinforcement the defence of the Sinai Front
by the IVth Army is assured.

General von Falkenhayn takes up the position that he
does not consider the defence assured, and that the further
reduction of Yilderim forces is to be deprecated under any
circumstances.

He consequently recommends that we on our side should
attack the British, and as far as possible surprise them,
before they are strengthened. He wishes to carry out this
attack with four infantry divisions, and the 'Asia' Corps.
Two of the four infantry divisions have still to be despatched
to the front.

I cannot yet decide to support the proposal, nor need
I do so, as the transport of an infantry division from Aleppo
to Bayak requires twenty days. During this period the
situation as regards the enemy will become clear, and one
will become better able to estimate the chance of success
of an attack.

I must, however, in any case be able to dispose of more
forces than at present, either for the completion of Yilderim,
or for the replacement of the very heavy losses which will
certainly occur in the Syrian attack.

I must consequently reiterate, to my deep regret, my
request for the return of the VIth Army Corps (which was
operating at that time in the Dobrudja) and for the despatch

of this Corps, together with the 20th Infantry Division,
commencing with the 15th Infantry Division.

In my opinion the Army Corps could be replaced by
Bulgarians, whose task is unquestionably being lightened
through the despatch of troops (British) to Egypt.

Should this not be the case, I would be ready to exchange
two divisions from the Vth Army for the two infantry divisions
of the VIth Army Corps, as the former are only suited
for a war of position, and would have to be made mobile
by the allotment of transport and equipment.

If these two infantry divisions were given up, the Vth
Army would have only five infantry divisions of no great
fighting value, a condition of things which is perhaps not
very desirable.

For the moment my decision is: Defence of Syria by
strengthening that front by one infantry division, and
prosecution of the Yilderim scheme.

Should good prospects offer of beating the British decisively
in Syria before they have been reinforced I will take
up General von Falkenhayn's proposal again, as far as it
appears possible to carry it out, having in view the question
of transport and rationing, which still has to be settled in
some respects.—Turkish Main Headquarters, ENVER.

II

Von Falkenhayn despatched the following telegram from Constantinople on August 25,
1917, to German General Headquarters:

The possibility of a British attack in Syria has had to
be taken into consideration from the beginning. Its repercussion

How Jerusalem Was Won

on the Irak undertaking was obvious. On that
account I had already settled in my conversations in Constantinople
during May that, if the centre of gravity of
operations were transferred to the Sinai Front, command
should be given me there too. The news now to hand—reinforcement
of the British troops in Egypt, taking over
of command by Allenby, the demands of the British Press
daily becoming louder—makes the preparation of a British
attack in Syria probable.

Jemal Pasha wishes to meet it with a defensive. To
that end he demands the divisions and war material which
were being collected about Aleppo for Yilderim. The
natural result of granting this request will be that true
safety will never be attained on the Sinai Front by a pure
defensive, and that the Irak undertaking will certainly
fritter away owing to want of driving power or to delays.

I had consequently proposed to the Turkish Higher
Command to send two divisions and the 'Asia' Corps as
quickly as possible to Southern Syria, so as to carry out
a surprise attack on the British by means of an encircling
movement before the arrival of their reinforcements. Railways
allow of the assembly of these forces (inclusive of heavy
artillery, material and technical stores) in the neighbourhood
of Beersheba by the end of October. The disposable parts
of the IVth Army (two to three divisions) would be added
to it.

In a discussion between Enver, Jemal, and myself, Enver
decided first of all to strengthen the IVth Army by the
inclusion of one division from the Army Group. This
division would suffice to ward off attack. The Irak undertaking
could be carried through at the same time. Judging
from all former experiences I am firmly convinced as soon
as it comes to a question of the expected attack on the

Sinai Front, or even if the IVth Army only feels itself seriously threatened, further troops, munitions, and material will be withdrawn from the Army Group, and Turkey's forces will be shattered.

Then nothing decisive can be undertaken in either theatre of war. The sacrifice of men, money, and material which Germany is offering at the present moment will be in vain.

The treatment of the question is rendered all the more difficult because I cannot rid myself of the impression that the decision of the Turkish Higher Command is based far less on military exigencies than on personal motives. It is dictated with one eye on the mighty Jemal, who deprecates a definite decision, but yet on the other hand opposes the slightest diminution of the area of his command.

Consequently as the position now stands, I consider the Irak undertaking practicable only if it is given the necessary freedom for retirement through the removal of the danger on the Syrian Front. The removal of this danger I regard as only possible through attack. V. FALKENHAYN.

III

Here is another German estimate of the position created by our War Cabinet's decision to take the offensive in Palestine, and in considering the view of the German Staff and the prospect of success any Turkish attack would have, it must be borne in mind that under the most favourable circumstances the enemy could not have been in position for taking an offensive before the end of October. Von Falkenhayn wished to attack the British 'before the arrival of their reinforcements.' Not only had our reinforcements arrived before the end of October, but they were all in position and the battle had commenced. Beersheba was taken on October 31. This appreciation was written by Major von Papen of Yilderim headquarters on August 28, 1917:

How Jerusalem Was Won

Enver's objections, the improbability of attaining a
decisive result on the Sinai Front with two divisions plus
the 'Asia Corps' and the difficulty of the Aleppo–Rayak
transport question, hold good.

The execution of the offensive with stronger forces is
desirable, but is not practicable, as, in consequence of the
beginning of the rainy weather in the middle of November,
the British offensive may be expected at the latest during
the latter half of October; ours therefore should take place
during the first part of that month.

The transport question precludes the assembly of stronger
forces by that date.

Should the idea of an offensive be abandoned altogether
on that account?

On the assumption that General Allenby—after the two
unsuccessful British attacks—will attack only with a marked
superiority of men and munitions, a passive defence on a
thirty–five kilometre front with an exposed flank does not
appear to offer any great chance of success.

The conditions on the Western Front (defensive zone,
attack divisions) are only partially applicable here, since
the mobility of the artillery and the correct tactical handling
of the attack division are not assured. The intended passive
defensive will not be improved by the theatrical attack with
one division suggested by General von Kress.

On the contrary this attack would be without result, as
it would be carried out too obliquely to the front, and would
only mean a sacrifice of men and material.

How Jerusalem Was Won

The attack proposed by His Excellency for the envelopment
of the enemy's flank—if carried out during the first
half of October with four divisions plus the 'Asia Corps'—will
perhaps have no definite result, but will at all events
result in this: that the Gaza Front flanked by the sea
will tie down considerable forces and defer the continuation
of British operations in the wet season, during which, in
the opinion of General von Kress, they cannot be carried
on with any prospect of success.

The situation on the Sinai Front will then be clear. Naturally
it is possible that the position here may demand the
inclusion of further effectives and the Yilderim operation
consequently become impracticable. This, however, will
only prove that the determining factor of the decisive operation
for Turkey during the winter of 1917–1918 lies in Palestine
and not in Mesopotamia. An offensive on the Sinai
Front is therefore—even with reduced forces and a limited
objective—the correct solution.

PAPEN.

IV

Letter from General Kress von Kressenstein to Yilderim headquarters, dated September 29, 1917, on moral of Turkish troops.

A question which urgently needs regulating is that of deserters. According to my experience their number will increase still more with the setting in of the bad weather and the deterioration of rations.

Civil administration and the gendarmerie fail entirely; they often have a secret understanding with the population and are open to bribery.

The cordon drawn by me is too weak to prevent desertion. I am also too short of troops to have the necessary raids undertaken in the hinterland. It is necessary that the hunt for

167

deserters in the area between the front and the line Jerusalem–Ramleh–Jaffa be formally organised under energetic management, that one or two squadrons exclusively for this service be detailed, and that a definite reward be paid for bringing in each deserter. But above all it is necessary that punishment should follow in consequence, and that the unfortunately very frequent amnesties of His Majesty the Sultan be discontinued, at least for some time.

The question of rationing has not been settled. We are living continually from hand to mouth. Despite the binding promises of the Headquarters IVth Army, the Vali of Damascus, the Lines of Communication, Major Bathmann and others, that from now on 150 tons of rations should arrive regularly each day, from the 24th to the 27th of this month, for example a total of 229 tons or only 75 tons per diem have arrived.

I cannot fix the blame for these irregularities. The Headquarters IVth Army has received the highly gratifying order that, at least up to the imminent decisive battle, the bread ration is raised to 100 grammes. This urgently necessary improvement of the men's rations remains illusory, if a correspondingly larger quantity of flour (about one wagon per day) is not supplied to us. So far the improvement exists only on paper. The condition of the animals particularly gives cause for anxiety. Not only are we about 6000 animals short of establishment, but as a result of exhaustion a considerable number of animals are ruined daily. The majority of divisions are incapable of operating on account of this shortage of animals. The ammunition supply too is gradually coming into question on account of the deficiency in animals. The menacing danger can only be met by a regular supply of sufficient fodder. The stock of straw in the area of operations is exhausted. With gold some barley can still be bought in the country.

Every year during the rainy season the railway is interrupted again and again for periods of from eight to fourteen days. There are also days and weeks in which the motor–lorry traffic has to be suspended. Finally we must calculate on the possibility of an interruption of our rear communications by the enemy. I therefore consider it absolutely necessary that at least a fourteen days' reserve of rations be deposited in the depots at the front as early as possible.

The increase of troops on the Sinai Front necessitates a very considerable increase on the supply of meat from the Line of Communication area, Damascus district.

How Jerusalem Was Won

V

The troops of General Allenby's Army before the attack on Beersheba were distributed as follows:

XXTH CORPS.

10th Division.

29th Brigade. 30th Brigade. 31st Brigade.

6th R. Irish Rifles. 1st R. Irish Regt. 5th R. Inniskillings. 5th Con. Rangers. 6th R. Munst. Fus. 6th R. Inniskillings. 6th Leinsters. 6th R. Dublin Fus. 2nd R. Irish Fus. 1st Leinsters 7th R. Dublin Fus. 5th R. Irish Rifles.

53rd Division.

158th Brigade. 159th Brigade. 160th Brigade.

1/5th R. Welsh Fus. 1/4th Cheshires. 1/4th R. Sussex. 1/6th " 1/7th " 2/4th R. West Surrey. 1/7th " 1/4th Welsh 2/4th R. West Kent. 1/1st Hereford. 1/5th " 2/10th Middlesex.

60th Division.

179th Brigade. 180th Brigade. 181st Brigade.

2/13th London. 2/17th London. 2/21st London. 2/14th " 2/18th " 2/22nd " 2/15th " 2/19th " 2/23rd " 2/16th " 2/20th " 2/24th "

74th Division.

229th Brigade. 230th Brigade. 231st Brigade.

16th Devons (1st 10th E. Kent (R.E. 10th Shrop. (Shrop.
Devon &R.N. Kent &W. Kent &Cheshire Yeo.).

169

Devon Yeo.). Yeo.). 12th Somerset L.I. 16th R. Sussex 24th R. Welsh Fus.
(Yeo.). (Yeo.). (Denbigh Yeo.). 14th R. Highrs.(Fife 15th Suffolk (Yeo.) 25th R. Welsh Fus.
&Forfar Yeo.). (Montgomery Yeo.
&Welsh Horse). 12th R. Scots Fus. 12th Norfolk (Yeo.) 24th Welsh Regt.
(Ayr &Lanark (Pembroke &Glanmorgan
Yeo.). Yeo.).

XXIst CORPS.

52nd (Lowland) Division.

155th Brigade. 156th Brigade. 157th Brigade.

l/4th R. Scots Fus. 1/4th Royal Scots. 1/5th H.L.I. l/5th R. Scots Fus. 1/7th Royal Scots. 1/6th H.L.I. l/4th K.O.S.B. 1/7th Scot. Rifles. 1/7th H.L.I. l/5th K.O.S.B. 1/8th Scot. Rifles. 1/5th A. &S. Highrs.

54th (East Anglian) Division.

161th Brigade. 162th Brigade. 163th Brigade.

l/4th Essex. 1/5th Bedfords. 1/4th Norfolk. l/5th Essex. 1/4th Northants. 1/5th Norfolk. l/6th Essex. 1/10th London. 1/5th Suffolk. l/7th Essex. 1/11th London. 1/8th Hampshire.

75th Division.

232th Brigade. 233th Brigade. 234th Brigade.

1/5th Devon. 1/5th Somersets. 1/4th D.C.L.I. 2/5th Hampshire. 1/4th Wilts. 2/4th Dorsets. 2/4th Somersets. 2/4th Hampshire. 123rd Rifles. 2/3rd Gurkhas. 3/3rd Gurkhas. 58th Rifles.

DESERT MOUNTED CORPS.

Anzac Mounted Division.

170

How Jerusalem Was Won

1st A.L.H. Bde. 2nd A.L.H. Bde. N.Z. Mtd. Rifles Bde.

1st A.L.H. Regt. 5th A.L.H. Regt. Auckland M. Rifles. 2nd A.L.H. Regt. 6th A.L.H. Regt. Canterbury M. Rifles. 3rd A.L.H. Regt. 7th A.L.H. Regt. Wellington M. Rifles.

Australian Mounted Division.

3rd L.H. Brigade. 4th L.H. Brigade. 5th Mtd. Brigade.. 8th A.L.H. Regt. 4th A.L.H. Regt. 1/1st Warwick Yeo. 9th " 11th " 1/1st Gloucester Yeo. 10th " 12th " 1/1st Worcester Yeo.

Yoemanry Mounted Division

6th Mtd. Brigade. 8th Mtd. Brigade. 22nd Mtd. Brigade. 1/1st Bucks Hussars. 1/1st City of London 1/1st Lincolnshire Yeo. Yeo. 1/1st Berkshire Yeo. 1/1st Co. of London 1/1st Staffordshire Yeo. Yeo. 1/1st Dorset Yeo. l/3rd Co. of London 1/1st E. Riding Yeo. Yeo.

7th Mounted Brigade (attached Desert Corps).

1/1st Sherwood Rangers. 1/1st South Notts Hussars.

Imperial Camel Brigade.

VI

There can be no better illustration of how one battle worked out 'according to plan' than the quotation of the following Force Order:

FORCE ORDER

GENERAL HEADQUARTERS,
22nd October 1917.

It is the intention of the Commander–in–Chief to take the offensive against the enemy at Gaza and at Beersheba, and when Beersheba is in our hands to make an enveloping attack on the enemy's left flank in the direction of Sheria and Hareira.

On Zero day XXth Corps with the 10th Division and Imperial Camel Brigade attached and the Desert Mounted Corps less one Mounted Division and the Imperial Camel Brigade will attack the enemy at Beersheba with the object of gaining possession of that place by nightfall.

As soon as Beersheba is in our hands and the necessary arrangements have been made for the restoration of the Beersheba water supply, XXth Corps and Desert Mounted Corps complete will move rapidly forward to attack the left of the enemy's main position with the object of driving him out of Sheria and Hareira and enveloping the left flank of his army. XXth Corps will move against the enemy's defences south of Sheria, first of all against the Kauwukah line and then against Sheria and the Hareira defences. Desert Mounted Corps calling up the Mounted Division left in general reserve during the Beersheba operation will move north of the XXth Corps to gain possession of Nejile and of any water supplies between that place and the right of XXth Corps and will be prepared to operate vigorously against and round the enemy's left flank if he should throw it back to oppose the advance of the XXth Corps.

On a date to be subsequently determined and which will probably be after the occupation of Beersheba and 24 to 48 hours before the attack of XXth Corps on the Kauwukah line, the XXIst Corps will attack the south–west defences of Gaza with the object of capturing the enemy's front–line system from Umbrella Hill to Sheikh Hasan, both inclusive.

The Royal Navy will co–operate with the XXIst Corps in the attack on Gaza and in any subsequent operations that may be undertaken by XXIst Corps.

How Jerusalem Was Won

On Z—4 day the G.O.C. XXIst Corps will open a systematic
bombardment of the Gaza defences, increasing in volume
from Z—1 day to Zx2 day and to be continued until Zx4
day at the least.

The Royal Navy will co-operate as follows: On Z—1 and
Zero days two 6-inch monitors will be available for bombardment
from the sea, special objective Sheikh Hasan.
On Zero day a third 6-inch monitor will be available so that
two of these ships may be constantly in action while one
replenishes ammunition. On Zx1 day 6-inch monitors will
discontinue their bombardment which they will reopen
on Zx2 day. From Zx1 day the French battleship *Requin*
and H.M.S. *Raglan* will bombard Deir Sineid station and
junction for Huj, the roads and railway bridges and camps
on the wadi Hesi and the neighbourhood. The *Requin* and
Raglan will be assisted by a seaplane carrier.

From Zero day one 92 monitor will be available from
dawn, special objective Sheikh Redwan.

From Z—1 day inclusive demands for naval co-operation
will be conveyed direct from G.O.C. XXIst Corps to the
Senior Naval Officer, Marine View, who will arrange for
the transmission of the demands so made.

XXth Corps will move into position during the night of
Z—1=Zero day so as to attack the enemy at Beersheba on
Zero day south of the wadi Saba with two divisions while
covering his flank and the construction of the railway
east of Shellal with one division on the high ground overlooking
the wadis El Sufi and Hanafish. The objective of XXth Corps
will be the enemy's works west and south-west
of Beersheba as far as the Khalasa–Beersheba road
inclusive.

How Jerusalem Was Won

Desert Mounted Corps will move on the night of Z−1=Zero
day from the area of concentration about Khalasa and
Asluj so as to co−operate with XXth Corps by attacking
Beersheba with two divisions and one mounted brigade.
The objective of Desert Mounted Corps will be the enemy's
defences from south−east to the north−east of Beersheba
and the town of Beersheba itself.

The G.O.C. Desert Mounted Corps will endeavour to turn
the enemy's left with a view to breaking down his
resistance at Beersheba as quickly as possible. With this
in view the main weight of his force will be directed against
Beersheba from the east and north−east. As soon as the
enemy's resistance shows signs of weakening the G.O.C.
Desert Mounted Corps will be prepared to act with the utmost
vigour against his retreating troops so as to prevent their
escape, or at least to drive them well beyond the high ground
immediately overlooking the town from the north. He
will also be prepared to push troops rapidly into Beersheba
in order to protect from danger any wells and plant connected
with the water supply not damaged by the enemy before
Beersheba is entered.

The Yeomanry Mounted Division will pass from the
command of the G.O.C. XXth Corps at five on Zero day
and will come directly under General Headquarters as part
of the general reserve in the hands of the Commander−in−Chief.

When Beersheba has been taken the G.O.C. XXth Corps
will push forward covering troops to the high ground north
of the town to protect it from any counter movement on
the part of the enemy. He will also put in hand the restoration
of the water supply in Beersheba. The G.O.C. Desert
Mounted Corps will be responsible for the protection of
the town from the north−east and east.

How Jerusalem Was Won

As soon as possible after the taking of Beersheba the
G.O.C. Desert Mounted Corps will report to G.H.Q. on the
water supplies in the wells and wadis east of Beersheba and
especially along the wadi Saba and the Beersheba–Tel–el–Nulah
road. If insufficient water is found to exist in this
area G.O.C. Desert Mounted Corps will send back such of
his troops as may be necessary to watering places from which
he started or which may be found in the country east of
the Khalasa–Beersheba road during the operations.

A preliminary survey having been made, the G.O.C. XXth
Corps will report by wire to G.H.Q. on the condition of the
wells and water supply generally in Beersheba and on any
water supplies found west and north–west of that place.
He will telegraph an estimate as soon as it can be made
of the time required to place the Beersheba water supply
in working order.

When the situation as regards water at Beersheba has
become clear so that the movement of XXth Corps and
Desert Mounted Corps against the left flank of the enemy's
main position can be arranged, the G.O.C. XXIst Corps
will be ordered to attack the enemy's defences south–west
of Gaza in time for this operation to be carried out prior
to the attack of XXth Corps on the Kauwukah line of works.
The objective of XXIst Corps will be the defences of Gaza
from Umbrella Hill inclusive to the sea about Sheikh Hasan.

Instructions in regard to the following have been issued
separate to all corps:

Amount of corps artillery allotted.

Amount of ammunition put on corps charge prior to operations.

175

How Jerusalem Was Won

Amount of ammunition per gun that will be delivered daily
at respective railheads and the day of commencement.

Amount of transport allotted for forward supply from
railheads.

The general average for one day's firing has been calculated
on the following basis:

Field and mountain guns and
mountain howitzers ...150 rounds per gun.
4.5-inch howitzers....120 rounds per gun.
60-pounders and 6-inch howitzers. 90 rounds per gun.
8-inch howitzers and 6-inch Mark VII. 60 rounds per gun.

This average expenditure will only be possible in the
XXIst Corps up to Zx16 day and for the Desert Mounted
Corps and XXth Corps to Zx13. After these dates if the
average has been expended the daily average will have to
drop to the basis of 100 rounds per 18-pounder per day and
other natures in proportion.

AIRCRAFT, ARMY WING.—Strategical reconnaissance including
the reconnaissance of areas beyond the tactical zone
and in which the enemy's main reserves are located, also
distant photography and aerial offensive, will be carried out
by an Army squadron under instructions issued direct from
G.H.Q. Protection from hostile aircraft will be the main
duty of the Army fighting squadron. A bombing squadron
will be held in readiness for any aerial offensive which the
situation may render desirable.

CORPS SQUADRONS.—Two Corps squadrons will undertake
artillery co-operation, contact patrols, and tactical reconnaissance
for the Corps to which they are attached. In the
case of the Desert Mounted Corps one flight from the Corps

squadron attached to XXth Corps will be responsible for
the above work. Photography of trench areas will normally
be carried out daily by the Army Wing.

VII

ORDERS FOR THE OFFICIAL ENTRY INTO JERUSALEM

1. The Commander–in–Chief will enter Jerusalem by the Bab–el–Khalil (Jaffa Gate) at 12 noon, 11th December 1917. The order of procession is shown below:

>   Two Aides–de–camp.
>   (Twenty paces.) O.C. Italian Palestine Commander–in–Chief. O.C. French Palestine Contingent(Col. Contingent Dagostino). (Col. Piepape). Staff Officer. Two Staff Officers. Staff Officer.
>   (Ten paces.)
>   M. Picot (Head of French Mission). French Mil. Brig.–Gen. Italian Mil. Att. American Att. (Capt. Clayton. (Major Caccia). Mil. Att. St. Quentin). (Col. Davis).
>   (Five paces.)
>   Chief of General Staff (Maj.–Gen. Sir L.J. Bols).
>   Brig.–General General Staff (Brig.–Gen. G. Dawnay).
>   (Five paces.)
>   G.O.C. XXth Corps, Lieut.–Gen. Sir Philip W. Chetwode,
>   Bart., D.S.O.
>   Staff Officer. Brig.–Gen. Bartholomew.
>   (Ten paces.)
>   British Guard.
>   Australian and New Zealand Guard.
>   French Guard.
>   Italian Guard.

2. GUARDS.—The following guards will be found by XXth Corps:

Outside the Gate—

How Jerusalem Was Won

British Guard: Fifty of all ranks, including English, Scottish, Irish, and Welsh troops.

Australian and New Zealand Guard: Fifty of all ranks, including twenty New Zealand troops.

These guards will be drawn up facing each other, the right flank of the British guard and the left flank Australian guard resting on the City Wall. The O.C. British guard will be in command of both guards and will give the words of command.

Inside the Gate—

French Guard: Twenty of all ranks.
Italian Guard: Twenty of all ranks.

These guards will be drawn up facing each other, the left flank of the French guard and the right flank of the Italian guard resting on the City Wall.

3. SALUTE.—On the approach of the Commander–in–Chief, guards will come to the Salute and present arms.

4. The Military Governor of the City will meet the Commander–in–Chief at the Gate at 12 noon.

5. ROUTE.—The procession will proceed *via* Sueikat Allah and El Maukaf Streets to the steps of El Kala (Citadel), where the notables of the City under the guidance of a Staff Officer of the Governor will meet the Commander–in–Chief and the Proclamation will be read to the citizens. The British, Australian and New Zealand, French and Italian guards will, when the procession has passed them, take their place in column of fours in the rear of the procession in that order.

On arrival at El Kala the guards will form up facing steps on the opposite (*i.e.* east) side of El Maukaf Street, the British guard being thus on the left, Italian guard on the right of the line, and remain at the slope. The British and Italian guards will bring up their left and

178

right flanks respectively across the street south and north of El Kala.

On leaving the Citadel the procession will proceed in the same order as before to the Barrack Square, where the Commander–in–Chief will confer with the notables of the City. On entering the Barrack Square the guards will wheel to the left and, keeping the left–hand man of each section of fours next the side of the Barrack Square, march round until the rear of the Italian guard has entered the Square, when the guards will halt, right turn (so as to face the centre of the Square), and remain at the slope.

The procession will leave the City by the same route as it entered and in the same order.

As the Commander–in–Chief and procession move off to leave the Barrack Square the guards will present arms, and then move off and resume their places in the procession, the British guard leading.

On arrival at the Jaffa Gate the guards will take up their original positions, and on the Commander–in–Chief's departure will be marched away under the orders of the G.O.C. XXth Corps.

6. POLICE, etc.—The Military Governor of the City will arrange for policing the route of the procession and for the searching of houses on either side of the route. He will also arrange for civil officials to read the Proclamation at El Kala.

VIII

The Proclamation read from the steps of David's Tower on the occasion of the Commander–in–Chief's Official Entry into Jerusalem was in these terms:

To the inhabitants of Jerusalem the Blessed and the people dwelling
in its vicinity:

The defeat inflicted upon the Turks by the troops under
my command has resulted in the occupation of your City
by my forces. I therefore here and now proclaim it to be
under martial law, under which form of administration it
will remain as long as military considerations make it

179

necessary.

However, lest any of you should be alarmed by reason of
your experiences at the hands of the enemy who has retired,
I hereby inform you that it is my desire that every person
should pursue his lawful business without fear of interruption.
Furthermore, since your City is regarded with affection by
the adherents of three of the great religions of mankind, and
its soil has been consecrated by the prayers and pilgrimages
of multitudes of devout people of those three religions for
many centuries, therefore do I make it known to you that
every sacred building, monument, holy spot, shrine, traditional
site, endowment, pious bequest, or customary place
of prayer, of whatsoever form of the three religions, will be
maintained and protected according to the existing customs
and beliefs of those to whose faiths they are sacred.

IX

No story of the capture of Jerusalem would be complete without the tribute paid by
General Allenby to his gallant troops of all arms. The Commander–in–Chief's thanks,
which were conveyed to the troops in a Special Order of the Day, were highly
appreciated by all ranks. The document ran as follows:

SPECIAL ORDER OF THE DAY

G.H.Q., E.E.P.,

15th December 1917.

With the capture of Jerusalem another phase of the
operations of the Egyptian Expeditionary Force has been
victoriously concluded.

The Commander–in–Chief desires to thank all ranks of all
the units and services in the Force for the magnificent work

How Jerusalem Was Won

which has been accomplished.

In forty days many strong Turkish positions have been
captured and the Force has advanced some sixty miles on a
front of thirty miles.

The skill, gallantry, and determination of all ranks have
led to this result.

1. The approach marches of the Desert Mounted Corps
and the XXth Corps (10th, 53rd, 60th, and 74th Divisions),
followed by the dashing attacks of the 60th and 74th Divisions
and the rapid turning movement of the Desert Mounted
Corps, ending in the fine charge of the 4th Australian Light
Horse Brigade, resulted in the capture of Beersheba with
many prisoners and guns.

2. The stubborn resistance of the 53rd Division, units of
the Desert Mounted Corps and Imperial Camel Brigade in
the difficult country north–east of Beersheba enabled the
preparations of the XXth Corps to be completed without
interference, and enabled the Commander–in–Chief to carry
out his plan without diverting more than the intended
number of troops to protect the right flank, despite the many
and strong attacks of the enemy.

3. The attack of the XXth Corps (10th, 60th, and 74th
Divisions), prepared with great skill by the Corps and Divisional
Commanders and carried out with such dash and
courage by the troops, resulted in the turning of the Turkish
left flank and in an advance to the depth of nine miles through
an entrenched position defended by strong forces.

In this operation the Desert Mounted Corps, covering the
right flank and threatening the Turkish rear, forced the
Turks to begin a general retreat of their left flank.

4. The artillery attack of the XXIst Corps and of the ships of the Royal Navy, skilfully arranged and carried out with great accuracy, caused heavy loss to the enemy in the Gaza sector of his defences. The success of this bombardment was due to the loyal co–operation of the Rear–Admiral S.N.O. Egypt and Red Sea, and the officers of the Royal Navy, the careful preparation of plans by the Rear–Admiral and the G.O.C. XXIst Corps, and the good shooting of the Royal Navy, and of the heavy, siege, and field artillery of the XXIst Corps.

5. The two attacks on the strong defences of Gaza, carried out by the 52nd and 54th Divisions, were each completely successful, thanks to the skill with which they were thought out and prepared by the G.O.C. XXIst Corps, the Divisional Commanders and the Brigade Commanders, and the great gallantry displayed by the troops who carried out these attacks.

6. The second attack resulted in the evacuation of Gaza by the enemy and the turning of his right flank. The 52nd and 75th Divisions at once began a pursuit which carried them in three weeks from Gaza to within a few miles of Jerusalem.

7. This pursuit, carried out by the Desert Mounted Corps and these two Divisions of the XXIst Corps, first over the sandhills of the coast, then over the Plains of Palestine and the foothills, and finally in the rocky mountains of Judea, required from all commanders rapid decisions and powers to adapt their tactics to varying conditions of ground. The troops were called upon to carry out very long marches in great heat without water, to make attacks on stubborn rearguards without time for reconnaissance, and finally to suffer cold and privation in the mountains.

How Jerusalem Was Won

In these great operations Commanders carried out their
plans with boldness and determination, and the troops of all
arms and services responded with a devotion and gallantry
beyond praise.

8. The final operations of the XXth Corps which resulted
in the surrender of Jerusalem were a fitting climax to the
efforts of all ranks.

The attack skilfully prepared by the G.O.C. XXth Corps
and carried out with precision, endurance, and gallantry
by the troops of the 53rd, 60th, and 74th Divisions, over
country of extreme difficulty in wet weather, showed skill
in leading and gallantry and determination of a very high
order.

9. Throughout the operations the Royal Flying Corps
have rendered valuable assistance to all arms and have
obtained complete mastery of the air. The information
obtained from contact and reconnaissance patrols has at
all times enabled Commanders to keep in close touch with
the situation. In the pursuit they have inflicted severe
loss on the enemy, and their artillery co–operation has contributed
in no small measure to our victory.

10. The organisation in rear of the fighting forces enabled
these forces to be supplied throughout. All supply and
ammunition services and engineer services were called upon
for great exertions. The response everywhere showed great
devotion and high military spirit.

11. The thorough organisation of the lines of communication,
and the energy and skill with which all the services
adapted themselves to the varying conditions of the operations,
ensured the constant mobility of the fighting
troops.

12. The Commander–in–Chief appreciates the admirable conduct of all the transport services, and particularly the endurance and loyal service of the Camel Transport Corps.

13. The skill and energy by which the Signal Service was maintained under all conditions reflects the greatest credit on all concerned.

14. The Medical Service was able to adapt itself to all the difficulties of the situation, with the result the evacuation of wounded and sick was carried out with the least possible hardship or discomfort.

15. The Veterinary Service worked well throughout; the wastage in animals was consequently small considering the distances traversed.

16. The Ordnance Service never failed to meet all demands.

17. The work of the Egyptian Labour Corps has been of the greatest value in contributing to the rapid advance of the troops and in overcoming the difficulties of the communications.

18. The Commander–in–Chief desires that his thanks and appreciation of their services be conveyed to all officers and men of the force which he has the honour to command.

G. DAWNAY, B.G.G.S.,

for Major–General, Chief of the General Staff, E.E.F.

X

The men of units forming the XXth Corps were deeply gratified to receive this commendation from their gallant Corps Commander:

184

How Jerusalem Was Won

SPECIAL ORDER OF THE DAY

BY

LIEUTENANT–GENERAL SIR PHILIP W. CHETWODE, BT.,
K.C.M.G., C.B., D.S.O., *commanding XXth Corps*

HEADQUARTERS, XXTH CORPS,
13th December 1917.

Now that the efforts of General Sir E.H.H. Allenby's
Army have been crowned by the capture of Jerusalem, I
wish to express to all ranks, services, and departments of the
XXth Army Corps my personal thanks and my admiration
for the soldierly qualities they have displayed.

I have served as a regimental officer in two campaigns,
and no one knows better than I do what the shortness of
food, the fatigue of operating among high mountains, and
the cold and wet has meant to the fighting troops. But in
spite of it all, and at the moment when the weather was
at its worst, they responded to my call and drove the
enemy in one rush through his last defences and beyond
Jerusalem.

A fine performance, and I am intensely proud of having
had the honour of commanding such a body of men.

I wish to give special praise to the Divisional Ammunition
Columns, Divisional Trains A.S.C., Supply Services, Mechanical
Transport personnel, Camel Transport personnel, and to
the Royal Army Medical Corps and all services whose continuous
labour, day and night, almost without rest, alone
enabled the fighting troops to do what they did.

SPECIAL ORDER OF THE DAY

How Jerusalem Was Won

HEADQUARTERS, XXTH CORPS,
31_st December 1917.

I have again to thank the XXth Corps and to express to
them my admiration of their bravery and endurance during
the three days' fighting on December 27, 28, and 29.

The enemy made a determined attempt with two corps
to retake Jerusalem, and while their finest assault troops
melted away before the staunch defence of the 53rd and
60th Divisions, the 10th and 74th were pressing forward
over the most precipitous country, brushing aside all opposition
in order to relieve the pressure on our right.

Their efforts were quickly successful, and by the evening
of the 27th we had definitely regained the initiative, and
I was able to order a general advance.

The final result of the three days' fighting was a gain to
us of many miles and extremely heavy losses to the enemy.

A fine three days' work.

CPSIA information can be obtained at www.ICGtesting.com
Printed in the USA
LVOW09*1910161213

365565LV00025B/1327/P